A HEART'S REVOLUTION

A HEART'S REVOLUTION

ROSEANNA M. WHITE

WhiteFire
——— Publishing ———

This is a work of fiction. All characters and events portrayed in this novel are either fictitious or used fictitiously.

Previously published as *Love Finds You in Annapolis, Maryland* with Summerside Press

WhiteFire Publishing
13607 Bedford Rd NE
Cumberland, MD 21502

ISBN: 978-1-946531-08-7 (print)
        978-1-946531-09-4 (digital)

In loving memory of Mary Proctor,
my first critique partner.

CHAPTER ONE

Endover Plantation, outside Williamsburg, Virginia
25 November 1783

Perhaps if Lark recited the pirate's code it would steal his attention. She could try standing on her head. Or if those options failed—as surely they would—she could throw herself to the floor before him.

Except Emerson Fielding was as likely to mistake her for a rug as to realize he ought to help her up. Lark indulged in a long sigh and cast her gaze out the window. The plantation lay dormant and brown. Most days saw Papa and Wiley in Williamsburg, swapping stories at R. Charlton's Coffeehouse. Emerson usually met them there, which was why this was the first she'd seen him in a month. Heaven knew he wanted only to see *them*, never *her*.

She wished her heart hadn't fluttered when he entered the room. Wished the disappointment hadn't followed so quickly when he barely glanced her way. Wished she had the courage to command his attention...and he the sense to give it without her command.

Life would be so much easier if she weren't in love with Emerson Fielding. But what young lady wouldn't be captivated by those dark eyes, the strong features, the height that left him towering above other men?

Today his hair was unpowdered and gleamed sable. He was in undress, his coat the common one he wore every day, unlike what he was sure to don for her birthday dinner that evening. His smile lit up his eyes, his laugh lit up the room.

Neither one did he direct toward her.

Lark's gaze flicked down to the emerald on her finger. Two years.

Twenty-four months. Seven hundred thirty interminable days. Not that she was keeping account.

"Hendricks ought to be at the coffeehouse about now," her brother said, standing. He tugged his waistcoat into place and tightened the band around his hair. "We have just enough time for a cup of chocolate with him."

She would not sigh again, it would be redundant. Why protest the usual, even if today was supposed to be distinctive?

As if reading her mind, Wiley flashed a twinkling gaze her way and grinned. "Of course, you will want to wish my dear sister happy returns before we head out, Emerson. I shall go fetch my overcoat and hat while you do so."

For the first time in the two hours he had been there, Emerson looked her way. And like every time he looked her way, she wished she had more to offer his gaze. Perhaps if she shared the golden-haired beauty of her mother and sister, his eyes mightn't go empty upon spotting her.

He smiled the practiced smile gentlemen were taught to wear in company, not the earnest one he shared with her brother. "Are you having a pleasant birthday, darling?"

An unexpected wave of anger crashed over her. "Do you never tire of using endearments you don't mean?"

Well, that earned a spark in his eyes. Not exactly one of delight or affection, though. "I take it you are *not* having a pleasant day. Well, perhaps I can brighten it." He reached into his pocket, pulled out a box covered in a scrap of printed calico.

She could manage no enthusiasm for what was sure to be another gift of jewels. He never seemed to grasp that she wanted no more *things*. She wanted his love—something he was either unwilling or incapable of giving. "What is it?"

His smile was right, teasing. But no secret knowledge nested in his expression. "Open it and see."

"You haven't any idea, have you?" She shook her head and looked out the window again as he strode toward her chair. His mother had undoubtedly foisted it upon him as he left, otherwise he wouldn't have remembered what the date signified.

She often wondered if his mother had also foisted that first gift of jewels upon him two years before.

His breath hissed out. "Of course I know what it is, but you shan't cajole it out of me. You will have to open it yourself to see."

The wrapped box appeared under her nose. She took it, careful to avoid brushing his outstretched palm with her fingers. It would only make awareness shiver up her arm, an unnecessary reminder of her unrequited attachment. Once she held it, though, she made no move to untie the ribbon.

Emerson shifted, impatience coming off him in waves. "Open it, Lark."

She shook herself. "But of course. I am certain you wish to hasten to your coffee and conversation. What will the topic be today? Congresses, constitutions, or crop rotations?"

Wiley would have appreciated the alliteration. Emerson greeted it with a rudely arched brow. Tempted to return the insult and roll her eyes, she tugged at the bow. Unfolded the cloth. Lifted the lid of the small wooden box.

Lessons in propriety had never covered how to handle a surprise like this. Lark gasped.

Emerson muttered a curse that proved he not only knew not what present lay inside, he disapproved of his mother's selection.

She leapt to her feet and shoved the glittering diamond necklace into his stomach. "Absolutely not. I cannot accept that."

His hand caught the box, but a war to rival the Revolution charged across his face. He wanted to take the jewels back, without question. But pride would not allow him. He held out the box. "Don't be ridiculous. I want you to have it."

An unladylike snort nearly slipped out. "Yes, that was apparent from your reaction. I will not, Emerson. Your sisters have told me of this necklace, and I shan't accept the most valuable possession in the Fielding family—especially when it becomes increasingly clear I will never be a member of said family."

Thunder darkened his complexion. "What madness is this? You are my betrothed, and you will accept the gifts I give you."

The emerald on her left hand felt heavy. "Perhaps what I ought to do is return the ones you have already given. They are naught but mockery."

She reached for the clasp of the bracelet that matched the ring. Her breath caught when his fingers closed around her wrist. He all but growled. "You will do no such thing."

"Prithee, why not?" Though she struggled to pull free, he held tight to her arm. "'Tis obvious you've no desire to make me your wife. For two years you have dodged every mention of nuptials, making a fool of me in front of our families and friends. For the life of me, I know not why you ever proposed. Release me."

He shook his head. "Calm yourself, Lark. Is that what this is about? The blasted wedding date? Deuces, I would agree to any date you want, if you would just be reasonable!"

"I have had my fill of reason. I want a morsel of your regard, and I will not marry you without it." She gave one more vain tug against his fingers. "I tire of being alone at your side, Emerson. I cannot subject myself to a lifetime of it."

Through the tears burning her eyes, she saw his face harden, then relax. His grip eased, but he did not release her wrist. Simply pulled it down and then held her hand. The warmth that seeped into her palm belied the cool words she had spoken.

Yet his smile was no more than it had ever been. "I have been remiss, darling, and I apologize. I assure you, you are my chosen bride. It has simply been a struggle to readjust to social life. After Yorktown…"

Anger snapped at her heels again, largely because of the compassion he called up with the mere mention of Yorktown. How could anyone—man, woman, or child—argue with one who had been at the dreadful battle? The moment a soldier uttered that word, all arguments necessarily ceased.

In this particular case she could not help but think he used it for that very purpose. "Emerson—"

"I shall make it up to you. Let us set a date this moment, and I will be the figure of devotion." The idea seemed to pain him—his smile turned to a grimace. For a man with a reputation as a charmer, he did a remarkable job of dashing her heart to pieces.

She sucked in a long breath. "I shan't hold you to the engagement. If you—"

"Not another word of such nonsense. Let us say the first Sunday in March, shall we? The worst of the winter weather ought to be over by then. We can announce it to our parents this evening."

It should have brought joy instead of defeat. It should have lit hope instead of despair.

He pressed the necklace back into her hands. "Take it, my darling. Wear it on our wedding day."

Before she could decide whether to relent or argue, he pressed a kiss to her fingers and fled the room as if the hounds of Hades nipped at his heels. Lark sank back into her chair and flipped open the box so she could stare at the large, perfect gems resting within.

Why did the thought of marrying her light such fires of panic under him? Lark rested her cheek against her palm and let her tears come.

She should have tried the pirate's code.

Emerson scraped the tavern chair across the wooden floor, fell onto its hard seat, and, for the first time in his memory, wished Wiley Benton would hold his tongue for five blasted minutes. He barely saw the familiar whitewashed walls, the wainscoting, the multitude of friendly faces. His mind still reeled, wrestling with images of those blinding diamonds—and the equally blinding tears in Lark's eyes.

What had Mother been thinking, blithely handing off the most valuable Fielding possessions? The diamonds—to Lark. It was beyond fathoming. They would overwhelm her. Eclipse rather than complement. And to have them abiding outside Fielding Hall for the next several months...

Still, he should not have lost his head. Then she wouldn't have lost hers, and he wouldn't have talked himself straight into a trap.

"What can I bring you gentlemen today?"

He looked up at the tavern's owner but couldn't dredge up a smile. No matter—Wiley would smile enough for the both of them. "Chocolate," his friend said.

"Make mine coffee, if you please, sir."

"That I will. And I shall direct Hendricks your way. He and the governor are chatting in the back corner."

"In a few moments," Emerson answered before Wiley could supply what was sure to be thankful acceptance.

As the proprietor stalked off, Wiley lifted his brows in that particular way that bespoke both humor and confusion. "What plagues you, man? You have been playing the dunderhead ever since we left Endover."

"I played it while there too." Indulging in a mild oath, he swept his tricorn off his head and plopped it onto the table between them. "I upset your sister."

"Lark?"

"Well, your other sister was hardly there to be upset."

Wiley took his hat off as well, his confusion plain on his face. "But Lark is so rarely in an ill temper. She especially shouldn't have been, given the good news of our cousin's delayed arrival."

Under normal circumstances, Emerson would have been amused at his friend's perpetual dislike of the family soon arriving from Philadelphia. At this moment he gave not a fig who was coming or when. "Apparently all it takes is overreacting when one sees one's mother wrapped up the family diamonds for her."

Wiley looked near to choking. "The ones your father goes ever on about? That had belonged to the countess?"

"The very ones."

Wiley let out a muted whistle. "I cannot conceive she accepted them. Especially if you seemed opposed."

"I had already insisted I knew what the gift was, though I did not. Then rather than returning just the diamonds, she grew angry and made to return *all* the Fielding jewels."

Wiley's eyes widened, and he leaned over the table. "What did you say to her?"

Emerson waved him off. "It hardly matters. I smoothed matters over, and we decided on a wedding date. The first Sunday of March."

Instead of seeming satisfied, Wiley's gaze went probing, and then accusing. "So simply? After shifting the topic away from the wedding each time my parents mentioned it the past two years? Frankly, Emerson, we have all doubted your intentions of making good on your promise."

"Of course I intend to make good on it." It was an advantageous match all round. The Bentons were a wealthy, respected family, perfectly equal to the Fieldings. Lark herself would make an excellent wife. She was well bred, well taught, not homely—if not as lovely as her sister, who was now Mrs. Hendricks. Sweet of temperament—today aside. He liked her well enough and expected he would come to love her in a decade or so, once they had a brood of children between them.

And she loved him, as his own sisters had pointed out two years ago.

Wiley narrowed his eyes. "Emerson, you know I would welcome you eagerly into our family, but I confess the longer this drags out, the more misgivings I have. You treat my sister no differently now than you did when she was a child, dogging your heels and sending us up a tree to escape her."

Perhaps that was the problem. She still seemed twelve to him, as she had been when he'd returned from England to fight for freedom from it. She still looked at him with the same blind adoration, still sat silently by whenever he was near.

That would change once they were wed though, surely.

"Emerson." Wiley's tone had turned hard, though barely more than a murmur. "I will see my sister happy. If you still dream of Elizabeth, if you cannot love Lark, then release her from the betrothal and let her find someone who can."

The name snapped his spine straight. Fight as he might against it, the image nonetheless surfaced of a woman as opposite Lark as one could find. Did he dream of her? Only in his worst nightmares. "Rest assured your sister is loved."

His friend's eyes narrowed. "If I did not know better, I would call that a cunning evasion. Loved she is. But I would have her loved by *you.*"

As would he. He could manage it, assuredly. He simply must put his mind to it, as he had to Newton's *Principia Mathematica* back at King William's School. "You have no reason to fear for your sister's heart, Wiley. I will be a good husband."

In three short months.

"You look more frightened than when we saw our first Redcoats advancing, muskets at the ready." Amusement laced its way through the frustration in Wiley's tone. "I would have many a laugh over this were it not my favorite sister that made you wince so."

"I am not wincing." Much.

"Benton, Fielding! There you are." Hendricks's voice came from the corner of the room, where the man had stood and waved a greeting to them. "I shall join you in a moment."

"We await you eagerly," Wiley replied with his usual grin. When he turned back around, it shifted and hardened into the expression few knew. But Emerson did, from the field of battle. It was the look that had always appeared on his friend's face moments before he let out a war cry and charged into the thick of things. "If you hurt Lark," he murmured so quietly Emerson could barely hear him, "I will kill you—or make you wish I had."

"I know you would. 'Tis not at issue." Twenty-five years of friendship had not been threatened by competition, an ocean's distance, or the ravages of war. He would not allow it to be distressed by one small, unassuming woman.

CHAPTER TWO

8 December 1783

Lark let her brother lead her around a muddy spot, then she cast her gaze out over the dormant fields. A few months past, they had been lush and green. A few months in the future, fresh life would spring up in the softest of shades. But for now all was dry and dead, unappealing to the eye.

She could commiserate well with the feeling.

"Perhaps they will meet with another delay. A bridge could be out. A river swollen. Perhaps the way is still covered in ice."

Lark laughed at Wiley's tone, hope coated in good humor. "Bad as this winter is thus far, there is no snow right now. I fear Aunt Hester and Penelope shall arrive today as planned."

"I fear it too." Her brother flashed a grin and pulled her closer. "But I fear for you even more than myself. I can escape with Father to the coffeehouse or tavern, and in two short days I shall depart for Annapolis. You, on the other hand, shall be forced to remain in our cousin's company hour after hour. Day after day. Week after week."

She let out a groan. Partly because Wiley expected it, but more because she dreaded the very thought. "Perhaps Charlton shall revise his policy and allow women to patronize his establishment, so I may come with you. Or if not, I could always don your old breeches and pretend to be a man."

Wiley gave her a playful nudge and then caught her before she could stumble off the path and onto uneven terrain. "You would faint in horror given some of the things men will say when not in the company of women."

"A risk worth taking."

He chuckled. "You could yet come with me to visit the Randels. Mr. Randel was quite insistent in extending the invitation to you, assuring me his daughter would enjoy the company of another young woman to hasten by the winter."

How was she to know if this Miss Randel would be any better a companion than Penelope? She had never met the family. "I cannot. Mother would never allow me with the Moxleys here, nor with the wedding looming so near."

She fell silent for a moment and soaked up the warming sunshine, the first they had seen in weeks.

"Prithee, Lark, tell me what distresses you." Wiley, it seemed, could always hear what she thought as well as what she said. "For a young lady who should be aflutter with plans for her nuptials, you are alarmingly melancholy."

With anyone else, she would have glossed over her feelings with a smile and wave of the hand. Not with her brother. "I feel as though my arms are bound and my feet on a tottering plank. Pirates at my back and a watery grave before me. No matter where I step, naught but misfortune awaits."

Wiley drew her to a halt and turned to face her, revealing the furrow in his brow. "I thought you loved him."

"I do. But he cares not for me, Wiley. He has proven it time and again over the last two years, and he proved it anew on my birthday." When she shook her head, she could feel the breeze tug at her hat. "Perhaps his words were right, but I know the look of a man in love. When Emerson looks at me…I think he sees only my shortcomings."

"You have no shortcomings." He chucked her under the chin and winked.

Usually she gave herself happily to his cheer. Not with this topic. "Then he sees me not at all."

Wiley sighed. "I wish I could assure you otherwise, but on this score I confess my own concerns. I want to be delighted about the match, yet I fear I will watch you both fall into misery."

Lark gripped his arm a little tighter. "You know him better than anyone this side of heaven. What ought I do to gain his affections? What *can* I?"

He shook his head and gazed into the distance. "I have no advice, Lark. I cannot fathom why he keeps such distance between you. I have spent these years hoping, praying my eyes deceived me or something would change. I told myself he *must* be exceptionally fond of you, or he would not have asked for your hand."

"You sound as though you are no longer so illusioned."

He patted her hand, as he had done when she was a child upset about some frivolity. "He insists he wishes to wed you. I cannot fathom why he would *not* want to, but his behavior has proven him anything but eager. It is unseemly, the way he has prolonged this betrothal. Certainly it would have been understandable during the war, or if he were traveling or building a home for you. But he has been a mile away this whole time. I know not how you suffered the insult so long, Larksong."

Though she knew it would be cold, she sank down onto the iron bench positioned under the bare trellis. "I was afraid to push, lest he run the other direction. Afraid to learn his heart belonged elsewhere. I am reaching the point where fear of an unhappy marriage is outweighing the fear of spinsterhood, however. Tell me truly, brother. Is he in love with another?"

"No." The answer came quickly, but not so quickly she thought it an overeager falsehood. "There was a young lady while he was in England, a gentleman's daughter. But when the war broke out and he confessed he would return to fight on the side of the Patriots, her father forbade a union. I thought the heartache might lead him into something rash when first he came home, but he has fully recovered from it. Of that I am certain."

And why, after a two-year engagement, was she only learning this now? From her brother, instead of her betrothed? "I can hardly take offense at something so long put to rest. Though the knowing of it would have been welcome."

"Lark." He sat beside her. His eyes, the same blue she shared, gleamed both bright and dark. Like a slip of moonstone caught in shadow. "If you have misgivings, if you feel the marriage would be a mistake, I pray you—cry off."

"I could never disappoint Mamma and Papa by ending it, Wiley. It would be my ruin, and theirs."

"Nonsense. They want you to be happy, as do I. I admit it may cause a stir, but soon enough another gentleman would step forward to claim you."

"I doubt that very much." She studied her hands, which had gone chapped and dry. "I have neither Mother's beauty nor Father's charm. The only thing to attract another suitor is the Benton name and the Benton wealth—but since an attachment based on those would carry no more affection than this one, why bother with the change?"

His finger caught her under the chin and urged her face around. "Listen to me, Lark. You are more than you think yourself, and any man who does not agree is a fool. You are lovely, you are sweet, you are full of wit. There is a man out there who will adore you, and you ought not settle for any other. Even Emerson."

The sentiment warmed her…but it answered none of her questions. For all his support, her brother would not be the one to feel it most keenly if she were to gain the stigma of a broken engagement. He would not be the one to feel the long gazes of the gentlemen at every ball, to hear the titters behind the ladies' fans. To awake each morning wondering if ever a day would dawn that would see loneliness banished.

"I will give it thought and prayer. But it is a hard decision to make. I do love him, Wiley, though oft I wish I did not. Only…I do not want to be a stranger to my husband, and that is what I feel like, even after knowing him all my life. I…" Having no idea what more she could say, she shrugged.

Wiley blew a long breath through his lips. "I shall be thinking and praying too, Larksong. Weigh well what you want, what you can live with. What will make you happy. And know whatever you choose, I will support you."

"I know you will, and I thank you for it." When a rumble intruded on her hearing, she lifted her face toward the drive. And sighed. "They have arrived."

"Quick, let us make our escape. If we hurry we can catch the post and be in Annapolis by week's end."

Lark chuckled and let him help her to her feet. "If only, my brother."

They wound their way out of the sleeping gardens and toward the side entrance of the house. Lark looked out over her home with a little sigh. She had seen the same stately drive, the same outbuildings all her life. The three-story brick abode with its elegant white columns had always been home.

Perhaps it always would be. She was grateful to have been born into one of the area's leading families, but to her mind the plantation was Wiley's legacy, not hers. Would she be relegated to living out her days here, though, the doting spinster aunt to her brother's eventual children?

They entered together and shed their hats. Lark positioned the lace of her mobcap back into place as commotion sounded at the front doors.

Mamma exited her drawing room, and she favored them with a smile that was resplendent, in spite of the advances of age. "There you are, darlings. Was your exercise pleasant?"

"Better than this will be, at any rate." Wiley's cheeky grin was all that saved him, Lark was sure.

Mamma narrowed her eyes playfully but otherwise scolded him not. "Come, they ought to be inside by now."

She led the way, but Lark was happy to move at the sedate pace her brother set. Her aunt Hester and uncle Moxley she liked well enough, but cousin Penelope… Perhaps she had changed in the year and a half since the Bentons had visited them in Philadelphia. If not, it would be an interminable winter.

They rounded the corner into the front hall but were still in the shadows of the flying staircase when their visitors came into view. Lark felt her eyes bulge when she caught sight of her cousin.

Penelope had always been beautiful, boasting the same flaxen hair and milky complexion as their mothers. Her eyes had always gleamed large and blue, and she had grown into a young woman with a shape to be envied. Lark had just never expected that shape to be so evident for all to see. "What is she wearing?"

Wiley attempted a cough to cover his laugh. "I believe, dear sister, the appropriate question would be 'What is she *not* wearing?' "

Lark pressed her lips down against a giggle. Knowing Penelope as she unfortunately did, she was sure the younger woman was in the height of fashion—she simply had no idea when the fashion had become walking around in one's undergarments, with one's hair hanging loose around one's shoulders as if fresh from bed.

Mamma had apparently put the question to her, though certainly with more tact. Penelope's silver-chime laughter rang out. "Isn't it lovely? New from France, where Marie Antoinette sat for a portrait in it. They call it a chemise gown."

"For obvious reasons," Wiley mumbled into Lark's ear.

She confined her response to a smile, since the Moxleys stepped forward to greet them. Her aunt embraced her first, and then Penelope pressed a kiss to her cheek.

Lark barely stemmed a sneeze at the scent of lavender that wafted from her cousin. "Lovely to see you, Penelope."

"Likewise, cousin. Did this fashion baby make it all the way down here? You really ought to try the style. The simplicity would not overpower you like those larger skirts do."

Lark forced a smile. "How kind of you to think of me. But no, yours is the first we have seen."

"'Tis a charming fashion," Mamma said. Lark couldn't be sure if she meant it. Her smile was bright, but she had always favored the extravagant styles. "And your hair is lovely like that."

"Well, one can hardly wear it piled high in a gown of such low profile—one would look terribly unbalanced." Another chime of laughter. "And I am all relief for you, Lark, that powdering is going out of mode, but for the most formal events. With your coloring, it always made you look so placid. Oh, but I am so sorry to have missed your birthday. Twenty! I never thought to be visiting you *here* when you turned twenty."

Penelope had most assuredly *not* changed.

Mamma cleared her throat. "Had you been delayed much longer, you could not have. The wedding will be the seventh of March. We will be quite overwhelmed with preparations these next months, so I am very grateful for your company, Hester dear. And I know Lark is glad to have a friend."

Indeed she would be, had a friend been present.

Penelope's gaze shifted in shade, though Lark knew no name for that particular glint within it. "Do you know, cousin, I have never even met your betrothed? I have heard others echo your claim that he is handsome, though."

Mamma clasped her hands together. "Oh, he is indeed. My darling songbird has charmed the most sought-after man in all Virginia. They will be joining us for dinner tomorrow before we send Wiley off to Annapolis the following morning, and you can all meet him and his family."

Penelope fluttered her lashes. "Oh, you are leaving so soon, Wiley? Would we had not been delayed so we might have enjoyed more of your company. But alas." Lark had no trouble at all interpreting that smug little smile on her cousin's face. "I am very much looking forward to meeting the Fieldings, Aunt Margaret."

In a move a stranger might have mistaken for friendly, Penelope linked her arm through Lark's. "You know, cousin, I quite admire you for this protracted engagement. To think of all the time you have had to become acquainted! You must be so very close by now. I confess I would lack the patience, but you are to be commended for your self-restraint."

As arrows went, that one had been both straight and true. Perhaps she ought to accept that invitation to the Randels' in Annapolis after all.

"What a monstrous little minx."

Lark smiled as Isabella Fielding, the eldest of Emerson's younger sisters, positioned herself close to her side and cut Penelope to pieces with her gaze. "Did you hear her insult my dress? And it straight from London! Send her directly back to Philadelphia, Lark, before she tries to steal all my beaux. Look at her, flirting with my brother as if you are not sitting right here."

Though Lark could grin at how quickly Isabella had seen through the sheen of Penelope's charms, that particular command was one she had no desire to obey. Since the moment Emerson had entered the room, her cousin had been batting her golden lashes at him and sending him a series of simpering, supposedly shy smiles.

Surely he responded only out of politeness. Had she not heard him and Wiley laugh time and again over mutual acquaintances who fell prey to asps like Penelope? He could not be interested in a woman like that. If he were, he would have chosen one of the many young ladies who had been playing the coquette with him all his adult life.

"However will you tolerate her until March?" The second Fielding sister, Sarah, had taken Lark's other side. "Perhaps you ought to have the banns read and move the wedding to January. Then you will have only Christmas to survive."

The third and final Fielding girl, Horatia, shook her head, her big brown eyes going wider still. "But Wiley will be away. And they could not possibly put the wedding together so quickly with all the guests they've invited. Why, General and Mrs. Washington will even be there!"

"Not that he will be the general then. Papa has said he is resigning his commission soon and retiring to Mount Vernon," Sarah said.

Isabella waved that away with her fan. "Just assure me the little monster has not been named a bride-maid."

Lark sighed. "Aunt Hester is already at work on her gown."

Isabella's eyes lit up with competition. "Then I shall have to make mine all the finer, so I outshine her."

If anyone could put the blond to shame, it would be Isabella. Though that meant Lark would be eclipsed by them both—and on what should be her day of days.

"Dinner is served."

Mamma and Papa stood at Ginny's announcement and led the procession out the drawing room door amidst laughter and continued conversation.

Emerson appeared at Lark's side, but his gaze didn't so much as touch her. He was far too busy studying the sway of Penelope's skirts. Distracting, to be sure, since one could see the movement of her legs under the cloth, but must he stare even as he offered Lark his arm?

She rested her fingers inside the crook of his elbow and drew in a long breath. "You look particularly well this evening, Emerson."

"Thank you, darling, so do you." Odd how a compliment could feel like an insult when it was so obviously unconsidered. "I imagine you are enjoying your cousin's company—she is a lovely young lady. Well spoken and pleasant."

From behind them, Isabella loosed an unladylike snort. Lark shot her a glance of amusement masked in reprimand. "She does have a way with words. And have you passed a pleasant week?"

"I'm sure."

Something knotted up inside her chest, where her heart should beat. Her cousin was beautiful, yes, and a practiced flirt. The same could be said of countless women—would his head be so easily turned by them all? Would she be forever known as the wife of the straying Mr. Fielding, if she married him?

She squared her shoulders. "Have you been terribly busy? I have not seen you since my birthday."

The reminder of their last encounter—and his promise to be the very figure of devotion—affected him not at all. "Quite."

Frustration brought her chin up. If he wouldn't pay attention to her, she could at least have a bit of fun at his expense. "Well. I have passed a busy week, learning the rules of a new trade. Did you know that to desert the ship or one's quarters in battle will be punished in death or marooning?"

"Mm."

Isabella choked back a laugh behind her. Lark smiled. "And one must always keep one's piece, pistol, and cutlass clean and fit for service."

"Certainly, darling."

"The true challenge will be in restraining my temper, however. It is strictly against the code to strike another while on board. Every man's quarrels are to be settled on shore, with sword and pistol."

"Yes, I—" Emerson finally looked down at her, his brows drawn. "Did you say something about swords?"

Surely she deserved credit for neither laughing nor rolling her eyes. "Of course not, darling, I said a woman has only her words. Hence why it is so important to have a good way with them."

He still frowned at her, but they had reached the dining room, so he made no reply. He led her to her usual chair, helped her sit, and then went around to his place across from her. Isabella leaned close to her ear. "How do you devise these things, Lark?"

She only grinned—which lasted until Penelope took the seat at Emerson's side. "What a delight it is to have you and your sisters with us this evening, Mr. Fielding. I feared my cousin had overstated the pleasures to be found in your company, but I ought to have realized guileless Lark is incapable of any exaggeration."

Was it unchristian to dream of plucking each and every golden strand from Penelope's head so Lark might strangle her with them? Undoubtedly. But perhaps if she left it at the plucking and refrained from the strangulation...

Emerson smiled at Penelope. "'Tis proving a pleasurable evening all round."

He obviously had no trouble following *her* conversation.

Oh, she must put aside the petty thoughts, the jealousy. They would only make her miserable without having any effect on the ones causing it. She allowed herself one look to her brother for fortification and otherwise made it a study to ignore the flirtatious banter occurring across from her. She paid no attention as Penelope laughed through the soup. She didn't listen at all as, over the meat, Emerson detailed his plans for expanding the Fielding plantation, though he had never seen fit to share his thoughts with *her*. She gave no heed when they lapsed into a discourse on whether the Articles of Confederation would suffice or if a constitution ought to be drawn up.

As if Penelope did anything but parrot the arguments Papa and Uncle Moxley had shared earlier in the day. Her cousin cared nothing for politics. Though Lark had a few opinions on the matter, if Emerson ever cared to hear them.

But he didn't. How much clearer could it be? Whatever his reasons had been for proposing, they had obviously included neither her looks nor her wit nor her disposition—he never acknowledged any of them with any insight. And Wiley, the one person who did, would be leaving come morning.

A servant placed her sweet before her, but she felt far too empty inside for that to fill her. Around her whipped five different conversations as everyone caught up, teased, cajoled, and huffed over differing politics. She had tried to put a word in now and then, but she had difficulty following the other four conversations when she was ignoring Emerson and Penelope so thoroughly.

Was this all life had for her? Being forever outside, removed?

Across from her, Penelope swept her lashes down. They glimmered like gold dust upon the cream of her cheek, then lifted again so her icy-blue gaze could pierce through to Lark's very soul. "You look pale, cousin. Are you feeling ill?"

All eyes shifted to Lark, though few had looked her way at any other time. She forced a swallow and shook her head. "I am quite well, thank you."

"Are you?" Isabella, at least, sounded genuinely concerned. "You barely touched your dinner, and your eyes are shadowed. Have you another of your headaches?"

Mamma leaned forward, worry etching her face. "Oh, Lark, you must speak up the moment one sets upon you, you know that. Activity only makes them worse. You ought to be in bed."

"Really, Mamma, I—"

"You do look pale." Papa frowned at her, that warm frown he always gave when about to insist on her better good.

Perhaps it was her imagination, but Aunt Hester looked nearly gleeful as she pronounced, "We cannot have you falling ill, darling, with so much planning to be done over the next weeks. You ought to retire. Nothing soothes a headache like some quiet."

Though her spine could be no straighter, she lifted her chin a notch. "I am well."

"We appreciate your hesitation to complain, dearest, but when one's health is at issue, one must relent." Mamma gave a nod that made the tower of her hair teeter.

"But, Mamma—"

"You know she would never voice a complaint in front of guests." Papa tapped a finger on the table.

"There is no complaint to voice, I am—"

"Do not be stubborn, darling." Emerson's voice rang cool, unconcerned. "You obviously are not feeling yourself. Your aunt is right, you should rest now to avoid illness later. We shall carry on without you."

Something inside her shrank, went cold.

Wiley pressed his lips together. "I highly doubt she is so beset she cannot finish the meal with us. It is the last I shall be with you for nearly two months, after all, and she has not seen her betrothed since her birthday."

Emerson's smile looked anything but reassuring. "I will be happy to return on the morrow."

Of course he would—and his glance at Penelope proved why.

Was it possible for one's blood to still in one's veins? She felt as though it had, as though she watched from afar off. Her presence was obviously unneeded. Woodenly, she stood. "Very well then. I bid you all good night."

The men all leapt to their feet, but even as she left the room, conversation resumed.

She clearly would not be missed.

CHAPTER THREE

Wiley waited until the collection of females adjourned, until the three older gentlemen were engaged in a heated debate on politics, before he took the chair next to Emerson at the table and leaned in close. "Do you take some perverse pleasure in playing the part of a fool, Fielding?"

Emerson paused with his brandy halfway to his lips. "Must we waste your last evening here with nonsense, Wiley?"

Wiley lifted a hand and pointed discreetly at the door through which the ladies had exited. "My cousin is a viper, and you have become her prey. Are you so blind you cannot see it or so stupid you do not care?"

Emerson brought the glass to his lips and took a sip. "Those are my only options? You will not grant that perhaps I enjoyed an evening of diverse company, but that I am in no danger of being declared blind or stupid or foolish?"

"You spent the past three hours flirting shamelessly with a known minx."

"I spent three hours," Emerson returned, leaning toward him, "engaged in conversation with a perfectly respectable young woman who will soon be my cousin. There is no harm in that."

"No harm?" Was the man mad? Wiley shook his head. He would have liked to pound a hand to the table but didn't relish the attention it would draw. "Did you not see my sister's face?"

"Of course I did. She was obviously pained—hence why everyone insisted she rest."

"It was not a headache, Emerson, it was *you*. You and your ghastly behavior. How can you not realize what you do to her? She wants only your affection, your attention once in a while, and you—you are too busy salivating over my cousin to even notice what it is you do!"

Emerson blinked, as if Wiley had lapsed into Dutch midway through his rant. "You are overreacting."

"I am not. Penelope...she has always been this way. A bat of her lashes, a sweet little smile, and she snatches whatever she wants. Whenever we have been in company, what she wants is inevitably what my sister has. Imagine the coup if she were to steal *you*."

"I am not a doll or a slate, Wiley. I cannot be stolen unless I wish to be—which I do not. I will marry your sister."

"Will you?" Wiley pushed away from the table and stood. "That will take more than an emerald and an agreement, Emerson. Something you are yet unwilling to give." He took a step toward the end of the table where his father sat with Mr. Fielding and Moxley. When Father looked his way, Wiley nodded. "Excuse me, sirs, I will go and check on my sister."

He strode from the room, but it wasn't until he had climbed the stairs and traveled the hall of bedchambers that he convinced his teeth to unclench. Blast it, he despised being in a foul humor. It didn't suit him. But now he would spend his entire trip to Annapolis worrying over this mess between Lark and Emerson—and now Penelope. Perhaps he ought to send his regrets to Randel and remain at home to be sure all fell into line.

He passed his own chamber and knocked on the next door. "Lark?"

"Come in, Wiley."

Well, she sounded herself, no tears clogging her voice. That was encouraging. Wiley opened the door and stepped inside, his gaze finding Lark at her writing desk. She had changed into everyday clothing and sat in a position familiar to her—paper and quill before her, a book open at the side.

He closed the door again and moved over to her secretaire. She looked up at him as he approached, giving him a view of her face. It was calm, though he wouldn't have called it serene. Resigned, perhaps. "How are you feeling?"

Her smile was small. "As well as I did before."

"So without a headache but emotionally ravaged?"

She set down her quill. "He knows her not like we do. I am sure he sees only the picture she is so careful to show."

"'Tis no excuse, Lark. He has seen through many another carefully crafted facade, I know not why hers should be any different."

"I am not making his excuses. Only trying to understand." She sighed and tapped the feather of her quill against the side of her paper. "Part of me wants to confront him. The last time I dared to, he set a date for the wedding. Perhaps if I were to be firm on this, he would decide to be a proper bridegroom. But is that what I want? Can I trust him, or should I end this farce and accept the consequences?"

"I wish I had an answer for you." Wiley glanced down at the page. "You have written him?"

"Nothing I intend him to read. I was working through my thoughts. My fears, my hopes. It would all be so much easier if I had been born beautiful, so that he fell in love with me as quickly as Hendricks did Violet. Why could I not have inherited Mother's fair complexion like the two of you?"

He smiled at the tease gleaming in her eye but then fell sober. Certainly, her coloring was different from his or Violet's, her hair having darkened over the years to be closer to their father's deepest brown. But to his eyes both of his sisters were lovely. Violet in a more exuberant way, but Lark…Lark had a quiet depth he had always loved. In her blue eyes dwelt the longing for things he well understood—knowledge, wisdom, a desire to be accepted for who she was. In her soul pulsed a spirit that grew tired of docility, one waiting to leap up, flag waving, and charge into battle.

He had been the same way and had been given the chance to fight for a cause in the Revolution. No longer was he the same man-child who had first gone to battle, and the changes, he felt, were all good… aside from those images that haunted him.

Lark needed the chance to spread her wings, to explore the world outside Endover and Williamsburg. She needed a cause to fight for—and he suspected that cause might need be her own liberty, her own freedom. The question, to his mind, was whether she could emerge from such a war without the nightmares he had brought home with him. Or whether one would even recognize the gift of victory without them.

He shook himself and motioned to the book on her desk. "*Don Quixote* again?"

"It was the only thing I had up here, and I daren't venture downstairs."

"Why ever not? You know well our darling cousin would never darken the door of the library, if she be the one you wish to avoid. Besides, the ladies are all gathered in the parlor with their stitching, and the men will be at their brandy and pipes for a while yet. You could sneak down and back up unseen. Come." He held out a hand to help her up. "Let us fetch you something newer. Have you read the ones I brought home last week?"

She stood, life entering her eyes. "Not all of them. And you know, 'tisn't such a bad turn. A book is far better company than Penelope."

He laughed and led her toward her door. "I readily concur."

They fell into silence for the trip down the stairs. What could he do to ensure his sister's happiness? To help her grow into the songbird that lurked under the quiet demeanor, that only peeked out now and then? A hard question, as he knew only what had worked for him. But he could hardly send her to school in Annapolis or place her under the tutelage of Mr. Randel. He couldn't convince her to come with him even for a visit, much less long enough to effect any changes.

She was right that she couldn't be carted off to the capital with a wedding looming, but Emerson was unlikely to take her there afterward. As much as Wiley had loved the "Athens of America," as they called the city, as much as he had taken to John Randel both in school and later in war, Emerson had never seen eye to eye with him.

He let out a sigh, silent lest his sister wonder about his thoughts. The library door was before them, cracked open. Flickering light spilled out, which was no great surprise. Their father always ended his days in there, so the servants would be sure to have the fire blazing in the hearth, a lamp lit.

Wiley opened the door and stood aside for Lark to precede him.

He regretted it when a shriek of horror spilled from her lips. He jumped into the room to see what had caused her distress and could not stifle the curse that sprang to his tongue.

Emerson stood before the hearth, even now disentangling himself from Penelope's arms. His eyes were wide, either from being caught or at the realization of what he was doing. Wiley was not certain which and frankly didn't give a whit. "Lark, go back to your room."

She made no move to obey. On the contrary, the hands that had flown to her mouth dropped, fisted, and fury lit in her eyes. She had found her battle. But he couldn't let her fight this one, not when the death toll was certain to include her heart. He stayed her with a hand on her shoulder when she would have charged forward, pulled her behind him. "Lark, go. *Now*. I will take care of this."

She turned on him, those blue eyes sparking like the hottest flame. "I will not. I will not suffer this."

For perhaps the first time since he returned home from Yorktown two years prior, he felt his face settle into the hard mask of Lieutenant Benton, rather than the carefree countenance of Wiley. "Trust me."

Her chin lifted, but not in stubbornness this time. Rather, in recognition of a fellow warrior. With one last withering glance over her shoulder, she fled the room.

Wiley settled his attention on the two parties beside the hearth. His gaze bore first into Emerson's guilt-stricken face. Emerson tugged at his waistcoat, his eyes shifting from floor to wallpaper to chair. Wiley transferred his glare to Penelope, who hadn't the sense to look contrite. Or perhaps she tried, but the smugness was far too pronounced to pull it off.

Blood roared through his veins. He was helpless to disobey when it ordered him forward, when it pulled back his arm. He relished the pain in his knuckles when they connected with Emerson's jaw.

"Wiley, no!" Penelope grabbed at his arm and made to put herself between them.

Wiley shook her off. "I ought to challenge you here and now, you swine."

His cousin put on a pout. "I appreciate the concern for my honor, but—"

"*Your* honor?" That nearly made him laugh. "I give not a fig for *your* honor, Penelope, assuming you have any. A woman who would deliberately try to steal another's betrothed is hardly worth the fight. But for my sister..."

"Wiley." Emerson stepped forward, palms out. At least he didn't move to Penelope's side. Wiley would have pummeled him if he had. "You would have every right, but please. 'Tis not what it appeared."

"So you were *not* kissing my cousin when you are betrothed to my sister?"

"I..." Emerson's face went red, and he motioned to Penelope. "She..."

"Threw herself at you? I have no doubt of that, but you made no effort to fight her off."

Penelope huffed, all show of demureness gone. "I did no such thing. I only responded to his advances, and while it was foolhardy, it is hardly my fault. Though now..." In a show worthy of the stage, Penelope flushed and dipped her head, her breathing fast and irregular. "I am shamed to think of how I let him touch me—"

"She is lying, Wiley. Nothing more happened than what you saw!"

"How can you say such a thing?" Tears clouded her eyes now. How could she summon them at will like that? "You cannot deny what happened. Oh, I am so distressed. I must go speak with Mother—"

"Don't even consider it." Wiley gripped her by the arm when she made to walk around him. "You think I cannot see your plan? You will tell some exaggerated tale to your mother so she cries out for him to marry you instead of Lark."

"Well he *must*, now!"

Wiley could all but see the blinders fall from Emerson's eyes. His face turned to a hard mask of fury. "You conniving little doxy!"

She tried on the pout again. "One can hardly blame me for trying to win you, Mr. Fielding. The moment I saw you, I knew in my heart—"

"Nonsense. You only decided you wanted what was Lark's, as Wiley said." Apology now flooded Emerson's expression. As if it weren't too late for that. "A useless maneuver, Miss Moxley. I am marrying your cousin."

He felt Penelope vibrate with rage. "You cannot!"

"In that much she is right." Wiley regarded his friend steadily. "You will not marry my sister now, Emerson. But you, dear cousin, will not shame her by letting it be known why."

Ah, there was the snake, eyes gleaming and lips ready to hiss. "You cannot keep me silent on something of this magnitude, Wiley, especially while you are away."

"Consider my trip canceled." He turned his face toward hers and prayed she had the wit to see he would do whatever it took to achieve her silence. "I will stay right here, and I will keep my gaze steadily on you. Breathe a word of this to anyone, and I shall be forced to confess I am the one with whom you were dallying. I whom you shall be forced to marry. I who shall see you pay for your disloyalty for the rest of your life."

She paled under the powder on her cheeks. "You would never. You detest me."

"Yes, I do. But not as much as I love my sister. So what say you, darling cousin? Is it worth the risk of being under my heel for the rest of your days?"

She jerked her arm away and sneered. "You are a wretch. You are all wretches, every one of you!"

He let her spin away, satisfied she would hold her tongue. She would have no desire to find herself wed to a man who saw right through her. A good thing, because he had no desire to wed a creature so selfish—though he would do it, if it would save the family this other, worse scandal.

"Wiley." Pain dripped from Emerson's tone and undoubtedly lined his face.

Wiley refused to be budged by it or even acknowledge it with his regard. He turned away. "You made your choice, Emerson. Perhaps someday we can repair our friendship, but you will *not* be my brother."

"Wiley!"

He strode from the room, ran up the stairs. Lark would need him. Having never seen her as furious as she had been in the library, he had no idea how she would handle this blow, but one thing was certain—she would not handle it alone.

Not bothering to knock, he let himself into her room. And halted.

Lark flew from her armoire to her bed, where a trunk rested at the foot, while their mother moved calmly about the room and Father leaned against the wall, arms crossed and frown deep.

"What is going on?"

Lark barely glanced at him. Mother offered a small, strained smile. Father straightened and cleared his throat. "Your sister informs us she and Emerson have had a falling-out and she wishes to call off the engagement. We cannot accept so rash a decision, of course—"

"But she obviously needs a bit of space and time to examine her heart," Mother finished for him. She put an encouraging hand on Lark's shoulder. "She will go with you to Annapolis after all, Wiley. She can stay until the first of February, then she must come home in time for the banns to be read."

Lark gripped a gown so tightly Wiley doubted the wrinkles would ever come out. "They will not be read, because there will be no wedding."

"You are overwrought, darling." Mother smoothed a wisp of dark hair from Lark's cheek. "Once you have some time to cool your temper, I am certain you will see the wisdom of keeping the wedding plans intact. One cannot call off a long-standing betrothal because of one quarrel."

"One quarrel?" Lark pulled away and tossed the gown into her trunk. "It is far worse than that, Mamma."

"Well then tell me what it is. Tell me why you fought."

His sister shook her head and strode to the secretaire, where a pile of boxes stood. If he weren't mistaken, they were the ones the Fielding jewels had always been delivered in.

She slid the emerald ring off her finger and put it on top of the boxes. "Just promise me you will not tell him where I go. Promise me."

His parents both sighed, exchanged a look. Nodded.

Wiley swallowed and glanced at each of them. While he applauded his parents for taking such quick action in getting Lark out of Williamsburg, he suspected Emerson would eventually sway them to his side. They were too determined to avoid the scandal of a broken betrothal.

"I will make sure of it, Larksong." He offered a tight, mirthless smile when her wide-eyed gaze sought him. "You will go with the Thomases tomorrow in my place, and I shall send a note to Mr. Randel posthaste letting him know of the change in plans. I will stay here and make sure Emerson does not discover your whereabouts." And ensure that Penelope held her tongue.

Mother sighed and rubbed at her eyes. "Wiley—"

"You will not sway me, Mother. Lark will be well cared for with the Thomases. I will see after her wishes here."

Father was shaking his head before Wiley even finished. "Be reasonable, son. It is too long a trip for her to take alone, in winter."

"The Thomases will be fine company and will certainly keep her as safe as I could."

"That is hardly the point!" Father paused, drew in a long breath. "If I am to send my unmarried daughter to Maryland so near Christmas, I will send her with someone dear to her."

Wiley arched his brows Lark's way.

Her hands clenched and unclenched; her nostrils flared. Then she moistened her lips. "As much as I would like to have Wiley's company, I would feel better knowing he was here with Emerson."

Father tugged rather forcefully at his waistcoat. "Absolutely not. Wiley will—"

"Now, just a moment, dear." Contemplation on her face, Mother came over to place a hand on Father's arm. "I'm certain Lark *will* feel more lonely without Wiley." She gave Father a pointed look. "And assuming Emerson did err, Wiley could certainly do good here, talking with him of it."

Wiley found his mother's motive rather too obvious, but he would take agreement in whatever form it was offered. "Exactly right, Mother."

Mother turned back to Lark. "But you must at least write him a letter, Lark, explaining why you have chosen to leave."

She raised her chin. "No. Let him wonder."

Wiley chuckled, even as he spotted the note she had already penned. It might do Emerson good to know what she really thought of him. "If you have everything packed, Lark, we had better see you to the Thomases tonight. They want to get an early start, and if you mean to attract no attention…"

Father looked pained. "I suppose that is best—we ought to keep it quiet as possible, and thank Providence arrangements have already been made with a family as respectable as the Thomases." Even as she looked at him, she was fastening her cloak. Father held her gaze firmly. "You must be sure. You have never been away from home, and if your brother will not be going…well, there is no turning back."

Her smile might not have been as bright as usual, but it was braver, and more determined. "I am done with turning back, Father. I want only to go forward."

Wiley hefted her trunk and motioned to the door with his head. "Then let's be gone."

Emerson probed the bruise on his jaw, his wince more from guilt than the physical throb. He had hoped to wake up and find the whole incident a nightmare.

He ought to have known the worst ones were always real.

What was the matter with him? Something, surely, or he would not have been such a fool. Had he really thought an evening's flirtation would mean nothing to Miss Moxley? He had barely stopped to think about it. It had been enough that she was pretty, attentive… that she reminded him so acutely of Elizabeth.

His eyes slid shut. That should have been his first warning.

"Here you are, Mr. Emerson."

He forced a smile for his stable hand and took the reins to his prized mare. "Thank you, Tommy." In one smooth movement, he mounted and urged the horse along the familiar trek to Endover.

Every time he blinked, Lark's horror-stricken face haunted him. He had seen tragedy enough in his days—men torn apart by ordnance and bayonet, ravaged by frostbite and starvation, broken by disease and exhaustion—but this was worse. When she had stepped into the library last night, it was as if he had seen her for the first time, and what met his gaze was a broken heart.

She had loved him. For the first time that struck him squarely, and only because he knew she did no longer. He had seen the death of her affection in her eyes seconds before anger had obliterated it. With its loss he had to wonder that it had ever been his. He had done nothing to deserve her affection, her devotion.

But he deserved the wrath and consequences. Still, he prayed God would grant him mercy and one more chance. Just one. He would do it honor this time. He would make things right, do what he ought to have done ages ago. Salvage the reputations of their families.

The mile between their homes seemed to stretch for eternity, yet when he arrived at the familiar columns of the Bentons' Great House, he wished it had taken longer still. He had not allowed himself to consider Wiley's wrath—hadn't wanted to. He'd seen it enough in the war, aimed at others. It was all the more disconcerting because it stood in such marked contrast to his usual amiable humor.

Would his friend truly have canceled his trip? Would he be there, barring the door? Or might he allow Emerson in to make his apologies to Lark and beg her forgiveness? For that matter, her parents had obviously been told there had been some kind of disagreement, given their avoidance of his gaze last night after the incident. They might themselves forbid him entrance.

He handed the reins to a servant, jogged up the few steps to the door. It opened before him, but the visage of the old servant holding it told him all was not well in Endover this morning. "What is the matter, Asa?"

The man shook his gray head. "Mr. Benton said you'd likely be by. They waitin' for you in the breakfast room, sir."

"Thank you, I shall head that way." He spared no time for passing off his cloak and hat, just charged in the appropriate direction until he entered the room.

Wiley indeed sat within, grim-faced and angry-eyed. His parents both occupied their usual seats, solemn and silent. Lark was nowhere to be seen, nor were any of the Moxleys. Clearing his throat, Emerson swept his hat off his head. "Good morning."

"Emerson." Mr. Benton stood, tugged down his waistcoat. "We imagined you would be by. Please, sit. We must speak with you."

In spite of his nod, Emerson couldn't convince his feet to budge. "What is it? Lark? I know she is angry and upset, but if I could have a moment to speak with her..."

"I am afraid that will not happen at this juncture. Emerson. Son." Benton drew in a deep breath and met his gaze. "She wishes to call off the engagement. We will not allow such a rash decision without due consideration, but we have granted her the time to contemplate it. She has left Williamsburg."

A stone of dread sank to the pit of his stomach. She had left? Left him alone to face the embarrassment of a broken engagement? "She...but sir, we can mend this. Where has she gone? She cannot yet be far, I will go after her."

"You will *not*. That is precisely why I have stayed here, to make sure of it." Wiley pushed forward an all-too-familiar pile of boxes. Onto the top he tossed a piece of stationery, folded but not sealed. "She left this for you."

He ignored the continued babble of Mrs. Benton, the low mumbles of Mr. Benton, as he reached for it. With his blood pounding he could barely hear them anyway. It was all he could do to hold the paper steady enough to read it.

> *I want only to be known, to be loved. Why, my darling Emerson, is that so much to ask? Is there something wrong with my person? With my company? If there is, why did you ever speak for me and give me hope you could love me? I see clearly now you cannot. Do not, at the least. Ought I to relinquish all my dreams, all my affections, and set a different course? Or resign myself to a life of loneliness with you?*
>
> *Yet I will not give up hope—hope that if not with you, I can find my purpose elsewhere. If that is what I must do, then so be it. I shall bid you farewell.*

His insides twisted. She had been so willing to love him selflessly, in spite of his showing her his worst. Now he had surely lost her, a young woman any man should be proud to make his wife. There was only so much she could forgive, and he had used up his allotment through the past two years of neglect. She would never allow him to discover what he had been blind to.

But he could not be content with this glimpse.

He turned to face her family. Wiley glared at him with condemnation, Mrs. Benton with pleading, Mr. Benton with a simmering detachment. Emerson forced a swallow. "Will you not give me some idea where she has gone?"

"We gave her our word," Mr. Benton said softly. "Give her the time she needs, Emerson. We are confident she will make the right choice and wed you happily."

Wiley's snort belied Mr. Benton's confidence. Emerson met his gaze, but it seemed a stone wall, insurmountable.

He sucked in a long breath. "I am afraid I cannot rest with this between us, sir. If you will not tell me where she went, then I will discover it for myself so I might hasten to beg her forgiveness."

He would, no matter what it took. He just prayed the Lord would preserve her person and soften her heart in the meantime.

CHAPTER FOUR

Annapolis, Maryland

Lark clamped down on quivering nerves. As the Thomases' carriage turned onto North Street, a biting wind gusted, slicing through the wooden sides, her cloak, and cutting straight to the bone. She moved her feet toward the once-warm brick, but it had been too long out of the fire and offered her toes no respite. Perhaps fleeing to Annapolis hadn't been the best plan. Perhaps she ought to have gone southward instead. Surely Wiley had some friend in Georgia who could have offered her sanctuary.

Mrs. Thomas shivered and pulled her fur wrap around her. "Why anyone would want to live upon the bay like this I can scarce fathom. That wind!"

Her husband grinned and tapped on the roof. "'Tis a blessing in the summer months, I expect. And here we are, Miss Benton." The man nodded toward the houses standing sentinel along the street. "Mr. Randel is at number 19, you say?"

So said the note Wiley had sent with her, which was tucked into her embroidery pocket. She nodded and swallowed against the anxiety building in her stomach. What if the Randels were not at home? What if Wiley's letter had not yet reached them? What if they were unwilling to take a stranger into their midst at this time of year meant for family?

Lark drew in a breath and forced her fears to a halt before they led her into thoughts of her own family, who were probably regretting allowing her to leave so near Christmastide. "I thank you again, Mr. Thomas, for seeing me safely here."

"Happy to do it, Miss Benton. We had the room, since your brother remained at home." The moment the carriage slowed enough, he opened the door and jumped out, not waiting for his servant. "Shall we make certain they are within?"

Lark smoothed a hand over the curls of their daughter, asleep beside her, and nodded. Mr. Thomas helped her down and poked his head back inside. "Will you wait here, my dear, or come in with us?"

Mrs. Thomas smiled. "Given that Henrietta is still asleep, we shall stay here. Good-bye, Lark. Enjoy your stay."

"Good-bye. And I shall, thank you." Beside Mr. Thomas, she headed up the brick walk.

The door flew open, and a blur of blue and cream streaked down the steps. Lark heard a bellowing, "Sena Katherine Randel, turn back this instant!" right before the blur plowed into her.

Her squeal blended with the shriek of surprise from the figure— presumably this Sena—as they tumbled together to the icy bricks. Not the reception she had expected, but at least she could be sure someone was home.

"Oh my." A gasp turned to laughter as the unfamiliar young woman sat up and pulled Lark with her, then dusted off a bit of snow stuck to Lark's cloak. "I suppose this is why Mamma and Mrs. Green caution me not to run everywhere I go. I'm terribly sorry, miss. Are you injured?"

"I am quite well." Lark couldn't help but smile into the laughing emerald eyes. This would be Mr. Randel's eldest child, who was, she believed, a year her younger. The one everyone supposed would be a friend for her. Strange how no one had mentioned that Sena was every bit as beautiful as cousin Penelope. More so, given the spark of good humor that lit her countenance. Why was Lark forever relegated to being the plain friend? Ah, well. At least Miss Randel looked prone to good humor. "Though next time you bowl me over, you could toss a cushion to the bricks first, and I would not object. Or perhaps aim me at a snow pile."

The young lady laughed again, and they pulled each other to their feet, Mr. Thomas and a plump, gray-haired woman lending a hand. Miss Randel dropped a polite curtsey. "What a way to meet someone. I am Miss Sena Randel, in case you missed Mrs. Green bellowing it."

"A pleasure to meet you, Miss Randel. I am—"

"Tut!" The plump woman—presumably Mrs. Green and most likely the housekeeper, given her dress—raised a hand and furrowed her brows. "I recognize those features, sure as day. You are Wiley Benton's sister, the Miss Lark Benton we have been expecting."

"Quite right. My brother's letter preceded me, then?"

A new figure emerged from the house, this time a gentleman. Mr. Randel, if her brother's descriptions could be trusted. He had fair brown hair pulled back in a queue and wore breeches and a jacket of excellent quality—but rumpled. He smiled much like his daughter. "Indeed it did, and we are much pleased to have your company. Now—our housekeeper has a memory better than any in these United States, but she seems to have forgotten to invite you in out of the cold."

"Oh, do forgive me! First the young miss flies out the door like a heathen, then the two of you go sprawling—it must have dashed my wits. Come inside, you poor dear." Gentle hands gripped Lark's elbows, though Mrs. Green scowled at Miss Randel. "And Sena, you will come too, after such an atrocious introduction, and I shan't hear another word of argument. Dashing off yet again without a proper escort... And no pouting—as Poor Richard says, 'If you would have guests merry with cheer, be so yourself, or so at least appear.' "

Miss Randel's lips twitched up. "Well, I shan't argue with Mr. Franklin, to be sure. It never gets me anywhere with so staunch a devotee as you defending his every word. Lead the way, Papa."

Mr. Randel held open the door, his gaze fastened on Lark. "Your brother's letter said we could enjoy your company at least through the end of January, perhaps longer. Have you a set schedule, or might we persuade you to remain with us through spring? Sena is in need of another young woman to keep her from trouble."

"No, I—that is, yes..." Lark sighed to a halt. "My parents gave me permission to stay only until the first of February, as they want me home in ample time for my March wedding. But I, in fact, have cried off the betrothal and hope they will come to accept that in my absence. If I must stay here through the proposed wedding date to assure it, I will."

"Indeed?" Mr. Randel motioned Mr. Thomas in as well, then

shut the door on the biting wind. He turned back to her with a grin. "To Mr. Fielding? Well. While I do not condone running from one's problems in general, I am in full favor of avoiding that particular gentleman wherever one may. We shall make every effort to shelter you from such a dreadful match and anyone in favor of it."

Miss Randel gasped and clutched a hand over her heart. "Oh, how thrilling! A fugitive in our midst. I imagine any day now the infamous Mr. Fielding will come banging on our door, demanding the return of his beloved. For once a little excitement will visit us!"

Lark felt caught between a grin and a sigh. "I am afraid that is unlikely, Miss Randel. For though I may have been his betrothed, I was never his beloved." After a week of sloshing through winter mud and dismal, cold rains, she had come to grips with that. His pride might sting when her family returned his jewels, but he would recover. And undoubtedly not waste a moment of concern over her, much less go through the trouble of finding her.

Her young hostess gaped as if such news were beyond comprehension. "Quite impossible, Miss Benton! My father cannot have been so right about him, especially concerning so lovely a lady as you."

Her father laughed and shook his head. "You ought not take it personally, Miss Benton. I have observed many a time Mr. Fielding is capable only of duty. Duty brought him to King William's School, duty sent him to Oxford, duty brought him back to the war. But there was never anything behind the duty, neither passion nor conviction to deepen it. He did only what was expected, *because* it was expected, which means he never excelled but rather was content to exist. I've little use for a man like that, and you surely deserve better as well. Say good riddance to him and enjoy the holidays here with us."

Yes, that was exactly Emerson's problem—she had been only a duty to him, never anything more. She nodded, grateful to Mr. Randel for putting words to it. "I shall, at that." When he grinned, Lark knew immediately why her brother liked this man so much—they were of a spirit, Mr. Randel and Wiley. Except that Wiley tended to look beyond the actual and search out the potential in a person— perhaps why he liked Emerson. Mr. Randel must be rooted more in reality.

Mr. Thomas shifted behind her and stepped back into the entryway. "Shall I bring in your things?"

"My man and I will assist you," Mr. Randel said. "Sena, why do you not introduce Miss Benton to your mother before the boys return with all their enthusiasm?" The two gentlemen headed out, a manservant behind them.

Miss Randel grabbed her hand and gave it a squeeze. Her bright green eyes sparkled with excitement. "How marvelous it shall be to have a friend with me for the holidays! I cannot tell you the thrill it gave me when we received your brother's letter. I think Papa had hopes of saddling your unsuspecting brother with me, but this is far better. A new friend! You must call me Sena, of course, and I hope you shall allow me to call you Lark."

"I would like that. Thank you, Sena."

Sena whipped her cloak off, and Lark followed suit, handing it to Mrs. Green. A moment later she followed Sena up the staircase. The ascent gave her a view of the bottom floor of the house, showcasing the lovely plasterwork and gleaming wood. Much smaller than Endover, but beautiful. "I cannot thank you all enough for having me."

"Oh, 'tis hardly a favor." Sena grinned over her shoulder. "Having another young lady in the house will be pure pleasure. I've three younger brothers, you see, and my dearest friend rarely ventures out. Nor does Mamma these days."

Cheerful company might be the perfect medicine for her as well. Lark smiled. "I know what you mean—my sister married five years ago, and it has been considerably more boring since then."

"I imagine you have friends in Williamsburg who will miss you, though."

A rueful chuckle slipped out. "Yes—but unfortunately, they are all Fieldings."

Sena linked their elbows when they reached the second floor. "You will have to provide me with an exaggerated tale of this broken engagement. I want only the boring details spared and every interesting one magnified. Have you someone to make a proper villain of? If not, I shall help you create a monster from some poor, ignorant neighbor."

How could Lark help but laugh? "I think you shall be satisfied with the villainy of my dastardly cousin Penelope, who tried to steal Emerson from me."

Sena's eyes went wide. "I despise her already. Here we are." She stopped before a partially opened door and knocked lightly upon it. "Mamma, are you awake?"

"Come in, Sena."

With another smile at Lark, Sena nudged open the door and stepped in. "I have brought you a gift."

Lark moved into the room too, which was bathed in soft golden light and a warmth that went deeper than one made by fire. Immediately at home, she drew in a peaceful breath and sought out the lady of the house.

Mrs. Randel rose from a settee, her smile as bright as Sena's, her round stomach proving why she didn't go often into society these days. "Oh, a guest! How marvelous. I am Martha Randel. You must be young Mr. Benton's sister."

"Lark Benton, madam." She dipped a quick curtsey and smiled.

Mrs. Randel approached and held out a hand for Lark to clasp. "How delightful. We were beginning to fear the weather would detain you forever. You are staying at least a month, are you not?"

Sena nodded. "She is escaping a betrothal with the infamous Mr. Fielding, you see, so must hide from him here. Hopefully through spring."

A glance at the matron showed she was amused at her daughter's theatrics. Lark smiled all the more. "For certain until February, hopefully into March as well."

When Sena clapped, Mrs. Randel chuckled. "See there, Sena dear. You asked for a sister for Christmas, and Providence provided—no matter what this baby is or when he or she arrives."

Commotion in the hallway drew them all out. Misters Randel and Thomas tromped up the stairs with wind-pinked cheeks, servant behind them. Her host smiled. "We shall have to put you in with Sena, Miss Benton. I do hope that poses no problem."

"'Tis quite fine, Mr. Randel."

"'Tis perfect, in fact." Sena ran ahead of her father to open the door to what must have been her room. "It shall provide us a means to giggle and dream without restriction."

"I have no doubt you would have found a way regardless, my sweet." He set down Lark's bag and turned back with a lifted brow. "If you wish to pen a note to your family letting them know you arrived safely, I have a missive to send off to Wiley myself."

"Thank you." Something akin to excitement, yet tinged with exhaustion, buzzed inside her. The Randels were more than she could have hoped for in conspirators. But oh, that no conspiracy had been necessary.

Emerson swept his tricorn off his head and stepped into the coffeehouse. Outside the sky was bleak and gray, the clouds swollen with impending snow. In R. Charlton's, however, men's voices raised in jest, rang out in laughter, and the smells of coffee and wood smoke lent the air a welcoming tang.

He wasn't in the mood for being welcomed. Especially since when he spotted his father and Mr. Benton at a table in the corner, they looked at him as though he wore a dunce cap.

Wiley, yet again, was nowhere in sight. As he had remained for the past week, whenever Emerson tried to find him. Though supposedly intent upon watching him, his friend had apparently deemed it sufficient to do so from a distance.

Or perhaps keeping Miss Moxley in line required all his attention.

Emerson scraped a chair out and plunked onto it, nodding at Father and Benton.

Mr. Benton's lips thinned. "I know you are distressed, Emerson. I am uneasy myself, given the weather that has descended upon us since Lark left. But we must trust Providence to keep her safe and rest in the certainty that this time will serve to endear your memory to her."

Not likely. Not until he could speak with her. Surely he could convince Wiley to disclose her whereabouts...if Wiley ever made himself available for questioning. "Please, sir, I must go to her. This is not a squabble that will pass with a little time and distance. We must sit and address it. Face to face."

Benton exchanged a glance with Emerson's father and sighed. "Mrs. Benton and I have discussed this at length, as have your parents, Emerson. No one will tell us what this disagreement of yours was about, but we cannot fathom it was anything so serious as to justify Lark's reaction. Hence our decision not to cancel the wedding. So far as anyone else knows, Lark merely took a scheduled trip to visit an old friend and had to seize the good weather while it held."

What could Emerson do but sigh and nod?

Another acquaintance hailed Benton, and he stood and took a step away to greet him. Father leaned in. "If I have learned anything through my years of marriage, it is that one ought not underestimate the stubbornness of an angry woman. I cannot convince Benton to tell me where she is, but you are right to think you must find her."

"I know. I will." He just had no idea how. No one in town had seen her on the morning in question, and he couldn't probe deeper without letting it be known he had no clue where his intended had gone.

He plunged a hand into his pocket and wrapped it around the ring he had slid on her finger two years ago. The night remained clear enough in his memory—the Bentons had thrown a splendid gala to honor her eighteenth birthday. He had walked into the ballroom with the ring in his pocket, his decision made.

Had he been ready to marry? No. Not with the war still so fresh in his mind, with the nightmares plaguing him every time he slept. Each and every night, a variation on the same theme. Rushing into battle, bayonet aimed at a random Redcoat…then the realization that the enemy he had just killed was in fact a friend from King William's School or Oxford.

It had happened in reality once. In his dreams, nightly.

No, he was in no condition then to take a wife. But when his parents suggested it might help him move forward and heal, it had seemed a fine plan. And who better to wed than unassuming little Lark? She would love him without demanding anything in return.

What a fool he had been. He had danced with her, made some compliment to her looks, though he had not spared any attention to what would have been a costly dress, hair that had probably taken hours to style just so. Had he even looked into her eyes as he led her to the quiet of the library and pulled out the emerald?

He remembered the sharp intake of her breath when he proposed. The shock in her "Of course, Emerson. *Of course*." The guilty relief when he ticked that item off his mental list of things to accomplish.

"Emerson." Mr. Benton had sat down again and leaned close, much like Father had done, his voice low.

"Please, tell me we are not making a mistake by keeping the wedding plans in place. What happened? What did you do?"

He ran a thumb over the smooth, flat stone in his pocket, let the gold circle fit onto the top of his finger. "It is more what I failed to do, sir. I never took the time to know her as she deserved." Surely if he had, that incident with Penelope never would have happened. Or if it had, she would have listened to his apologies.

Her father frowned and shook his head. "Lark is not usually so given to frivolity. Why did she not realize there would be time for that after the wedding?"

"I suppose she thought if I had not done so in the last two years, I wouldn't in the next two." With his free hand, he pinched the bridge of his nose. She was undoubtedly right. He might have told himself he would come to love her naturally over time, but he'd had no intention of making it so, not if it required effort. As with Newton's *Principia* at King William's School—he had never fully understood it, just learned enough to secure the marks he needed in class. It had all faded as soon as he left academia. He would have done the same with Lark, been content to merely appear devoted without ever opening his heart to her.

Not now. Now if she gave him another chance, he would use it wisely. If she rejected him again, let it be for the scars within he would show her, rather than for the lack of showing.

CHAPTER FIVE

Lark gazed out the window, its edges laced with frost, and into the still morning. One lone wagon rattled down Tabernacle Street, but otherwise she could see no one out yet. From other windows in the house she could see the State House's dome, but her current view afforded her nothing but the empty street and acres of snow-covered green across from it.

Hunched in the cold fog was the crumbling silhouette of an abandoned mansion. From her brother's descriptions of the city, she knew it must be Bladen's Folly—the mistake the former governor was most notorious for. Given the hulk of the shadow, she could see how large it was meant to be. But now it stood broken and empty, naught but a vacant dream.

Lark pulled her shawl tight and rubbed her hands over her arms. Perhaps Governor Bladen had overreached his budget in commissioning the mansion, but she could hardly condemn him for it. He had been the leader of the Free State—why would he not want everyone to see what he had attained? Yet decades later, everyone laughed at him.

Just as everyone would laugh at her for thinking she ever had a chance at holding Emerson's heart. She was as foolish as Bladen, building dreams that exceeded her allotment.

"Trying to make out the Liberty Tree?"

Lark spun around as Sena reentered the room in her dressing gown, wearing a smile. Lark lifted a brow. "Pardon?"

Her new friend joined her at the window and pointed to a stretching shadow near the would-be governor's mansion. "The Liberty Tree—there, on the corner of Bladen's Folly's lot. The Sons of Liberty met there to plan out our part in the Revolution. There they plotted the Annapolis Tea Party and the sinking of the *Peggy Stewart*. And before that, the first Methodist sermon in Maryland was delivered under its boughs by Joseph Pilmoor." Sena let out a happy sigh. "The British destroyed all the Liberty Trees in the other states, but ours remained out of their reach. 'Tis the last one standing. A symbol of all our nation represents."

A symbol of liberty, so near one of folly? Lark drew in a long breath and nodded. Fitting. Perhaps she had made a mistake, but now she was free of it. Free of the bonds of what would have been a loveless marriage, free of her own insipid longings. "I would like to see it up close at some point."

"We shall walk that direction on the next fair day. But today..." Lark grinned as Sena twirled away from the window. "Today, I shall introduce you to my dearest friend, Kate, and her brother. You will adore them, Lark, and they you. Kate is a bit shy, but I know she will take to you. It is always such fun to be the means by which others become friends." When a maid silently entered, Sena whirled to a halt beside her armoire and opened the door to it, pulled out a lovely striped dress in the Louis XVI style.

Soon afterward they descended to the main floor of the house and toward the unmistakable sound of three young boys in the holiday spirit. Lark had met Johnny, Will, and Mark at dinner the night before and had not been surprised to find that the young men—aged thirteen, eight, and five—were even more mischievous than their sister.

Life with the Randels ought not to be dull.

The sideboard boasted a few platters of steaming food, and Lark helped herself to a cup of coffee. Mrs. Randel was not within, but the patriarch sat at the head of the table, the *Maryland Gazette* before him.

"Anything interesting, Papa?" Sena asked as she picked up a plate.

Her father lifted one corner of his mouth. "To me? Quite. To you? I somehow doubt it. Only record amounts of snow, temperatures below zero in New England, and delegates still refusing to come to Annapolis because of it. No pirate attacks, no princes in disguise, no knights attacking windmills..."

"Dull as always."

Lark chuckled and helped herself to a warm corn cake. "What is wrong with the world, that there are no longer knights-errant waging war against wayward windmills?"

"Exactly my question." Sena slid a sausage onto her plate. "You have read *Don Quixote*."

"Several times. 'Tis one of my favorites."

Johnny made a face and shoveled a heaping bite of bread into his mouth. "I despise that book."

His father smacked him lightly with his newspaper. "If your mother saw you talking with a mouthful..."

Johnny swallowed and grinned. "She would forgive it, given the topic. She dislikes *Don Quixote* as much as I."

Breakfast passed in similar conversation. Lark laughed with the others, chimed in with a word here or there, and felt a part of it all despite not knowing these people yet a full day.

So very different from that last meal with the Fieldings and Moxleys.

Mr. Randel folded his paper and stood. "Sena, might I assume you and Miss Benton will be paying a visit to the Calverts this morning?"

"Absolutely, Papa. I must introduce Lark and Kate."

He nodded. "Ask them to dinner on Christmas. None of the rest of their family has returned to the city, and I know it will be lonely for them."

Lark could only attribute the tears in Sena's eyes to her habitual exaggeration. Why else should the invitation be so striking?

"I will, Papa. Thank you. I know they will appreciate it."

Mr. Randel nodded, but his expression was a bit odd.

Lark couldn't hope to determine why. She drank the last of her coffee. "I have heard of the Maryland Calverts—are your friends related?"

Sena's face went sober for the first time since she bowled Lark over the previous afternoon. "Indeed. They are not direct descendants of Lord Calvert, mind you, but close enough. Close enough."

Close enough for...what? To be blamed for the family's ties to England? Perhaps. It made as much sense as anything. But who was she to look down her nose upon someone for their associations? "Well, I look forward to making their acquaintance."

"Which you shall do soon." Sena shook off the sobriety and smiled. "Let us go check on my mother, then head over. Now that I've a proper companion, we needn't even trouble a maid or Papa to see us there."

Mr. Randel sighed as he headed for the door. "But you are only to go there and back. No running about the town without escort, Sena. Do you understand?"

Lark could hardly fathom why he felt the need to issue such instruction…until she saw the gleam of mischief in Sena's eyes when she said, "Oh, of course, Papa. Of course."

Edwinn Calvert reread the missive for the seventh time, but still the words did not change. His request had been denied. Again. And this time without such politeness as he had received before. Without a mask of manners to soften the slap.

Perhaps, a clerk from the governor's office had written, *you ought to have considered this before you cast your allegiance where you did.*

Edwinn rubbed a weary hand over his aching forehead and rested his elbow on the desk at which he sat. Not his desk, not his room. Not his house.

At this rate, he might never see his own home again.

"Bad news?"

Edwinn looked over his shoulder as Kate entered the room. His sister offered an encouraging smile, but her cheer could not change facts. He sighed. "They still refuse. I know provisions were included in the Treaty of Paris, but at this point I have my doubts they ever intend to return our property. The war has been over for two years already, and still…"

Gentle fingers rested on his shoulder. "I know. And if they will not, then we keep on as we have been doing. Return to the plantation or purchase a more modest home here."

Yes, but another home would not be *their* home. The one their grandfather had built, the one they had been raised in. And he couldn't take them back to the plantation, where Kate all but faded away and stopped speaking. Not to mention they needed to preserve what silver they had left to live on, and to provide a dowry for Kate.

Assuming anyone in these new United States would deign to marry the bashful sister of a Tory. His reasons for remaining loyal to the Crown were never heard—they all just saw his allegiance and judged. No listening to reason, no prospect of understanding. Were it up to his neighbors, he would be forced from the land entirely, shipped off to England or up to Canada.

Kate craned forward to look out the window. "There comes Sena—with a friend, it looks like." Her delicate brow creased with worry. "I do not recognize her."

A corner of Edwinn's lips twitched up. "Well, you know Sena. She could trip over a brick and declare it her newest friend." He made his voice quiet, encouraging. "Go ahead out and receive them, Katie. You know she would never bring anyone here unless she thought her someone you would like."

Kate turned those trusting, loving eyes on him and blinked. "Will you join us? You mustn't stay in here brooding."

What was he to do but pat her hand and dig up a smile? "I shall be out forthwith. I only want to write a letter to Uncle Calvert first."

Kate loosed a long breath and nodded. "They will see reason eventually, Edwinn. The Calverts helped build this country—they will not hold our ancestral estates from us forever."

He nodded his agreement...but was none too sure.

As his sister glided from the room, Edwinn considered the stationery and quill before him. Instead of picking it up, he stood. His hand reached for his cane as he slid over to the many-paned window. Through the slight waves in the glass he could see the frosty, wind-bitten world. The trees, all devoid of leaves. The sky, a low-hanging gray today. The citizens, dashing about with cloaks and hats through snow piles from the last storm.

Those years during the war that had forced him away from Annapolis, he had felt like a wanderer. Oh, he knew he made the right decision in leaving—the Patriot stronghold was no place for a "Sympathizer of the Crown"—but the plantation in the wilds of Maryland had never felt like his own, and Kate had no friends there whatsoever. They had hastened back to the city as soon as the war was over.

But their home…it was no longer their home.

Father God, I know not where to go from here. Is it Your will I live out my days like this? If so, I will. You have been gracious enough to provide the silver to keep us, even as tenants. But please, help me to find a way to become part of society again. Help my old friends to see I am the same man I was before the war, that it was not cowardice that led me away from their cause.

He leaned on his cane and sighed. A cloud of condensation fanned across the glass of the window, then faded away. When the wind gusted down the street, a draft whistled in. The cold made his leg throb.

Feminine laughter rang out from the drawing room. That, at least, brought a smile to his lips. In spite of the opinions of Annapolis's gentlemen, Kate still had her dearest friend at her side, the one person other than family to ever draw her out. Which meant that though he might feel the pangs of ostracism, she did not. Praise the Lord for that.

Edwinn turned from the window and sat down again, resting his cane against the desk. It took only a moment to pen the latest news for their uncle. He'd let the ink dry while he paid his respects to Sena and her companion, then send it off in the post.

Giggling met his ears as he stepped from his study. He smiled and moved across the entryway to the room opposite. His cane tapped with every other step, but the young ladies didn't seem to hear him. He entered unnoticed, giving him a moment to take in the scene.

Kate sat on the settee, her hand clasped in Sena's, both with heads thrown back in laughter. He always enjoyed seeing them together, his sister with her russet curls yet even temperament, Sena with her dark locks and sense of adventure. Perhaps an unlikely pair, the spirited and the shy, but ever since they were children, they had been inseparable.

Except during the war, of course.

He kept himself from looking at Sena overlong. She would be an easy young lady to admire, but what was the use? Her father now counted Edwinn an enemy. Instead, he set his gaze to wandering to the stranger, who sat on Kate's other side. He drew in a long breath. She had hair of a warm brown, eyes of an endless, deep blue. A face more sweet than stunning…and sorrow lurking behind an affable mask.

How well he knew that feeling.

Perhaps she felt his gaze, for her eyes turned from the girls to him. What was that, that made him feel as if he knew her, though even her name was a mystery? The faintest hint of a blush infused her fair cheeks.

Edwinn offered a smile and then cleared his throat and forced his gaze back to Kate and Sena. "Good morning, ladies."

"There you are, Mr. Calvert." Sena's brilliant smile tempted him to let his thoughts dwell on her. "Allow me to introduce Miss Lark Benton of Endover Plantation, near Williamsburg. Lark, Kate's elder brother, Mr. Edwinn Calvert."

Of nowhere. No longer of Calvert Street, no longer at the Briers Plantation. He bent at the waist. "A pleasure to make your acquaintance, Miss Benton. I do hope you are enjoying Annapolis."

She nodded and smiled. "I only arrived yesterday, but I am sure I will enjoy it immensely, thank you."

A smile played around the corners of Kate's mouth, proving this new acquaintance was one she liked. Perhaps one she could grow comfortable with. "Lark will be staying with the Randels until spring."

Spring? She would be here for months, then. Long enough for Kate to warm to her, though otherwise it could hardly affect him. No matter how sweet her features, how alluring her eyes, he was beyond seeking romance in every lovely new acquaintance.

These past years had taught him that if the Lord called him to wed and start a family, he would have to travel into British territory to find a wife. And given how near he was to thirty, and the leg that made travel so uncomfortable…bachelorhood would have to suffice.

Yet the lecture did little to quiet the whisper of wistfulness. Was it so wrong to wish for a companion? To wish he had the freedom of other, Patriot men, to pay court to the young women around him and discover what match the Lord might have in store for him?

Edwinn renewed his smile and took the chair across from them. "The three of you will have ample time for mischief, then." To Miss Benton he added, "It is inevitable when in the company of these two."

Her smile was like the unfurling of a rose. "I determined as much the moment Sena knocked me to the sidewalk yesterday afternoon."

A chuckle slipped out. "Bowling over visitors now, are you, Miss Randel?"

"It was all Mrs. Green's fault, chasing me with a rolling pin as she was." Sena's eyes gleamed.

Miss Benton laughed. "She had no rolling pin."

"She must have dropped it in the bushes before you saw her. She was determined I not leave the house without escort, though no one could be spared to come with me, and I was determined to reach Kate before another snowstorm struck." Her attempt at a serious face gave way to a grin. "Well, perhaps she had only a metaphorical rolling pin. Still, I would not have run directly into Miss Benton had I not been so set on escaping her and her infernal Poor Richard quotes. She was screeching, 'Glass, china, and reputations are easily crack'd, and never well mended' from the moment I descended the stairs."

He'd heard stories enough of Mrs. Green to laugh with the ladies, though he had met the Randels' housekeeper—a distant cousin of Mrs. Randel—only a few times.

"Well, we are glad to have you in our fair town for a while." Kate graced the visitor with a small but warm smile and stood to meet Mrs. Haslip, who entered with the tea service. "Everyone likes chocolate, correct?"

After the chorus of agreements, Sena grinned again. "I have yet to tell you the most exciting part of Lark's presence, Kate. She is a runaway!"

Coming from anyone else, that pronouncement might have shocked Edwinn into dropping the silver cup of steaming chocolate Kate handed him. Given its source, he merely sipped and waited for an explanation.

Kate, however, always fed her friend's dramatic bent. The moment her hands were free, they flew to cover her mouth. "A runaway?"

He suspected the flush in Miss Benton's cheeks had little to do with the hot drink she now held. "'Tis hardly the proper word for it. And it is nothing interesting."

"Nothing interesting?" Sena accepted a cup and arched her brows. "My dear, you have broken off an engagement and let your family secret you away in the middle of the night—what could possibly be more interesting than that?"

"Your betrothed has no idea where you are?" Kate poured the last cup for herself and settled between the other ladies once more. She gazed down into her cup. "Will he not worry?"

Indeed. Edwinn sipped again, not sure if he ought to hold such a thing against this young woman…or if perhaps it spoke to the urgency of her arrival here.

Miss Benton focused her gaze on her chocolate. "I cannot think he will be overconcerned, and my family approved of my coming to Annapolis to gather my thoughts. My brother was a student of Mr. Randel and served under him in the war. I posted a letter assuring everyone I arrived safely, and I am certain they will let Mr. Fielding know I am well if he asks. But had I not left…" She shook her head and blinked rapidly. "Many would say I ought to have borne the situation. But I could not."

"Well of course not! Her betrothed was a genuine villain and betrayed her in the worst way imaginable."

Miss Benton greeted Sena's pronouncement with a crooked grin. "He is not a villain, Sena, only…not in love with me."

His first thought—the man was a fool—gave way to one far more certain and more of his spirit than his mind: she still loved this man, villain or not.

And why should that make him want to sigh? He didn't even know her. And if she knew him, it would undoubtedly not work to his favor, given that her brother was a Patriot soldier. Her family would be no more welcoming to him than Mr. Randel was. Which meant one more could-have-been that would never be.

Edwinn succumbed to the sigh and set his chocolate on a table. The Lord obviously had some purpose in bringing this fetching young lady into his life, in opening his senses to her so quickly. And obviously, it was for no purpose other than to be a friend.

So be it.

"You are very brave." Kate drew in a wistful breath and cradled her cup in her hands. "I would never have the courage to end an engagement, if ever I manage to procure one."

"Had I not, I suspect my cousin would have managed to end it without my input. But I cannot think you will have a hard time finding a husband, Kate." Miss Benton smiled with oblivion. "You are so lovely and sweet."

His sister blushed. "I thank you. But I am not invited anywhere—"

"Oh!" Sena all but leapt up and settled on the very edge of her cushion. "That reminds me. Papa asks you both to come on Christmas."

For a moment, only the tick of the mantel clock filled the room. Kate met his gaze, a world of meaning in her eyes. Mr. Randel had never forbidden her entry to his home—being a fair man, he had not held her responsible for Edwinn's politics—but *he* had not been welcome at Randel House since the Revolution.

What did it mean, this invitation? Simply that John Randel was showing Christian kindness for Christmas? Or were perceived wrongs finally forgiven?

Either way, his lips curved up. "We would be delighted. After church?"

"That will be perfect."

Perfection he was unsure of—but hopefully it was a promise of things to come.

Chapter Six

Lark pulled her cloak tighter and stared up with awe at the elegant abode. "I do not understand, Sena. If this is the Calverts' house, then why...?"

Her friend pursed her lips and blew a breath out through them. "I doubted you would realize. Their property was seized during the war."

That brought Lark's eyebrows together. "Seized? But why?"

They started walking again along Calvert Street—named after Kate's family, apparently—back toward the Randels'. Sena shook her head. "Why else? Edwinn remained loyal to the Crown."

Lark came to an abrupt halt and spun back to look at the columns of the house. "He is a...a Tory?" Shouldn't she have realized the moment she met him? Shouldn't it have been emblazoned across his forehead, or apparent through a stubborn glint in his eyes, a haughty demeanor? But Mr. Calvert had been the epitome of gentle manners, even humility. The way he had teased his sister and Sena—that look he had given her when he first came in—surely those were not the marks of a Tory.

There had been families loyal to King George in Williamsburg, of course, but most of them fled when independence was declared, many returning to England. She had met none since the war ended. Hadn't thought any would dare show their faces.

Sena urged her onward when a gust of wind whipped over them. "And no one will forgive him for it, though he and Kate are the best people I know. Do you not agree?"

"They are wonderful." She had never met a young lady as sweet as Kate, though indeed she had been very shy, especially at the start. And Mr. Calvert—he was nearly as handsome as Emerson with his auburn hair and strong features. When he had looked at her, it was as if he saw her. Really saw her, and approved of what met his gaze.

Why could Emerson never look at her like that? In all the years they had known each other, not once had he shown as much interest as Mr. Calvert did in that single look. No man ever had. And why should this one, now? Even if her heart were ready for someone else, her family would never approve of a Tory.

Sena bumped her shoulder into Lark's and grinned. "I think Edwinn liked you as well. Did you notice the sparkle in his eye whenever he looked your way?"

She also noticed a certain something in Sena's tone. "I think, moreover, *you* are rather fond of *him*."

Though she laughed, Sena's gaze darted away. "Foolishness. I admire him greatly, but some things will never be. Dreaming of them is useless."

"Words I know well…but it never stops us, does it?"

Her friend's sigh rivaled the wind. "No, it never does. I admit I have entertained a fancy or two, but that is all it is. All it *can* be."

Lark turned her face toward Church Circle. She could see little of it through the buildings between, but even had she been closer, there would be little to meet her eyes. They had walked past it on their way to the Calverts' temporary home on West Street, and Sena had already shared the history of St. Anne's parish. The original church had been too small and had been torn down—right before the war. With all the supplies used for Fort Severn instead of the new church, the circle named for it sat empty, little but a foundation and piles of snow-covered scrap to show where the only church in Annapolis belonged.

The congregation met in the theater now, and they were saving the money to begin construction again. But in the meantime, God's house was only a vision.

Perhaps that, too, was a metaphor for life, like the Liberty Tree and Bladen's Folly. Sometimes man's best-laid plans resulted only in shambles. Sometimes pursuing a worthy vision resulted in losing what one had to begin with. She had no doubt a new St. Anne's would eventually be built. But in the meantime…

Eventually, Sena would find the right match. Eventually, Lark would find a new path. But in the meantime…

"Did he fight for the crown?" Lark asked as they turned up North West Street. "Is that how his leg was injured?"

"Edwinn? Oh no. He had a riding accident when he was a boy, before Kate was even born—he is eleven years her elder. He could not fight at all. Some say that is why he made the choice he did, that since he could not fight he aligned himself with England because she was the presumed victor. It is not true, of course."

"No?" Lark pulled her cloak tight and bent her head, hoping the brim of her bonnet would protect her from the wind.

"No." Sena's voice went soft. "He believes in our nation, Lark, think not otherwise. He loves Annapolis, loves Maryland, loves the entire country. He just could not justify revolting against his lawful ruler. Papa tried to talk him into joining the Patriot cause, even if he could not join the army, but he kept quoting that verse from one of the epistles…you know the one, it speaks of obeying one's rulers, even if unjust, because they were put over you by God. He thought we ought to find our independence through political channels, not with muskets and bayonets."

Though the bite of the wind made her eyes water, Lark raised them so she could meet Sena's gaze. "But politics achieved nothing."

"Papa pointed out as much." Sena's lips twitched up. "Edwinn insisted that, though they may treat us ill, it was the Lord's place to punish them for it, not ours."

Lark halted again and buried her hands deeper into her muff. "So what, then? He thinks all those who fought for our independence were sinning? He would judge them all—my brother, your father"—Emerson, too, though she would not mention his name—"for standing up for their land of birth against a tyrant?"

Eyes sparkling, Sena chuckled and motioned her onward. "On the contrary—when asked that question, he quotes that part of another epistle which says something of how one must obey one's own convictions, or one sins, though another may not be convicted of the same thing. He has never once accused others of sinning by fighting. He only maintains it would have been wrong for *him* to disobey the king. But of course, no one listens to that. They insist he is a cowardly traitor, self-righteous and judgmental."

A frown creased Lark's brow. It might have been her first reaction, but pondering it...that supposition did not at all fit the genteel man she had met. "What of Kate? Did she support her brother?"

"Well of course she supported him, though this being Kate, she never once voiced her opinions. Her silence on the matter was enough to keep Papa from growing angry with her, but he and Edwinn have not spoken—other than one heated argument when the Calverts returned to Annapolis—since the war began. Which is a shame. Edwinn was one of Papa's prized pupils, one of his favorites and friends. Only your brother has rivaled their closeness."

What a strange thought. Her brother and Mr. Calvert, so similar in their master's affection, yet ending up on opposite sides of the most crucial of fights. Had they ever met? Were they perhaps at school together?

They came to the corner of North West and Tabernacle Streets, and that impish grin possessed Sena's lips. "Would you like to see Bladen's Folly? I found a way inside."

"Inside?" Despite sound reason—and Mr. Randel's instructions to come straight home—Lark followed after her. "It looks positively ramshackle. Is it safe to go in?"

"Of course not. What would be the fun if it were?" Laughing, Sena took off at a run.

Lark had little choice but to lope after her. Heavens, she hadn't run down a public street since she was a child.

They sprinted past a gentleman who only arched his brows and called out, "Good day, Miss Randel. Miss."

Sena craned her head without slowing. "Good day, Mr. Boone. Give Mariah my greetings."

"Do at least watch your step, there are still patches of ice and snow." The gentleman shook his head and kept on.

Lark struggled to pull in a deep breath. Her stays did not assist in the effort. "Why do I have the impression this is a normal activity for you?"

Obviously not having any breathing troubles of her own, Sena laughed. "There is nothing as glorious as running. There it is. Hurry, there will be less wind inside."

Well. If she fell through a rotten floorboard, at least it would be an interesting story to tell.

Wiley stood at the rear of the ballroom and looked with disinterest at the festive gathering. Most of the holiday balls would take place in the month following Christmas, but a few had started early.

He was in no mood for a celebration, but his parents had insisted he come. He hadn't the heart to refuse them. They were missing Lark, and he must do what he could to ease their hearts—otherwise they might insist on calling her home prematurely.

Her letter had arrived that morning, and he had been every bit as relieved as his parents to see that she was well. Winter had borne down upon them with unprecedented ferocity since she left, and worry had been inevitable.

But she was safely arrived and already enjoying her hosts. He hadn't met Randel's daughter in recent years to know if they would take to one another, but apparently they were fast friends.

Excellent, and exactly what Lark needed. A friend unrelated to Emerson, a town that had not known her since birth. New ideas, new experiences. By the time she returned, she would be her own person. He knew her well enough to imagine the results, and the thought brought a smile to his lips.

"And why are you grinning at that particular set of blond curls, Wiley Benton?"

Wiley blinked and looked to Isabella Fielding, who had appeared at his side. "Hmm?" Directing his gaze back where it had been, he realized cousin Penelope was within his line of sight. "Ah. Only because I enjoy dissecting her choice of victim, I assure you. Have you noticed which men she flirts with?"

Isabella cocked her head so her carefully arranged curls cascaded over one shoulder. "The wealthy ones."

"Not just that—the wealthy ones who are only *visiting* Williamsburg. She intends to find a husband, I think, who will take her far away from us." Apparently his cousin took his threat seriously. The thought did wonders for his humor.

Isabella grinned and edged an inch closer. "Well, it is good to see you have not decided to pursue a family alliance, Mr. Benton."

He chuckled. Isabella was every inch the flirt Penelope was, only she managed it with a sanguine disposition. "Did the thought make you jealous, my dear Miss Fielding?"

She had one of the most fetching grins. Obviously he must flirt back, to give her the chance to flash it regularly. "More like concerned, dear sir. She is obviously a sly sort, and I should hate to think of you falling for her tricks. But given how little we have seen you lately… Why, my brother is in the pits of despair over how much you have kept at home, and during the first respite from bad weather in weeks!"

Ah, so that was her game. Wiley sighed. "Emerson put you up to this, did he?"

She gave an exaggerated bat of her black lashes. "Whatever do you mean, Mr. Benton? Can I not speak to the most handsome man in the room without an ulterior motive?"

"Certainly you can—but you have obviously sought out *me* for reasons most ulterior." He glanced over her head and spotted Emerson easily enough. He stood glowering in the opposite corner. Watching them.

Isabella's coquetry fell away, leaving her face sincere and sweet. "I am worried for him. He will not say what happened that night, but obviously something did, for Lark to leave so suddenly. He is gone to pieces over it—and you, refusing to see him. You are his closest friend, a brother. Why are you angry with him?"

For a moment he merely set his jaw and stared her down. Her eyes were without guile, her face genuinely pleading. His gaze flicked to where Penelope giggled across the room. He kept his voice low, as she had. "You want to know what happened? Lark and I caught your saintly brother in an embrace with my cousin."

She hissed out a breath. "What? Emerson, with that—that—?"

"Precisely. Perhaps Lark could have borne it, had she been secure in his affections. Perhaps it would have been excuse enough to know Penelope instigated it. But after the way he has ignored her for

years, and the thoughtlessness he shows her every time they meet…
I could not bear seeing her in such misery. So we sent her away."

"I should think so!" She rolled back her shoulders and lifted her
chin. "If my idiot brother is going to act like that…well, let him enjoy
a full taste of the consequences. I cannot believe he would—ooh."
Pressing her lips against a growl, she directed a piercing glare Emerson's way. "How could he be so brainless? Does he not realize Lark is
the most wonderful young woman to be found?"

"Apparently not. But do tell him your opinion on the matter."

She raised her chin still more and spun away. "You can be certain
I shall." After one step, though, she halted. "She is safe? This weather…"

"Safe and well."

"Good. Thank you, Wiley."

Watching her flounce away, he had to grin. No matter what Emerson had intended with that little ploy, Lark had one more ally.

He almost felt sorry for his erstwhile friend. Almost.

Emerson clasped his hands behind his back as Isabella made her way
through the crowd, exchanging a smile with one acquaintance, a
laugh with another. Why didn't she hurry? She knew how anxious he
was; that was why she had agreed to try to charm some information
out of Wiley.

He was unsure what it meant, the two of them frowning and
whispering. But Wiley had at least spoken to her, which was more
than could be said for him. Surely—please, Lord—she had learned
something.

Finally she arrived at his side. And proceeded to hit him in the
arm. Only a minor sting, but still. "What was that for?"

"As if you must ask." Leaning close, she seethed. "How could you
be such a dolt? *Penelope*?"

He winced, sighed. Why had he thought Wiley would keep it
secret? "It was a mistake, Izzy, one I regret. But a fleeting one. It is she
who followed me, she who—"

"And *you* who had spent the evening flirting with her. I noted then you were acting poorly, and now?" She paused to huff. "Much as I want Lark for a sister, I cannot wish such a marriage on her. She would do well to stay away until our parents resign themselves."

That dagger sliced more acutely than the blade that scarred his side at Yorktown. He cradled her elbow and led her out of the ballroom. "Where is she? Please, Izzy. I cannot make things right if I cannot apologize."

"I daresay your words have lost their meaning, Emerson." She pulled her arm free of his hand. "I did not ask, lest I be tempted to tell you once my anger has cooled. You brought this on yourself."

He raised a hand to his eyes, rubbed. "Yes. I know I did. But I must at least know she is well."

"He promises she is."

He ought to be grateful for that much. But it wasn't enough. He must find her, must lay his heart bare before her and prove to her he was not truly the blockhead he had acted. "She needs to come home. It is Christmas, and she ought to be spending it with her family. She knows no one outside Williamsburg, so what must she be going through now?"

For a long moment, Isabella only stared at him, agape. Then she loosed a breathy laugh. "*Now* you concern yourself with her feelings? Had you bothered to do so two years ago—"

"I know." It came out harsher than he intended. "Do you not think I realize that?"

"At this point I'm not convinced enough of your brains to give you credit for any realizations." With a well-placed stomp on his toes, she stormed back into the ballroom.

At least she had used the ball of her foot and not the heel. Small blessings.

In no mood to return to the ballroom with its energetic harpsichord playing Christmas hymns and carols, Emerson headed for the verandah. Perhaps the cold evening air would soothe the flames of regret and shame.

Stepping off the porch, he followed the shadowed path of crushed oyster shells. In the distance he could barely make out the dark slither of the James River, the acres of dormant fields before it. He'd been to this neighboring plantation often enough to know he might find a moment's peace in its gardens. But when he stepped past the hedge, he spotted another already pacing the labyrinth.

When he recognized the figure as Wiley's, he sighed.

His friend looked up and undoubtedly scowled. "Hunting me down again?"

"No, actually. Will you stomp off if I come nearer?"

There was just enough light from the hanging lanterns to catch the hint of a smile on Wiley's mouth. "I may, if you say something insufferable. But at the moment my mood has improved a bit, after seeing your sister snarl at you."

"Yes, thank you for that." He drew in a breath, marveling at how even this brief exchange made him feel better. Wiley might be behind this disappointment, but Emerson had no one but him to turn to with it. He stepped into the meandering labyrinth and traced its shape with his steps. "You probably missed her stomping on my toes."

Wiley chuckled. "I can well imagine it. You deserve every ache."

"I do. And not just to my feet."

From his spot deeper along the path, Wiley halted and sighed. "Your aches can be nothing compared to Lark's. You crushed her, Emerson. You pushed and pushed for the past two years, then this last…" He shook his head and balled his fists. "She is strong. But sometimes strength requires pushing off from the cause of pressure rather than withstanding it."

What was he to say to that? He nodded, but Wiley would know he agreed only with the sentiment, not with the result. "I want to make things right with her, Wiley."

"And you can. When she comes home, after the proposed wedding date has passed. You can make things right—but you will not wed her."

Emerson looked from the last sliver of moon left in its phase to the decorative lanterns glowing where they hung around the garden. The one, natural but providing no light tonight, the other crafted with deliberation and illuminating the darkness. "We can mend things. We could still have a good marriage."

"No. You love her not."

Emerson's eyes remained locked on the flame within the glass and metal housing. "I will. I want to."

Wiley stepped over the plants separating their portions of the path and into the space before Emerson. "You had your chance."

"But—"

"I say this as your friend." Wiley's face went intent, serious. "Let it rest. Help convince our parents the bond is severed, and move on with your life."

Did he actually expect him to do that? Emerson shook his head. "I cannot. She is my intended. I want to marry no one else."

Wiley's eyes turned stony. "Then marry no one. You do not love her; you act only out of pride and expectation. For once in your life, Emerson, pay heed to your heart rather than your duty."

He forced a swallow. The accusation should have piqued him, but instead it resonated with something within. "For once in my life, Wiley, I am. Please. Tell me where she is."

Still and silent, Wiley held his gaze. After a brief eternity, he sighed. "I cannot. She wants nothing to do with you, and I will honor her wishes."

"If you but tell me where to find her, I will change her mind. Change her wishes."

A wisp of a laugh escaped Wiley's lips. "And that, my friend, is why she does not want you to know her location. We all know you can be charming when you want to be. But charm is not enough for a sound marriage."

"Of course not." Not that he had contemplated that truth before this disaster. "But if I can speak to her, we can work through this. Establish a foundation built on something sturdier."

Wiley sighed. "I will pass along your wish to apologize. That is *all* I will do—and you ought not to expect acceptance from her. Her feelings would not have healed yet."

That was more than he had expected. Emerson drew in a long breath. "And what of you, Wiley? Have you forgiven me?"

Wiley's lips twitched. "Well, you *have* seemed genuinely miserable. Though I suppose if I forgave you completely, that would not please me so much."

Emerson smiled. "You will be better able to enjoy seeing it if you stop avoiding me."

"True." Wiley quirked a brow. "Let us strike a deal. I will cease avoiding you, if you cease asking me to intervene with Lark."

"'Tis fair." Difficult though. Yet if Emerson were going to be without his bride, he might as well be without her with his friend. He extended a hand, which Wiley shook.

Relief flowed through him. But under it still roiled the conviction that he must find Lark, must set things right.

How in the world would he achieve that without prying information from Wiley?

CHAPTER SEVEN

Lark held the cloth close to the window to catch the light and aimed her needle at the hem. Her best dress had seen better days—namely, any day preceding this Saturday past. She had been all excitement to join the Randels at the official ball held in honor of General Washington before his resignation, had dressed in her finest, and had been nearly as giddy as Sena to go to the beautiful Caroll estate abutting Acton's Creek.

Over the course of the evening, she had broken a heel from her slipper, received a bump that sent wine onto her skirt, and ripped the hem when an oblivious dancer stepped on it.

Still, her lips pulled up in a smile. She had never seen the likes of that ball. To be sure, Mr. Caroll was the wealthiest man in the country, so it was to be expected. But a more jovial gathering she had not beheld in many a year. Between the men at their cards and the women laughing along with the music, movement and color had filled her vision with every turn of her head.

And when they stepped outside to return home in the early hours of the morning, the city had been glowing in an illumination, in recognition of the general. Lanterns and candles and lamps shone from shop windows, public houses, and private dwellings, casting their golden glow upon the buildings and streets and surely reaching all the way to heaven.

As she stitched the tear closed, Lark decided a torn hem and sore toes were a fair price to pay for the privilege of taking part in such a celebration.

The Randel boys whooped their way into the room, dragging her attention from her sewing. Johnny led the parade in an oversized tricorn, a wooden sword belted to his waist. "There is the mighty Delaware, soldiers!"

Mrs. Randel looked up from her own mending with a soft smile. "Might you valiant troops ford the river from the other room?"

"But Mother—"

"Better still," their father interrupted from behind his book, emerging enough to display an arched brow, "go review that Latin I assigned you. You will find it most apropos for the season."

Will huffed and planted his hands on his hips. "But Father, school is out for the holiday. Why must we do lessons? None of the others will be."

"None of the others have the misfortune of being the schoolmaster's sons. The three of you may work together on it. I imagine with little Mark helping, you shall be done in no time."

The youngest frowned. "I hate Latin."

"And I needn't any help." Will raised his chin. "I'm better at it than Johnny, even."

The eldest gave his brother a shove. "You are not. But we are both far ahead of anyone else, which only means we are bored in class. Come, Father, let us play."

Mr. Randel raised his book again, but Lark caught the wink of a grin. "Education takes no holidays, my boys. It is only a few lines to keep your wits sharp. Off with you. I expect to see a translation when I return from the State House."

The three spun for the door, mumbling, and nearly ran into Mrs. Green. She shook her head at them. "Now children, you know what Poor Richard says. 'Genius without education is like silver in the mine.' You may all be smart as whips, but without your father's instruction, it would be worthless. Run along now."

Lark cast a quick glance beside her and caught the indulgent roll of Sena's eyes. In her week with the Randels, she had heard no fewer than a dozen of Mr. Franklin's adages spill from the woman's lips— perhaps closer to two dozen.

Mr. Randel lowered his paper once the boys were clear of the room. His grin still hovered around the corners of his mouth. "Did your brother complain of me like my sons do, Miss Benton?"

She chuckled and double-checked her last stitch. Invisible. Perfect. "No, just of my incessant begging that he share with me all he had learned. There were several times when he mumbled about not wanting to come home from school only to play teacher to a speck of a girl who had no need of Latin or mathematics."

"You surely had tutors." Mrs. Randel gave her the same soft smile she had bestowed on her own children. "Did they not indulge your desire to learn?"

"Not always in the subjects I wanted. Left to my own devices, I would be poorly equipped for running a house and far better at the more masculine subjects."

Sena grinned and tossed the stocking she had been mending into the basket at her feet. "You ought to have grown up with us, Lark. Papa would have filled you to bursting with every subject you could possibly want to learn about, and then some. He always eschewed the idea that females need only learn of dance, music, drawing, and some literature. He taught me the same subjects as my brothers."

"And why not? You are every bit as good at them as they." With a glance at the mantel clock, Mr. Randel straightened. "We ought to be on our way soon, if you ladies would like to ready yourselves."

Mrs. Randel sighed. "How I wish I were not so conspicuous. I would love to accept the invitation. Mrs. Green, you ought to go in my place. I know you admire General Washington greatly."

"I do, that, but such occasions are not the thing for me. Besides, you will be in need of a respite, so who would keep an eye on the boys if I went?" The housekeeper waved the suggestion away and tidied the table between her two employers. "Let the young ladies go with Mr. Randel and enjoy themselves. I will expect a full recounting when they return."

"You shall have it," Sena swore. Most likely with a few embellishments, if Lark knew her new friend a whit.

A tingle of excitement swept through her. She put her dress and needle down and stood without hesitation. Whoever would have thought she, of all the members of her family, would manage to be present when General Washington resigned his commission? Not her father, his longtime acquaintance, or her brother, who had served under him in the war, but her. Little, insignificant Lark Benton.

"I still cannot believe he will resign," Sena said as she led the way from the room. "He could have retained his commission and ruled the nation from the helm of the military. He could have had any title in the world. And instead he will retire to Mount Vernon and live quietly."

Lark followed her friend up the stairs to their shared room. "He is a great man."

"Not only that, but a good one." Pushing open the door, Sena bounced inside and scooped up her bonnet. "I am so glad you are here for this, Lark. We will someday be able to tell our grandchildren we witnessed one of the most important acts in our nation's history."

Lark smiled, even as a pang pierced her. Grandchildren. Dare she hope to ever have any of those, now? Marriage did not seem to loom in her future. But she could tell her sister's children about it, and the nieces and nephews Wiley would someday give her.

They took turns in front of the mirror, positioning their bonnets just so, then went back downstairs for their cloaks and muffs. The weather was still frigid, but the walk would be brief.

Sena's mother joined them at the door. "You two look lovely."

With a pirouette, Sena laughed. "All the important men in the nation will be there. Perhaps I shall catch myself a noteworthy husband."

Her mother sent her gaze heavenward. "If that were your goal, my dear, you would be wed already. But since matrimony will require taming that adventurous spirit of yours…"

"Or I could marry an adventurer. There are wilds yet to be explored, Mamma. Perhaps I shall go off in search of the Northwest Passage."

Mr. Randel appeared with hat and cloak and shaking head. "I know a few frontiersmen, if you would like me to introduce you, my dear. Perhaps they, with their less civil ways, would have better luck controlling you than I do."

Sena laughed and looped her arm through her father's. "For that, I shall refuse to marry for another while yet, to torture you the longer."

Lark let her mouth relax into a smile. Out of control or not, when Sena decided she was ready to wed, no man would be able to resist her. Although she had to wonder if her friend was not ready, or if her heart was more firmly attached to Mr. Calvert than she admitted.

Oh, why did love and wisdom in love not coexist more often? Why could they not decide with their minds where their hearts inclined? She would have been able to forget Emerson long ago, were that the case. Then his dark eyes would not be filling her dreams every night, nor would the taunting images of him with Penelope.

Well, enough of him. She twirled her cloak about her shoulders and squared them. She didn't need Emerson Fielding to have a full life.

As if reading her mind, Mr. Randel sent her a twinkling grin and opened the door. Cold air rushed inside, and the three of them stepped onto the stoop and descended the stairs with waves of farewell for Mrs. Randel and Mrs. Green. Mr. Randel led the way to the right, up North Street, and Lark fell in beside Sena directly behind him.

"After this," Sena whispered, "I would like to introduce you to another friend of mine. We will have to stop in the Market Place first to pick up a few things, if that meets with your approval."

"By ourselves?" Though she whispered, her gaze darted to Mr. Randel.

Sena grinned. "Papa would feel he must refuse if we asked, but he does not mind me venturing out without escort nearly so much as he pretends. Especially now that I have you with me. Really, are you not better than a maid or servant boy?"

Lark had her doubts about that but felt reckless enough not to argue the point. Never in her life had she dared go to market with only another girl near her own age. Might it not be exciting? She nodded her assent.

The white dome of the State House loomed majestic before them, and Lark couldn't resist tilting her head back to see its full splendor. At the top waved the latest design of the nation's flag, with its vertical field of blue spanning the height of the stripes, and its thirteen white eight-point stars. "Oh, it is the first I have seen the new flag."

Mr. Randel turned round with a smile. "Mr. Shaw's design, of course. He is responsible for the furniture within the Senate Chamber as well."

They joined the confluence of other fashionable families pattering up the marble steps and past the columns, through the tall wooden doors. Mr. Randel turned to them again. "You ladies must repair to the gallery with the other womenfolk. I shall see you after the proceedings."

"Of course, Papa. I see Mrs. Alderich going up now—we shall join her."

Lark looked up into the rotunda as they passed through it, drawing in a breath of appreciation at the detailed designs worked into the plaster and the bountiful windows in the top part of the dome. They then entered the stairwell room and headed up to the gallery. The Senate Chamber lay before them as they took their spots at the rail with the other ladies. At the farthest end of the room there was a dais with a broad leather chair upon it, a clerk's desk and chair at its side. Light streamed in from a wide bank of windows, opposite a fireplace with flames licking high and bright.

Men swarmed the room, all in their best dress, hats tucked under arms and cloaks tossed over shoulders. Lark scanned the collection in search of General Washington but saw his figure nowhere.

"There is Thomas Jefferson." Sena pointed directly below them, to where the statesman stood with a hand held behind his back, chatting with his fellow Virginia representative, young Mr. Monroe. Lark drew back a bit—both men were familiar with the Fieldings, and she had no intentions of inadvertently giving away her presence here. Chances were slim that they'd recognize her, but not impossible. She had been introduced to both before.

"I wonder if Mr. Hamilton will be here." Sena looked over the crowd with interest. "He and Papa are excellent friends."

"Oh?" A smile twitched Lark's mouth up. "I have never met him, but I have heard rumors."

Sena's brows arched up in obvious delight. "What kind of rumors?"

"Let us just say Mrs. Washington has named a tomcat at Mount Vernon Hamilton after him, given his ways with females."

Sena laughed, bright if muted. "I am not surprised. Though Papa has not had much chance to talk with many of his friends since the war. I know he misses the old Tuesday Club days."

"Tuesday Club?"

Sena grinned. "That was what the gentlemen called their boasting and drinking parties. Alexander Hamilton was the news-bearer and practically haunted the post road for the latest official gossip. They met most often in public houses, but occasionally at the members' homes. We hosted a time or two when I was very small. I remember sneaking down to watch."

"I can only imagine what you overheard." Lark chuckled, remembering well Wiley's warnings about the coffeehouse—how much worse would gentlemen be at a gathering such as Sena described?

"Oh, what wits they all were! They would read poetry and essays they had written, sing ridiculous songs they had composed, have mock trials...." Sena's smile faded a bit. "All that ended with the war. Papa is practically starved for intellectual gatherings, I think. He keeps mumbling about putting another club together. Perhaps after the babe comes."

A ripple of murmurs moved through the crowd below, and a moment later another man stepped in. Lark drew in a long breath. Taller than most any other in the assembly, General Washington was unmistakable. His hair was powdered and perfectly arranged, his military uniform precise, each button gleaming. Behind him were four men also in military dress, whom she assumed to be the general's aides.

A bell might as well have rung through the chamber. The chatter died, and the men all made for their places. The congressmen took their seats about the room in armchairs. A quick count told her there were about twenty present, plus the onlookers gathered wherever they could find room. Mr. Randel stood with a bevy of gentlemen from town.

Lark's eyes followed Washington as he strode across the floor to the chair positioned to the right of the congressional president. A hush blanketed them as he sat, so she could hear the far-off chime of a clock striking noon.

The president, whom she knew to be General Mifflin, rose from his seat and turned to Washington. He cleared his throat and lowered his chin a notch, but it did nothing to hide the bob of his Adam's apple. "Good day to you, General. We welcome you here today most graciously. The United States in Congress assembled are prepared to receive your communication."

As Washington stood again, Lark's fingers wrapped around the railing. She and Sena both leaned into it, getting as close as possible to the proceedings.

The general reached into his pocket and pulled out several sheaves of paper folded together, took his time in smoothing them out. Though Lark couldn't see his face, she saw the rise of his shoulders as he drew in a breath. Did even he, arguably the greatest man in these United States, need steadying from time to time?

"Mr. President." The general's voice rang out to fill the room, deep and steady...but tight, as if barely restraining emotion. "The great events on which my resignation depended having at length taken place, I have now the honor of offering my sincere congratulations to Congress, and of presenting myself before them, to surrender into their hands the trust committed to me and to claim the indulgence of retiring from the service of my country."

Lark blinked back tears. She heard several sniffles from behind her.

Washington paused a moment, shifted slightly. "Happy in the confirmation of our independence and sovereignty, and pleased with the opportunity afforded the United States of becoming a respectable nation, I resign with satisfaction the appointment I accepted with diffidence; a diffidence in my abilities to accomplish so arduous a task, which, however, was superseded by a confidence in the rectitude of our cause, the support of the supreme power of the Union, and the patronage of heaven."

Lark's fingers tightened still more as she tried to stem the tide of... what was it? Pride, perhaps, in her nation and one of its leaders. In the realization that he spoke the truth, that theirs was a country so young, yet so blessed by the Lord. A country won through the courage and faith of countless good men.

"The successful termination of the war has verified the most sanguine expectations; and my gratitude for the interposition of Providence and the assistance I have received from my countrymen increases with every review of the momentous contest."

He went on to commend those who had served, those who

served still. With each syllable, it seemed as though his emotion grew. Yet rather than choke off his words, it filled them until they resounded within Lark.

"I consider it an indispensable duty to close this last act of my official life by commending the interests of our dearest country to the protection of Almighty God and those who have the superintendence of them to His holy keeping."

He separated one page from the rest and held it out. Lark nearly gasped when she saw his hand tremble. "Having now finished the work assigned me, I retire from the great theater of action, and bidding an affectionate farewell to this august body under whose orders I have so long acted, I here offer my commission, and take my leave of all the employments of public life."

"Oh, I wish he wouldn't," Sena murmured, fingers pressed to her lips.

Lark well understood that sentiment. What kind of spirit must it take to be so deserving of honor that one could control an entire country if one chose, yet of such humility that one would refuse?

General Mifflin accepted the first paper, then the rest when Washington handed them over. He swallowed hard. "The United States in Congress assembled receive, with emotions too affecting for utterance, the solemn resignation of the authorities under which you have led their troops with success through a perilous and doubtful war."

Sena gripped Lark's elbow. "Come. Let us go before the masses can blockade us."

"Will your father not worry if we leave without him?"

Sena's answer was to lean over the railing, apparently catching her father's eye. After sending a wave and a smirk below, she grabbed Lark's hand. "There, he now knows we are off in search of trouble. Hurry."

If she argued here, it would draw undue attention. Better to go along now and then try to reason with Sena once they had gained the out-of-doors. They had to cut a path through the women, but once they were on the stairs, they ran into no one else—that is, until they reached the bottom and plowed directly into a group of men.

This was becoming far too familiar a sensation in this town. At least this time someone caught her before Lark could become acquainted with the floor. She glanced up to utter her thanks, only to have the words lodge in her throat.

General Washington gave her a small smile and put her gently back on her feet then glanced at Sena. "Ah, Miss Randel. I ought to have known where there is mishap, you would be involved."

Sena curtsied, her cheeks pink. "My apologies, sir. Might I present my friend, Lark Benton of Williamsburg?"

"Benton?" He turned back to Lark with interest. "Of Endover?"

Lark could only nod.

He smiled. "Give your father and brother my greetings. And of course, my wife and I shall see you all at your wedding in March."

With a nod, he and his aides hastened away. Lark gripped Sena's arm to keep her knees from buckling. "George Washington knows who I am."

"More, Lark—he thinks he is going to your wedding. The one you cried off."

Flutters took flight in her stomach. "Oh dear."

"Indeed. Luckily, I know how to combat that particular 'oh dear.' Follow me, my friend."

Anything would be better than contemplating that would-have-been wedding. And really, what could Sena have in mind that would be so terrible?

Behind them Lark could hear the rising noise of the assembly breaking up. She hurried with Sena under the rotunda and out into the brisk air. Because she couldn't resist looking, she saw Washington and his men striding quickly toward the right, but Sena pulled her straight down the hill.

She had come to expect that her friend rarely walked anywhere, but she had not yet grown accustomed to the half run required to keep up with her. They shot down Cornhill Street so fast Lark feared tripping over an icy cobblestone; she didn't dare look up to see what they passed. Shops, taverns, residences, she assumed. At its end was an open area directly before the docks.

That was enough to instill reason and fright back into Lark. "Sena, we ought not go into Market Place by ourselves. We can go back and fetch a maid first, or a page boy."

"Have you not noticed how understaffed we are? There is no one to spare for following me about. Over here." Sena pulled her toward a market space and into a building filled with foods from the Caribbean. The ripe scent of tropical fruit teased Lark's nose and made her mouth water. Her friend headed straight for the pineapples and purchased one with barely a pause before dashing out again.

Casting only one longing look toward the oranges, Lark followed. Then halted. Her gaze landed on a row of Negroes near the docks, lined up along with assorted barrels and crates as men in fashionable dress walked the lengths of them, surveying them like horses.

Her stomach clenched. Having grown up on a plantation, she understood the reality of slavery. She listened to her father debate the inhumanity of it with his neighbors, had heard him swear that he would free all they owned upon his death, and that importation of Africans ought to be illegal. But she had never given it serious thought, as it seemed an institution that would soon wither away. She had certainly never seen an auction before. Had never beheld the emotions rampaging across the slaves' faces as they were bought and sold.

A shackled mother gripped the hand of a child, as if willing Providence to uphold the bond. Perhaps they would remain together. She knew Papa made an effort to preserve families, though some of their neighbors deliberately broke them up for reasons she had never understood. This mother's fear seemed to seep from the dock over to where Lark stood, churning and bubbling into her own deepest hurts until tears burned her eyes.

How well she knew the terror of pending loneliness; but what must it feel like to fear one might never see one's own child again? How much worse would that be than what she had suffered?

"Lark?"

She shook her head and made herself look away, back to Sena. Why, even in this land of freedom her brother had fought for, were so many denied the choice to pursue liberty? How could the same men who revolted against one tyrant play the part with others? Was her father right, that it would soon fade away? Or would the voices of opposition win the day?

Lark met Sena's gaze and found the girl sober and still. "I know," her friend whispered, nodding toward the auction. "There is a reason we have so few in our employ. Papa abhors slavery, but our finances only permit a few paid servants. With him being at war so long, and getting paid so little for it, our family's legacy is stretched thin. But we would all rather do without the help than further the slave trade."

Lark shook her head. "It is largely how things are on a plantation, though most Virginians admit it is a barbaric practice. I have heard them say it will die a natural death now that we are our own nation."

A strange little smile flitted over Sena's mouth. "Let us hope so, though I have my doubts. Shall we go?"

Arguing seemed petty now. Lark nodded. "Where, exactly, are we going?"

Sena motioned to the area of town behind Middleton Tavern, which seemed to be a line between the wealthy and the smaller, dirtier homes. "My friend Alice lives right over there."

Lark didn't mean to frown. But how did Sena know someone from that section of town?

Her friend smiled. "You are wondering how I met her. She was my neighbor growing up, until she fell in love with a sailor and married him despite protests from her family. Society says I ought to pretend we were never friends, but I cannot do that to her. She lost enough of her past, thanks to her choice of husband. There is no reason for her to lose me, too, when I care little for what people think of our continued friendship."

Sena headed toward the left, where Middleton Tavern stretched long and red, its now-brown gardens extending behind it all the way to the water's edge. Beyond it, the houses looked gloomy and tired under their inches of old snow, the air less crisp, and the people walking the streets nowhere near fashionable. Everyone appeared respectable enough, but…

"Alice lives just over here." Sena led her down an alleyway and up to a clapboard building. She knocked upon its rickety door but didn't await a reply before entering. "Alice? 'Tis Sena."

"Back here."

Lark let her gaze wander as they entered. Though neat and tidy, the house was without the luxuries to which she was accustomed. It lacked the symmetry typical of a Federal-style home like hers and the Randels'; there was no style to the plaster, no shine to the wood. Sufficient, but a testament to how far from their social equal this Alice had fallen.

A child squealed from somewhere in the back of the house, and the voice that had greeted them scolded gently. Sena grinned and strode toward a back room. The kitchen, Lark realized as they entered. At Endover, their kitchen was separate from the house and boasted a new cast-iron cookstove. Yet this was a cheerful little room, with its roaring fire and fragrantly bubbling cauldron, with its bread rising on the table and a little girl pouting at a plate of carrots.

A woman stood at the hearth swinging the crane back over the fire. Obviously, this was Alice. But whatever Lark had expected, Alice was not that. She stood tall and statuesque, and though her clothing was plain and serviceable, it could not hide the perfect figure or grace of each movement. Just as the cotton mobcap could not dim the shine of the woman's scarlet locks. Her face was stunning—was everyone beautiful but Lark?—and the smile that lit her countenance proved this was not where Alice belonged. Surely she could have married anyone she pleased. Why had she chosen a destitute seaman?

"Sena." Even in that single word of greeting, culture came through. "I hardly expected to see you again before Christmas. And bringing a visitor!"

"This is Lark Benton, of Williamsburg." Sena set the pineapple on the table, dropped a kiss upon the little girl's head, and went to embrace Alice. "I wanted to drop in and check on you. Has Matty secured the new position?"

Alice's beautiful face went tight with concern. "We will not know until he gets back from this voyage. I pray so. If he were to captain the ferry, he would be home so much more—but then, I am not sure it would satisfy his love of seafaring." She brightened again and smiled at Lark. "Forgive me, I should have greeted you first, Miss Benton. I am Mrs. Alice Mattimore."

"One of the dearest women in Maryland." With a flash of dimples, Sena grinned and bent down on the opposite side of the table. When she stood again, she had a sleeping baby in her arms. "The little golden-haired angel scowling at her vegetables is Callie. This precious sleeping bundle is little Hugh."

"I just put some coffee on. Please have a seat."

Lark pulled out a rough-hewn chair, offering a smile to Callie. The girl ignored her and poked at a carrot, her gaze on the pineapple. Lark could hardly blame her for that preference.

While Sena and Alice chatted about acquaintances she had never met, Lark settled into the hard chair and surveyed the spartan kitchen. She wouldn't have the first idea how to keep house in this fashion, with no servant in sight and the barest of necessities at hand. What had made this choice worth the consequences? Did Alice love this sailor-husband of hers so much? Surely her parents had not approved the marriage.

The greatest rebellion Lark had ever made was in insisting they cancel the wedding and threatening to stay here past their agreed-on date to be sure of it. What would Papa and Mamma do if she did? They would be saddened, angry, perhaps come here to try to force her home. But they could not—would not—force her to marry against her will. And so they would forgive her, the strain would eventually dissipate, and she would live quietly at Endover the rest of her days.

But to make a decision like Alice's? One that would estrange her from her family forever?

Lark traced a line of wood grain on the well-worn table. She was not at all sure she had the courage to stand for any belief at so great a cost.

And was not at all sure that wasn't a great lack on her part.

CHAPTER EIGHT

Emerson stretched out in his favorite leather chair, feet propped on a footstool, gaze locked on the crackling fireplace. Within those dancing flames he saw nothing but hope burning up like paper tossed into the blaze. In the other room his sisters all laughed as they hung evergreen boughs and mistletoe and gossiped about the wassailing in town, but he might as well have been a continent removed.

Why celebrate this year, when he finally realized what gift he had held, only after he'd lost it?

"There you are. Emerson, really, stop sulking. It is Christmas Eve."

He arched a brow at his mother. "Sulking? You call it sulking when one's betrothed takes flight and her family refuses to share where she has gone?"

Mother sighed and settled on the footstool beside his feet. Her hair was styled and powdered to receive the family that would be staying with them tonight, her dress ornate and new. She still cut an impressive figure, could still turn heads. She turned his father's regularly, anyway.

Why had he never paused to realize that was a crucial part of his parents' relationship? Why had he never let his head be turned by Lark? Mother's beauty wasn't overt, but it went deep. As Lark's surely did, had he ever bothered to look for it.

He was an oaf. A fool. A veritable dunderhead.

Mother sighed and patted his knee. "You must stop punishing yourself, Em. What's done is done. The important thing is that when you find her, you make amends."

"'When'? More like 'if,' I should think."

That spark of confidence in her eye could be nothing more than maternal love, for he surely had done nothing to earn it. "You will find her. And when you do..." She reached into the embroidery pocket of her skirt and pulled out a small box. "Her Christmas gift."

Emerson sighed even as he accepted it. When he removed the lid, he felt no surprise at the diamond bracelet that went along with the necklace Lark tried to refuse. Why would his mother think it would make any difference?

His mind drifted back to her birthday disaster. Her rightly accusing him of not knowing what gift he gave, him adamantly denying it and then proving her right. A smile tugged at his lips. Had he ever seen such spirit from her as when she shoved the necklace into his stomach? Not since she was a child. At the time it had only baffled him, but now...

She wasn't so unlike Wiley, not if that were a glimpse of her true self. And Wiley had always been his closest friend. Why, then, could he not be her friend too? If she would hear him out, forgive him, they could start afresh with a solid foundation.

His gaze dropped to the bracelet. Firelight sparkled in the heart of each gem and sent miniature rainbows dancing over the walls. It nearly lit a hope within him, until he realized these jewels represented part of the problem. Handed to him by his mother, as every other gift had been since Lark's eighteenth birthday. Mother had invited him to pick out gifts from their most valuable pieces, but he had declined. Said he trusted her judgment.

Hadn't wanted to be bothered.

Deuces, it was a wonder Lark hadn't turned tail and run long ago. What kind of man couldn't be bothered with gifts for his bride? What kind of man ignored her?

Not the kind he wanted to be.

He closed the box and handed it back to his mother with a smile. "Thank you, Mother. But if ever again Lark accepts a gift from my hand, it will be one I choose for her."

She nodded, as if that were exactly the response she had intended all along. Perhaps it was. "Good for you, Emerson. Good for you. Now." She stood, lifted her chin, and gave him that look that had kept him in line as a boy. "Hie yourself into the drawing room with the rest of the family. There is holly to be hung."

Loneliness crept in like fog along the James River. Lark did her best to ignore it through the church service, during the walk back to Randel House, but it hovered behind her shoulder all morning and pounced when she took a seat in the corner of the parlor.

What was she doing away from her family on Christmas? Much as she liked the Randels, she was not one of them. As they passed around small gifts they had selected for one another with the greatest of care, she had to wonder if Wiley or Mamma had thought to bring out the ones she had made for everyone. As this family made the appropriate exclamations of excitement and gratitude, she envisioned her parents and Wiley and the Hendrickses gathered at Endover doing the same.

And a mile away, Emerson would be with his kin too. He would make merry as if nothing had changed this year. As if he had not betrayed her, had not broken her heart.

As if he weren't the reason she was now a hundred fifty miles from home on this sacred day.

Tears burned her eyes, forcing her to squeeze them shut to avoid crying before the entire Randel family. Perhaps she ought to make her excuses and retire to Sena's room.

When she sensed someone settling on the chair adjacent to hers, she knew the opportunity for escape had passed. Figuring it was either Sena or her mother who had come to investigate her silence and tightly shut eyes, Lark opened them again with a sigh, prepared to assure them she was well.

But it was no Randel who sat smiling beside her. Edwinn Calvert and his sister had apparently arrived, for the gentleman was the one in the chair, giving her a look of such sympathetic concern she felt her cheeks flush scarlet in response. "Oh, Mr. Calvert. I did not hear you come in."

He chuckled and waved a hand at the rumbustious boys. "I expect you could not, over the young Randels' enthusiasm. Happy Christmas, Miss Benton. I hope you do not mind me claiming a seat so near you—it seemed the safest spot in the room."

"You are welcome, of course." She smiled at him for a moment, though quickly directed it toward the gathering at large. Something about this man…his looks inspired her to gaze longer at him, and his expression was so kind, so inviting. She wanted to bask in his attention enough that she knew she mustn't. At this point in time it would be nothing but a balm over the wound Emerson had inflicted, not appreciation of him for his own sake.

Besides, the glance Sena sent his direction proved her friend was far more interested than she wanted to be as well.

She could hardly be rude, though. "Have you and Kate enjoyed a pleasant morning thus far?"

He hummed and rested both hands on the silver handle of his cane. "We have. Quiet until now, but nevertheless pleasant. Still, we are deeply moved to have been invited to Randel House." His gaze locked on hers, earnest and sincere. "Miss Randel would have told you why the invitation was surprising."

Why did that make her flush again? It was not her business being discussed, nor her questions that had led to Sena sharing his story. And obviously he felt no need to be embarrassed about it, so why should she?

Logic which did nothing to cool her cheeks. "You know her well enough to realize she likes little better than a good story."

He chuckled again, all bighearted humor, and sent his gaze Sena's way. "And where one is not forthcoming, she has no qualms about creating one. But she and Kate are far too close for her to have exaggerated ours, I think. I am sure she gave you a fairer version than warranted."

"Can one be too fair?" With the arch of her brows, she let her smile bloom. "I would say you give her too much credit, but I think that impossible. She deserves all one could possibly spare."

"She is fast to gather friends. And thankfully, she holds fast to them once they are hers." He nodded to where Sena laughed and pulled Kate in for a quick embrace, then turned his evergreen eyes back on her. "Yet however good a new friend, they cannot replace one's family on a day such as this. You must be missing them."

Away flew her hope that he hadn't noticed her melancholy. She folded her hands together. She hadn't the elegant, tapered fingers of cousin Penelope, nor the ability to set the world to rights with a single touch, like Violet and Mamma. Still, it would have been nice to have someone with her today to hold her hand, to assure her she had a place. "It is difficult, but for the best."

She wouldn't enjoy herself in Penelope's company anyway.

Another hum from Mr. Calvert, then he leaned forward slightly. "Might I pray with you, Miss Benton? I have the feeling you are in need of the reassurance of our Father's arms about you today."

Her head snapped up as her brows furrowed. Certainly she had requested prayers before—from her reverend, or from trusted, older family members. But never in her life had a young man offered to pray for her of his own volition. How in the world was she to respond to that?

Mr. Calvert inclined his head. "I do not mean to make you uncomfortable. I will simply—"

"It is quite fine." Why, after all, should prayer be a means of discomfort? She prayed daily. Religiously, one might say. She forced herself to relax. "I would appreciate it."

Nodding, he glanced at the rest of the assembly, who paid them no mind at all, then turned back to her. He didn't bow his head or clasp his hands, only let his eyes slide shut. Lark didn't even do that— how could she, when she glimpsed the emotion that washed over his face? Perfect peace, perfect contentment. As if by merely praying, he were…home.

"Dear Father in heaven," he began in a whisper she could scarcely hear, "I thank You and praise You for this holy day and all it represents. For sending Your precious Son to come as a babe and walk among us, so ultimately He could become our propitiation and our salvation. I thank You for this most holy remembrance, and for the chance to share it with friends old and new, and with my dear sister."

Here he paused, drew in a long breath, and tilted his head as if listening to something at a great distance. "Lord, we come before You now to ask that You pour out Your peace and assurance upon Miss Benton. She understandably feels the loneliness that comes of being away from her own family, among friends only new, at this time; but You, Father, have been with her always and are with her still. Help her to feel Your presence, now more than ever, and to see Your hand moving in these strange and unexpected circumstances that have brought her to our city. Almighty Father, heal the wounds on her heart, on her spirit, and on her self, that she might see the intrinsic value You have bestowed within her. Reveal to her the purpose You have so perfectly ordained for her life. We ask this in the name of Your only begotten Son, Christ Jesus."

Tears stung again, but they were different this time, and she made no effort to clear them. She echoed his "Amen" and then let her breath shudder. "Thank you, Mr. Calvert. That was…that means more than you could know. Or perhaps you can, as you seemed to know exactly what to pray."

"Forgive me if I sounded too familiar." A smile flitted across his face, ending in a hint of a grimace. He repositioned his leg, set his cane beside him. "Though I confess, you seem less a stranger to me than you are. Perhaps it is only because I can empathize with your feeling of being away from home, uncertain about the future."

"Perhaps." She ignored the shiver of awareness those words inspired and watched Will and Mark charge their miniature cavalry pieces into heated battle on the rug in front of their parents. Then she looked at her companion again. "Sena mentioned you attended King William's School. My brother did as well. Wiley Benton."

"I am afraid I was at Yale College when he arrived, though Mr. Randel mentioned him often before…"

Before the war, and their break. He didn't say it, but he didn't have to. Lark could read the pain of it in his eyes. At least until he shook it off and refreshed his smile.

"Miss Randel mentioned your brother and her father served together in the army, is that correct?"

"He was in Mr. Randel's unit, yes, both Wiley and…" She pressed her lips together against Emerson's name.

"Ah. Your betrothed, perchance?"

Lark snapped her spine straight and lifted her chin. "My *former* betrothed, Mr. Calvert."

"Of course." The man looked to be fighting back a smile, which made no good sense at all. "Is that how you met him? Through your brother?"

And what made him think Emerson was a topic she wanted to discuss? Yet he asked with such gentleness, as if he truly cared about the answer. She sighed. "I have always known him. His family's plantation is adjacent to ours."

"Ah." Again, such enlightenment, and he nodded as if that shed brilliant light upon her situation. "I suppose it was a natural and well-received alliance, then. It is always good to have bonds with one's closest neighbors."

Well. That might indeed explain Emerson's desire to marry her. She had yet to find a better reason. "Yes, I…undoubtedly."

His lips twitched again. "Nothing to do with fonder emotions, then? Nothing to do with love?"

Hardly an appropriate line of conversation with a man she'd only met once before. She turned her face to the window, though she didn't look out it.

Yet…she might have met Mr. Calvert only once, but he seemed no less familiar to her than Emerson. "Nothing at all. One can hardly love a stranger, can one? And that is all he ever wanted to be."

Somehow his gaze snagged hers again. What was it his eyes put her in mind of? Summer on the plantation. Deep green, mature life, blanketed by warmth. Not the spark and leap of flame, but the steady, whelming heat of the Lord's season of growth.

He shook his head. "I cannot fathom it. How could he possibly want to remain a stranger with you?"

Heat suffused her cheeks again. Was he flirting with her, or only being kind? She had no practice in discerning the difference. It sounded little like the kind of flirtation her friends and brother employed, but she couldn't be sure. She breathed a laugh. "You would have to ask him that, sir."

Mr. Calvert grinned. "When he comes banging on Mr. Randel's door in search of you, I shall."

She opened her mouth to assure him that particular event would never occur, but Sena and Kate descended upon them, effectively putting an end to the conversation.

Just as well. It was an unsuitable conversation at any rate.

"Happy Christmas, Lark." Kate sat beside her and smiled. She hesitated a moment, gnawing on her lip, then held out a small, wrapped parcel. "I have brought you a small token of welcome."

Eyes flying to the gift, Lark felt the stain of embarrassment yet again. "Oh, you ought not to have, Kate. I have nothing for anyone—"

"Nonsense. It was just an extra something I had lying around my secretaire. Here, please."

Fearing refusal would damage this overture of friendship, Lark accepted the package and guessed it to be some sort of book. "Thank you. It was very sweet of you to think of me." She carefully untied the string and folded back the paper, smiling when she saw the leather-bound journal. Her own had been left at home in the haste of her departure, and already she missed the chance to sit and write her thoughts. "Oh, 'tis perfect."

Kate sighed in seeming relief. "I'm glad you like it. My diary is a critical part of my prayer life, and I thought perhaps, with all you are going through..."

"Yes. Thank you." She glanced from Kate to Mr. Calvert. All this talk of faith and prayer—Lark had always considered herself a faithful Christian. But perhaps she still had something to learn in that regard, something to make her beam with such certainty, even when all was in turmoil.

How strange to find such an example of the Lord's goodness in two people she would once have considered the enemy.

A knock sounded from the front door, and a moment later Mrs. Green entered with a frown. "It looks to be more wassailers. I cannot imagine why they would come on the holy day itself."

Sena stood, pulling Kate and Lark up with her. "Well, we shall do our Christian duty regardless of their belatedness. Come, ladies, let us purchase some of their wassail."

No one either objected or stood to go with them, so they three headed for the door. Lark had never much cared for the wassail the poor usually brought around, but everyone knew one was obliged to buy it whenever it was offered. A way to offer charity, to have the satisfaction of knowing the children of the wassailers would eat the next day, without offending anyone's pride with alms.

Sena took a moment to liberate a few coins from a drawer before opening the door. She jingled them together and revealed the triangular pieces with a shake of her head. "I thought Papa had exchanged all these fractioned *reales* for Chalmers's shillings. Ah well. Hopefully the wassailers will not mind."

She peeked out the window, and her smile went from polite to brilliant. She threw open the door. "Alice! Come in, come in. I thought perhaps I had not been at home when you stopped on your wassailing…but you have no wassail."

The redhead stepped inside with a strained smile, her children bundled up and huddled against her. She glanced at Lark, Kate, then steadied her gaze on Sena. "Hugh has been sick. Just a cold, but it has kept us in, and too busy to make any. But you had said to be sure and stop, and—I would not to have intruded on your Christmas, except that I was afraid you would worry that I had not come by."

Given the circles under Alice's eyes, Lark was not surprised when Sena studied her friend intently. "Something is wrong. Something more than a cold. The children?"

"No, no, they are well, other than the sniffles." With a sigh, Alice adjusted Callie's woolen hat.

"Your husband?"

Lark's heart twisted within her when she saw the tears flooding Alice's eyes.

The woman's nostrils flared. "'Tis but the delays from this terrible weather. He ought to have returned weeks ago. I kept myself from worrying until now, but he is always home for Christmas, always." She looked down, turned partially toward the door. "The best I can hope for is that his ship is iced into harbor. The worst…"

"Alice." Kate stepped forward and placed a hand on her arm. "I will redouble my prayers on your behalf."

Alice wiped at her damp cheeks and offered a halfhearted smile. "Thank you for that, sweet Kate. And for indulging me in my need to see a few friendly faces before I go to dinner with my husband's family and listen to all their worries. I had better make haste, though. Sena." They clung to each other for a moment. "Thank you for everything."

"Nonsense, I have done nothing. Try not to worry, Alice. All will be well."

Looking far from convinced, Alice and her silent children left again. Sena looked none too convinced herself when she turned back around. She shook her head. "I cannot think what she will do if he is away much longer. During the war he did well privateering, but since then… I think his last shipment barely brought in enough to cover expenses. She has begun taking in mending."

Mr. Randel stepped to Lark's side, though she had no idea how long he had been in the entryway, how much he might have heard. Enough, given the lines around his mouth. "Do you think her parents would take her and the children in until Mr. Mattimore returns?"

At that, Sena loosed a scoffing laugh. "You know her father as well as I, Papa. Matty's may try, but they are no better off." Her expression changed into a plea. "Papa…if her pride would suffer it, have we a position to offer her? Just until Matty comes home."

Mr. Randel sighed and lifted a hand to rub at his forehead. "I wish we could, my dear, but our household budget—"

"I will give my pin money to the cause." Sena batted her lashes. "And all of it I have been saving for a new gown. Please, Papa."

Though he smiled, Mr. Randel shook his head. "Sena, it will take more than one young lady's pin money to make a difference in this situation."

Lark sucked in a breath, her mouth opening before she quite knew why. "What about two young ladies' pin money?"

He arched a brow her way. "I applaud your generosity, Miss Benton, but you do not even know Mrs. Mattimore."

"I know enough." Enough to admire her for her decisions and to pray she had the strength to make her own in like fashion. "Please, sir, if it would make it feasible, then consider it. My parents sent me with far too much, and…and I cannot help but wonder where I would be had they not supported me in my decision to leave Williamsburg for a while. I should hope someone would have helped me. Can I do less, here?"

His sigh sounded like capitulation. "We shall see. I will have to speak with Mrs. Green before I can agree to anything. Perhaps if we pinch our pennies elsewhere, and if she will agree…well, we shall see."

The lamps seemed to brighten with Christmas cheer.

CHAPTER NINE

Edwinn looked up from his book when he heard the knock upon the outer door. Undoubtedly it would be Sena for Kate, Miss Benton probably with her. Rarely did anyone else visit. The light footfalls of their housekeeper sounded in the hall, and Edwinn debated for a moment whether he would join the young ladies today. He always enjoyed their company, but he had been in a strange sort of mood since Christmas, and he had no choice but to attribute it to the hours he and Kate had spent at Randel House.

They had shared a meal with the family, had lingered afterward, and while Kate had seemed perfectly at home and was treated with the highest warmth, Master Randel had not once spoken to him, had not even looked his direction. Obviously nothing had been forgiven. Why, then, the invitation at all?

He would probably not be the best company for his sister and her friends today. Better to stay with his book and perhaps take the time to pray a bit more.

Mrs. Haslip stepped into the room. "A guest for you, Mr. Edwinn."

"For me?" He frowned as he placed his marker in his book. "Who is it?"

"Mr. Randel." She smiled. "Shall I show him in?"

"Randel?" Edwinn set the book upon a table and stood. "Yes, of course."

A moment later the guest blustered into the room, whipping off his navy riding coat and tossing it haphazardly onto a chair. Edwinn straightened his spine. "Master Randel. What an unexpected surprise. Would you sit?"

"'Mister' will suffice, Calvert, as it has been years since you were my pupil. And no, thank you." Randel marched over to the window, toyed with his watch chain, and then spun back around. "It is Martha. The babe is coming."

"Ah." Edwinn lowered himself back to his chair. "Is all well?"

"Is all ever well in a birth?" Randel shoved a hand through his hair and strode over to the mantel. "How is one ever to tell, with all that moaning and groaning, and being forbidden from the room? I had to escape before I went mad."

"And you came here?" Edwinn winced, especially when his guest spun on him. "I did not mean…I am only surprised. You have not sought me out since I came home to Annapolis, except to tell me to go to England."

This time Randel winced. "Wounds were still fresh. Edwinn, I…I fear for my Martha, and I know no one as faithful as you. I was hoping you would pray for her. Mark's birth was so difficult—what if this one…?"

Edwinn stood again and hobbled over to his former teacher, his once-friend, and placed a hand on his shoulder. "Of course I will pray, but there is no reason to fear the worst. She is a strong woman."

"That matters little in these things." Randel pinched the bridge of his nose and let out a wobbling breath. "My apologies. I should not burst in here spewing fear at you, expecting you to do anything for us, when I have treated you as I have these last few years."

His hand slipped back down to his side. Was he apologizing for bursting in…or for that treatment? Swallowing hard, Edwinn wished he had brought his cane on this small trek so he might lean on it. "I harbor no ill will against you. In your eyes, I aligned myself with tyranny."

Randel narrowed his eyes. "And I maintain your reasoning was poor and your decision faulty."

"For you it would have been." Edwinn let his lips twitch up. "For me, it was the only decision I could make in good conscience. I still believe revolution was not the answer—that said, this is my country, and I pray blessing upon it."

The breath Randel loosed left him looking deflated. "Your ability to do so is what brings me here. I cannot grasp how you would manage to pray so diligently for those who have treated you ill, but I know you do exactly that. And so I come, though it leaves me feeling as though I ask for charity."

"Charity is the greatest of virtues, greater even than faith and hope. Would you deprive me of the chance to exercise it?"

A smile tugged the corners of Randel's lips up, and the light in his eyes changed. "You always excelled at debate." The beginnings of a smile did not last long. He waved at the room. "I suspect it will be of no assistance in your current dilemma though. The government is not feeling kindly toward Tories these days. You ought not to be surprised if Calvert Hall is never returned."

Edwinn limped back to his seat with as much grace as he could force into his aching leg. "I am prepared for that possibility. Though it pains me to think of my family's legacy lost to us forever, it does not pierce me nearly so much as the thought that I shall live out my life friendless." He sat, arched his brows. "I suppose you will tell me it is but the consequence of my decisions."

His guest followed him and took a seat on the couch, though the anxious jittering of his knee made Edwinn think it was only out of politeness. Randel sighed. "It is that. But I daresay if you are patient, you shall begin to see a softening from old friends who realize you have not changed. I confess, Calvert, such constancy is unexpected in a man of such youth."

Edwinn had not felt particularly young in many years. Not since his parents both passed away when he was twenty-one, leaving him the sole caretaker of little Kate. He pushed that aside. "Is that what your invitation for Christmas was, sir? A softening? Or merely a gift to your daughter, who wanted her dearest friend with her?"

Randel studied him for a long moment, but Edwinn refused to flinch or glance away. The elder gave a small shake of his head. "Kate is not the only Calvert Sena admires. You too are her friend, Edwinn."

He knew as much, but hearing Randel state it made a strange sensation flit through him. "You have a daughter of unmatchable heart, sir."

"She is unmatchable in more ways than that."

Something about that slanted glare made Edwinn try to straighten his already upright spine. "Sir, if you fear I have designs on Sen—

on Miss Randel—"

"I am not sure I do fear it as much as I would have a year ago." Smiling, Randel stood again, paced. "Not that I am giving you leave to court her, mind you."

Was it embarrassment or unrealized expectation scorching Edwinn's face? He had never dared entertain any notions about Sena. Even if by some miracle Mr. Randel *would* approve, he would have no chance with her. He knew that. His nature would be more appealing to a quieter sort like Miss Benton, surely—though she was just as unattainable. They all were, all the lovely Patriot women.

But to hear it proposed, even if denied... If Mr. Randel were aiming at a new method of torture for the Loyalist, he had designed a good one.

Edwinn cleared his throat. "Of course you are not. I wouldn't— that is, your daughter is certainly worthy of any attention, but I would never dare—"

"Where are your clever debating skills now, Mr. Calvert?" Randel laughed and paced to the window again.

Edwinn drew in a sharp breath and grinned. "They are realizing you have cleverly deflected my question to *you*, Mr. Randel. About Christmas."

"Ah." Randel's smile faded. "Too much has changed in these seven years. The society that once fed my spirit has fractured and shifted, has gone from men interested only in wit and words to leaders of armies, and now of governments."

Edwinn folded his arms over his chest. "You yourself led a goodly portion of that army."

"And I cannot regret it. But I can regret the changes it has forced upon us." He looked out the window for a long moment. "Our city is changing too. With every inch Baltimore grows, we shrink. And with construction of the new capital city underway along the Potomac... I fear we shall dim still more, until we are naught but a remembrance. A provincial backwater once again. Already there are murmurs of moving Maryland's capital to Baltimore, though pray God it never happens. But the day may come when I have nothing but memories left of those gilded days before the war. Why cling to the bilious ones?"

Edwinn was not the only one who felt the pangs of all these changes? Of the loss that accompanied the inception of a nation? "A good question, sir, since bilious thoughts only embitter us."

Randel nodded without looking his way. "When Miss Benton arrived, it made me think of her brother, and of the man to whom she had been betrothed. Benton I held in greatest esteem, Fielding I never cared a whit for, yet the two were inseparable. I offered her sanctuary with nary a qualm, but then that evening I considered what I was doing and wondered if I am guilty of what I always told my pupils never to do—judging without full knowledge. How am I to know if Mr. Fielding is still the passionless boy he had been? Had I not begun to see changes in him during the war, even if I denied them to myself?"

Mention of Miss Benton and her betrothed made something go tight within Edwinn's chest. A reminder, perhaps, of what the Lord expected of him where she was concerned. "And yet he obviously acted amiss, to force her to Annapolis to escape him."

"But that is the thing." Randel pivoted, pointed. "The Emerson Fielding I know was too devoted to his overinflated sense of duty to act on *any* impulse, be it licit or illicit. Perhaps it meant he did what he must, but he never acted beyond the call of duty. At least until Yorktown. You remember Alexander Baldwin?"

The sudden question made Edwinn blink, search his memory. "He was two years behind me in school."

"And two years ahead of them. One of the only other Tories I taught. Fielding felled him at Yorktown. He did not realize it, of course, until the bayonet had already pierced."

The thought sliced Edwinn. He hadn't known Mr. Baldwin well, but they had been friendly enough. Enough that it hurt to realize he was dead, and at the hands of someone he now had a connection to, however tenuous.

Randel's eyes slid shut. "He said nothing to me, but I overhead him talking to Benton about it, heard the agony in Fielding's voice. And rather than try to comfort him as a good commander would, I actually thought, 'Perhaps this will teach him the price of war, teach him to be either hot or cold but not lukewarm,' and left him to his pain."

"Did it? Teach him, I mean?"

When Randel opened his eyes again, they were blank with dark memories. "I cannot say. Both he and Benton suffered minor injuries in the battle and went to their homes to recover when peace was declared. I have seen neither since, and Benton does not expound on such things in his letters. Not about Fielding, anyway." He blinked, straightened, smiled. "All this to say, Lark's arrival has made me remember and reconsider. To realize that if we as a nation and a people are to move past the war and its penalties, we must keep our eyes trained ahead, not dwell on the injuries of the past."

Edwinn gripped the head of his cane where it leaned against his chair. "Is that your way of saying you forgive me?"

Randel lifted his brows. "Do you admit you did something that needs forgiving?"

Edwinn chuckled. He couldn't help it. "Forgiveness, and the need of it, is something that belongs to the subject, not the object. It matters not if I was right or wrong, only that you perceived me as being so and were hurt by it. Similarly, forgiving me will not change me, but you. A certain tutor of mine taught me that distinction in a theology class at King William's School."

Randel smiled only slightly and held Edwinn's gaze for a long moment. "I hurt you as definitely as you hurt me. More, probably, because I was your mentor and teacher yet turned against you when you held fast to your beliefs, which I first helped instill in you. Yet you have already forgiven me, have you not?"

Edwinn inclined his head. "It hurt. It still hurts when I consider it. But yes, Master Randel, I have forgiven you."

"And I still disagree with the way your beliefs manifested themselves. I still believe our cause was just and the Almighty supported us. But I cannot dispute what He may have spoken to your heart, as it pertains to you. Yes, Edwinn. I forgive you."

Edwinn's logic must have been faulty, for a burden lifted from his shoulders with those simple words. For the first time in seven years, he felt nearly home. "Thank you." Faced with such emotion, he had little choice but to clear his throat and change the subject. "Shall we pray for your wife?"

They prayed together as they hadn't done since Edwinn's school days, and then the elder stood. No doubt he was as eager to return to his laboring wife as he had been to escape. He paused, however, at the door. "As for the other matter…perhaps in fact I *would* approve, were you to pay court to my daughter. If ever your thoughts inclined that direction."

At the moment, Edwinn's thoughts could incline nowhere. They were far too muddled a mess.

Emerson strode away from the house with a furrowed brow and headed for the post office a few doors down. The matter he had sought out Mr. Thomas for was far from urgent, but it was unusual to find the lawyer's house completely vacant. If anyone knew when the family might be back, it was Mr. Tillman, the postmaster.

The older gentleman looked up when Emerson entered, the gray wisps of his hair floating above his head as if blown by some breeze. His wig, as usual, sat on the table at his elbow like a sleeping pet. "Emerson, good day. No post yet today, but I have a few letters for your father from yesterday."

"Thank you, Mr. Tillman." Emerson leaned into the table—careful to avoid the wig—and watched the man sift through mounds of papers. How he kept it all straight, Emerson couldn't determine. "Did you enjoy a good Christmas?"

"Oh, most excellent. Rose and her little ones made it in from Jamestown, and it was a blessing indeed to see the children again. They have grown so these past months!" Mr. Tillman pulled a few letters from the stack. "And you? I imagine you were lonely with Miss Benton traveling this year, eh?"

Emerson's heart thudded in a tired, sluggish way. "Miserably. Speaking of traveling, do you know if the Thomases have gone away for the holiday? I stopped by their house to ask Mr. Thomas a question about a lease and found it shut up tight."

As he slid the Fielding mail onto the table, Mr. Tillman pursed his lips and scratched his largely bald head. "Well now, let me think. They stopped in a while back to let me know they'd be visiting Mr. Thomas's brother, and they went early enough to see General Washington resign his commission, I believe. Yes, left early on the tenth. To Annapolis. They ought to be back by the end of January, weather permitting, if your business can wait that long."

"That should be soon enough, indeed. Thank you, Mr. Tillman." Emerson slid the mail into his pocket and nodded.

"Happy to help, though young Benton could have told you as much. He was planning on traveling with them before his trip was canceled, as I recall." Ah, that was right. And recall he would—the postmaster knew the comings and goings of everyone within fifty miles of Williamsburg, Emerson was sure. "You have a good day now, and give your family my regards. And if I might give a word of wisdom, you may want to send your miss a sweet-filled letter of your own soon."

Had he any idea where to send such a letter... "Wise words indeed, Mr. Tillman. I asked Wiley to convey my sentiments in his letter to her the other day, but I will certainly be writing her independently soon." He hoped. Perhaps he would be able to claim to the postmaster he had lost the direction and have him put on it the same one Wiley used.

"Wiley's letter?" Tillman toyed with one of the plaits of his discarded wig. "Neither he nor his parents have sent anything recently, but to that Randel fellow in Maryland."

He hadn't written her as promised, then? Emerson barely kept from sighing and forced a smile instead. "Perhaps he has yet to send it. I will ask him. Good day, Mr. Tillman."

He stepped back out into the weak sunshine and strode toward his horse, hitched outside the Thomases'. A few steps from his mare, he halted.

The Thomases had departed the day following the Penelope incident. Gone to Annapolis, where Wiley had planned to go.

Annapolis, where lived one Mr. Randel, to whom Wiley had recently sent a letter.

"Of course. *Of course.*" Leaping into the saddle, Emerson dug his heels into his horse's sides and took off for home.

For the first time in weeks, he had hope to match his purpose.

Chapter Ten

Lark ambled along Tabernacle Street and enjoyed each slow step. Though the air was brisk, the sun was warm, and her blue cloak soaked it up and warmed her shoulders as she walked.

This was the first time she had ventured out alone, but it had seemed appropriate. The Randels were all caught up in the arrival of the newest addition, the tiny and perfect Annabelle. Lark had praised the babe in abundance all yesterday, after the girl's arrival during the night before. Had taken her turn cradling the infant and had ignored the questioning ache in her heart. Had laughed with Sena over the joy of having, finally, a sister.

But today she thought the family might enjoy an hour with no strangers underfoot, so she had tucked the newly arrived letters from her family into her pocket and donned her cloak. She walked across Tabernacle and stepped onto the browned grass of Bladen's Folly's lawn. Remaining within sight of Randel House and her guardians, she crossed in front of the abandoned mansion, smiling at the memory of her and Sena's foray into it the week before, and headed for the bare-limbed Liberty Tree. It stretched high above her, its spindly fingers seeming to touch the clouds. She pulled out the blanket she'd tucked under her arm and tossed it, still folded, to the base of the trunk.

Once settled against the tulip poplar, she extracted the letters Mr. Randel had handed her earlier that morning. The first was in her mother's hand, and she opened it with a smile.

It faded as she read Mamma's urging to resolve her anger with Emerson and come home as soon as the weather allowed, stressing that the wedding would be in March as planned. She said how much they missed her, how determined they were to see her make amends with her betrothed.

Guilt battled determination in Lark's chest. She wanted to honor her parents, to obey them…but if they persisted in this, what choice did she have but to stay here, where they could not force her to the church and let expectation rule her?

She picked up the second letter. Her name was scrawled on one side of the folded paper in Wiley's script, which brought the smile back to her lips. She unfolded it and read.

Dearest Larksong,

Already we miss you terribly, as you can well imagine. Christmas felt empty without you here. Knowing Mother is writing you as well, I imagine she will do her best to convince you home, back to your duties as a betrothed woman. I urge them continually to put a halt to preparations for the nuptials, though I have honored your silence in the specifics of the break. I did explain the situation to Isabella Fielding. She stomped on her brother's toes. I assume you can see me grinning in delight as I recall it.

I avoided Emerson until said stomping, but we came across each other afterward. Lark, I must be honest. He is a frightful mess over this. I will not take his side, and I would never betray your confidence, but I feel compelled to tell you I believe him wholeheartedly repentant. Not just for the incident with Penelope, but for the prior two years he wasted. I have never seen him like this, not even in war.

There, message delivered. I told him I would let you know how heartsick he is, on the condition that he stop asking me where to find you. You ought to have seen him when he agreed, all but whimpering at the hopelessness of discovering your whereabouts without my cooperation. You would have cackled in delight.

Yet, if you feel yourself softening, I would not argue with you coming home earlier than planned. This seems to have jarred him from a long-standing stupor, and I believe when next you see him, it will be a different, better Emerson that greets you. Too late though, I fear, and your heart is too precious for me to put it in danger of another ache.

Find your heart's desire, Larksong, and fly after it, wherever that leads you. If by chance it brings you home again soon, then I will welcome you.

Most affectionately,
Your brother, Wiley

Lark pressed her lips together and lowered the paper to her lap. Not the letter she had expected, to be sure. Wiley might be Emerson's closest friend, but he had never been blinded to the man's flaws or swept away by his charms. For her brother to take his part even this much, Emerson must be miserable indeed.

She fisted her hand in the fabric of her cloak to keep from balling up the missives. Two weeks of misery was nothing compared to what Emerson had put her through. She wouldn't fly home, back to his arms, because he moped about for a few days.

Her eyes slid shut, and the sunlight painted swirling rainbows upon her lids. It wasn't just about her continued anger. That was only over the Penelope incident, and it would fade. Eventually. But the bigger issue remained, the one that had made her question the betrothal before her doxy of a cousin ever arrived.

They might have known each other all their lives, but they were strangers, she and Emerson. He knew nothing of her heart or mind and had never wanted to. And what did she really know of him?

She rested her head against the tree. Was it so terrible that she wanted more than a facade of a marriage? Was she being unrealistic? Childish? Ought she hire a companion, a carriage, and go home? Ask Wiley to fetch her? Return to her repentant former-betrothed and agree to give him another chance, let her parents preserve their dignity?

For a moment, she let that possibility swim through her mind, let it travel the river of her thoughts and dreams, whirl through the pool of her duties and expectations. But then she opened her eyes and saw the broken shell of a governor's mansion sitting atop the gentle knoll.

No. She would not go home and settle for what her family wanted her to do, she would not build a marriage on Emerson's guilt and her own fear that no other man would ever want her. Not when the truth remained that *he* did not want her, either. Better to be alone in a new town than alone in her own home. Better to wait and see if something more awaited her than to resign herself to nothingness.

What was it Mr. Calvert had said in his prayer? *Reveal to her the purpose You have so perfectly ordained for her life.* That was what she wanted, that was her supplication. She longed to have purpose.

And she would stay right here in Annapolis until she found it. If Emerson needed to assuage his guilt, let him do so before the Almighty. She never wanted to see him again.

Wiley's whistle died on his lips when he saw the commotion at the Fieldings' stables. Maybe a carriage being loaded with trunks was not, in itself, cause for a lump of dread to form in his stomach. But the fact that Emerson was the one striding from house to outbuilding, a valise in hand…

He swung off his mount and hurried toward his friend. "Emerson. What the devil is going on? Are you away on business?"

No, that look his friend shot him was not good. Not good at all. Hope mixed with determination, and a bit too much certainty. Emerson handed off the bag to a stable hand. "Oh, just a trip for personal matters. Hopefully short. I feel the sudden urge to visit our alma mater, Wiley, and pay my respects to Mr. Randel."

Wiley bit back a curse. "Mr. Randel, you say? The two of you never much liked each other."

"No, but you and he always did, didn't you? I cannot believe I missed it this long. You did not just cancel your trip, you sent her in your stead. They had even invited her to begin with, had they not?" He shook his head. "She merely traveled with the Thomases as *you* had planned to do."

Wiley swept his hat off his head and dashed it to the ground. "Emerson—"

"You wonder how I finally pieced that together?" His friend offered his usual charming smile, the one Wiley hadn't seen since…

well, since it was aimed at Penelope. "Chance—no, Providence—led me to Mr. Thomas's door for some legal advice today. But of course, he wasn't home—though I had forgotten that—so I asked after him at the post office. And once Mr. Tillman began talking...well. He is always a fount of information, is he not?"

Wiley's dusty hat looked pitiful on the ground. He picked it up with a sigh and brushed it off. "And you think the proper response is to rush after her? Emerson, I wrote her as I said I would, and I told her I thought you sincere in your desire to make things right. Mother has urged her to come home as well. Give her a chance to respond."

"No." Something else burned in Emerson's eyes now, something closer to need. "I cannot rest until I see her again, until I can speak to her myself. I cannot sit idly by now that I know where she has gone."

Wiley shook his head. "Emerson, she will not receive you. Not yet. Give her time to heal. Write her a letter—"

"It is not enough." Yet he reached into his pocket and pulled out what looked suspiciously like one. Though it appeared a bit worn, so it was surely not one he had just written her. "This letter she wrote has shown me a glimpse of the young lady I ignored, and I must know more of her. More than ink and paper can tell me, more than the miles between us allow."

"Oh. Hmm." Several choice words flitted through Wiley's mind. Most of them pertaining to what his sister might do to him if she realized he had given Emerson the note she had written only for cathartic purposes. He took a step back from her imaginary rage and folded his hands behind his back. "You kept that."

Emerson looked at him as if he were a madman. "Of course I kept it. What did you think I would do, toss it into the fire?"

Wiley hadn't really thought that far ahead when he carried it downstairs along with the jewelry. He had only wanted Emerson to see what he had lost, and why he had lost her. "I had hoped so. She... well, to be honest, she wrote it for her own benefit, not for me to give to you. Before we went down to the library."

"Before?" Emerson's hand fell limp to his side, his expression one of a man who had been stripped of his last shred of hope. "She felt this way *before* she saw what she did?"

Well, deuces. Wiley hadn't meant to make him feel worse. "Since her birthday, though I suspect it had been brewing a while before that."

Emerson's shoulders sank. "So even had I not been a complete dunderhead with your cousin, she might have cried off."

"Hence why you need to give her time to sort through things. 'Tisn't only about her justified anger, 'tis about what she desires in general."

Emerson's shoulders rolled into alignment again. "No. Hence why I need to make all haste to Annapolis and bring her home. We must address this."

Wiley sucked in a breath and blew it back out in a gust. "There is no talking you out of it, is there? Short of tying you down for the next three months."

"None."

"Then I will come with you. If you convince her to return home, you cannot travel together alone."

Emerson quirked a brow. "My mother has already considered that, Wiley, and has sent me with a letter for a friend of hers—an upstanding widow from Annapolis who has been wanting to visit. She would make a better chaperone than you. Besides, your original reason for staying here still holds. You must keep an eye on Penelope."

Blast, he was right. Who knew what stories the little minx might come up with if both he and Emerson left? They could return to find a very different wedding in the planning. Wiley sighed and set his hat back onto his head. "Emerson...try not to be an idiot, will you?"

Emerson offered a crooked smile. "That is my foremost goal as well."

"Go with God, then."

"Thank you. I shall return soon, my friend, with your sister."

Wiley clasped his hand, but he couldn't stop the shake of his head. Somehow, he didn't think Emerson would find it so easy when he knocked on Randel's door. Now that Lark had taken a stand, she wouldn't be easy to budge.

CHAPTER ELEVEN

Lark spun through the last steps of the cotillion, petticoats flashing, and laughed as the music came to a boisterous end. Out of breath and feeling pleasantly flushed, she curtsied to her partner and made no objection when he offered to fetch her some punch.

"You are such a good dancer." Sena linked their arms together with a grin and spun them in a quick circle. "You put me to shame. It is no wonder all the best partners seek you out."

Her cheeks grew hotter, but Lark laughed. She wasn't so sure of the reason—for all she knew Sena had put all her gentlemen friends up to it—but she had indeed found herself the center of much male attention at the collation and dance this evening. Strange and new. And elating.

"Here you are, Miss Benton." Mr. Selby handed her a cup of punch with a small bow. "Could I bring you anything else? A coconut jumble perhaps, or a little sugar cake?"

"I thank you, Mr. Selby, but no. This is all I need." She took a sip to prove it.

Sena tilted her head. "Off again, are you, Mr. Selby?"

The gentleman bowed and smiled. "Only for a moment, Miss Randel. My mother is beckoning, no doubt wanting some refreshment as well. I shall return forthwith."

Lark smiled him away and turned to Sena to express her amazement at the evening's progression, but she halted when another bevy of young men approached. Gracious, Sena seemed to be acquainted with the entire continent.

"There you are, gentlemen!" Sena grinned and pulled Lark closer to her side. "Allow me to make introductions. Lark darling, these are Misters Alderidge, Forrister, and Litchfield, and that fellow hiding behind them is dear Mr. Woodward. All former pupils of my father, soldiers of the bravest mettle, and devoted Annapolitans. Gentlemen, Miss Lark Benton."

One of them stepped forward—Mr. Litchfield, was it?—and held out a hand. When she placed her fingers upon his, he bowed over them while directing a saucy smile her way.

Acrobats leapt in her stomach. Ever since she had been old enough to attend balls, she had been betrothed to Emerson. No one in Williamsburg had ever flirted with her. Even if a man took her hand, it was nevertheless to someone else he would direct his grin. She scarce knew how to respond, but with a small smile.

"Pleasure to make your acquaintance, miss." Though he released her fingers, his expression remained interested. Interested! In *her*. "I confess we all wondered who the lovely young woman with Miss Randel was, especially when we saw how you dance on the air. In spite of its arriving with another snowstorm, this new year obviously agrees with you."

A laugh tickled her throat. "All twenty hours of it, yes."

"You must be new to our fair town," another of the men said. Forrister, perhaps? He had a dimple that flashed when he smiled. "Certainly I would remember had I seen you here before."

"Always the charmer, Mr. Forrister." Sena chuckled. "She is from Williamsburg. Mr. Woodward, you spent some time there, did you not?"

The three in front parted to give their friend room to answer. Mr. Woodward, Lark saw, was a young man of slight stature and had a scholarly look about him. Somehow, she couldn't imagine him charging across a field of battle with a musket in hand. "A few months," he said softly, "when I was a boy. I enjoyed my time there very much."

Sena stood on tiptoe, gaze on the other side of the room. "Excuse us, gentlemen. You can all convince Miss Benton of your wit and winning personalities in a few moments. I must introduce her to Charlotte Griffith."

When they had gone a few steps, Lark grinned. "A friend of yours you must introduce me to, yet who is in your society? Well, this is a first."

Sena shot her an amused glance. "She is no Kate or Alice, but we have always been friendly enough. I suppose it seems as though I have two separate lives, does it not?" Her brows wiggled. "It is true. I am really a spy, but pretending to be a young lady of respectable society. A pirate captain, secretly undermining the community by infiltrating their youth and filling their minds with nonsense."

"Dastardly." Fanning herself, Lark tamped down another laugh but let the grin spill forth. "Little do you know I am also a pirate captain, from an enemy vessel no less, here to undermine your undermining. Beware, Cap'n Mobcap. I shall not see this community undone. I rather like it."

"Captain Mobcap?" Sena tossed her head back in a laugh. Dark curls danced around her shoulders. "We ought to write that down and weave a yarn for the boys."

"Aye, we should." Lark stepped out of the way of a quick-moving adolescent boy and took another sip.

Sena waved at someone and led Lark around a table full of sweets. "Here we are. Charlotte, you look beautiful this evening. I brought a new friend to introduce. Lark Benton of Williamsburg."

It seemed Lark had heard herself being introduced more in the past few weeks than in all her life before. She smiled at Charlotte. "Good to meet you, Miss Griffith."

"Oh, you may call me Charlotte. Any friend of Sena's will surely be mine as well." Charlotte grinned and absently smoothed a ruffle on her dress. "I was wondering who the newcomer was, causing such a stir with the menfolk. I suppose 'tis too much to hope you are a penniless nobody they will lose interest in within a day."

Sena shook her head with sparkling eyes. "Too much to hope indeed."

"I feared as much." Charlotte gave a dismissive wave with her fan. "I ought to be used to such things—there is always someone new distracting them from those of us always here. Sena somehow holds their attention, but we cannot all manage that. Though perhaps if we all employed her antics…"

"Not all could manage *that*, either." Sena looked as though she would like to stick her tongue out at her friend.

Lark's smile faded. Though the idea of causing a stir with the men had given her heart a little jolt, the truth of Charlotte's observation sobered her. She was a novelty, nothing more.

Charlotte seemed to realize her comment had bordered on insulting. She winced and offered a conciliatory smile. "You are right, Sena, and I meant it not to come out so… You are a delight. More a delight than most of us can hope to be. And Miss Benton, one can see your sweet spirit from across the room. I am so glad Sena brought you over. But"—eyes sparkling, she leaned close—"if you are searching for a beau, there is no better option than my own darling brother, seen there by the doors. He cuts a fine figure, does he not?"

Before Lark could look for him, Sena laughed. "Clever, Charlotte. Direct her to the one young man you could have no interest in yourself."

"I thought it the perfect plan."

Lark laughed and settled into the conversation—one she could participate in with ease. Yet as she spoke of gowns and bonnets, handsome men and coquettish women, she couldn't help but think all their words amounted to nothing. No talk of faith and prayer and purpose. No serious topics.

No wonder Sena led two separate lives.

"Ah, there is my brother now." Charlotte reached for an approaching young man and introduced him.

Mr. Griffith bowed to her and held out a hand. "If I might have this dance, Miss Benton?"

She placed her fingers in his with a murmur of agreement, but a flash of dark hair in her periphery stole her attention, and her head swiveled.

Not Emerson. Of course not. He was in Williamsburg. Not here, at this New Year's celebration, but in his own home with his own friends. As he should be.

She smiled again at Mr. Griffith—a handsome man with lovely brown eyes that did *not* put her in mind of Emerson's—and followed him back to the dance floor.

Freedom sang through her, and only now did she realize why. Emerson was not here. Emerson was no longer a concern. For the first time, she didn't have to wonder if he would look her way at a ball, if he would notice or even care if she danced with anyone else.

He would not be in a corner with the other young men, ignoring her, would not therefore make it clear the obligatory two dances they shared were only given because of expectation.

Until now, every time she took to the floor with someone else, she had fought back a mixture of longing that Emerson would see and be jealous, and worry that he would think her forward. Both concerns butting heads with the nagging thought that he wouldn't notice at all. More often than not, that had been exactly the case. And when notice he did, he certainly didn't seem to care. Because he was secure in her affections?

Hardly. Her affections had never seemed to enter his mind at all.

But no matter now. He could neglect her no longer, and so her night would not be stained with realization of it.

Perhaps that was why the evening shone so bright.

Emerson watched the once-familiar streets of Annapolis, buried now in snow, roll by his carriage window. Over the years since he lived here, new houses and businesses had sprung to life, while some he had known were boarded up and abandoned. Though the war never touched the city, it had clearly felt the effects.

Annapolis had never been home, though he spent most of his adolescence here. His lips quirked up as he remembered the dread of coming back to this place as a boy. It meant the end of holiday, the start of school once again. Much better were the times he had gotten to leave it, with those weeks of unstructured days stretching before him.

This time was different. This time he breathed in the Maryland air with a smile and thanked the Almighty for getting him here safely, in spite of the snowstorm that had raged through yesterday. He would have a room secured by noon, be at the Randels' soon after. A few hours baring his soul to Lark, a visit to his mother's friend… With any luck, the three of them would be leaving again in the morning, before more bad weather could strike.

A short while later, Josiah pulled the carriage to a stop outside Middleton Tavern, and Emerson jumped down. He gave his servant a grin. "You take care of the horses, Josiah, while I secure the lodgings."

"Sounds good, Mr. Emerson." The cheerful man gave a wave and climbed down from the driver's bench.

Emerson strode into the inn and quickly located the proprietor. "Good day, sir. I am in need of lodgings for me and my servant."

The burly man nodded. "Any idea how long you intend to stay?"

"Ah." Best to be reasonable. "At least one night, possibly more."

"Well, we've a fine room available in the rear of the building, overlooking the gardens."

"That will do quite nicely." He would settle into it, then seek out Lark.

As he followed the man up the stairs, he prayed she wouldn't slam the door in his face.

"Girls, would you do a favor for me?"

Lark and Sena looked up from their stitching. Mr. Randel had stepped halfway into the room, Annabelle bundled in his arms. Sena smiled. "What is it, Papa?"

"I promised Mr. Lloyd I would look over a speech for him and need to return it to the State House this afternoon. But your mother just fell asleep, Mrs. Green is out with the boys, and Rory is on another errand for me.... Could I trouble you to deliver it? I realize the streets are still snowy—"

"Trouble?" Sena leapt up. "I thrive on it. Of course we shall go. Is there a session today for us to eavesdrop on?"

Mr. Randel chuckled. "As if you would find that particular eavesdropping interesting. Just leave the papers with a clerk and leave the poor statesmen alone."

Lark stood to run after Sena, who had already vaulted up the stairs. Lark had barely reached the bedchamber before Sena was whirling round again. At least she had grabbed Lark's cloak and bonnet as well as her own. They attired themselves on the return trip down the stairs and paused at the bottom to attach the pattens to their leather boots.

When they looked up, the manservant's son waited beside Mr. Randel.

Sena sighed. "Papa, there is no need to inconvenience Little Rory with this. The State House is all of two steps away."

"And the last time you went to it—with *me*, no less—you slipped away to pay a visit to Mrs. Mattimore in a side of town I would just as soon you not go to alone." He clapped a hand on the gangly boy's shoulder. "If you intend to do the same today, which I deem highly likely given your friend's lack of reply to our offer of employ, you will go with escort."

Lark smothered a grin at the exasperation on Sena's face. Exasperation that soon pulled up into mirth as she accepted a bundle of papers from her father. "You know me too well, Papa."

He opened the door for them, and Lark and Sena stepped out, Little Rory a step behind them. Tying her bonnet under her chin as chilled air swept over her, Lark let Sena dash ahead. "And our hurry today is what? Are we going to sneak onto the ferry to pay a visit to an outcast friend on the Eastern Shore? Perhaps keep tryst with your pirate crew?"

Sena laughed and waited for her on the walkway, grinning at their young escort. "Little Rory is more fun than Papa would like to think, so all options are open. Who can tell what adventure we might stumble into?"

"With you, my dear friend, only the Lord Himself can know."

"Spontaneity fends off boredom. And hurrying fends off the cool air. I maintain my approach to life is the proper one, and the rest of society just has yet to realize it."

Lark replied only with a laugh, since they were even then hurrying up North Street. Approaching the State House this time didn't cause quite the reaction it had before. There were no other residents approaching, dressed in their best, no men in army uniform, no expectation of General Washington arriving any moment. As they circled around to the entrance, the place felt barren and quiet.

A flash of something caught Lark's eye as Sena pulled her toward the door. Deep brown hair, a familiar stride—nonsense. Lark shook her head, but she couldn't keep her shoulders from tensing. When would she stop imagining Emerson every time she turned around?

When would that dual hope and fear stop pouncing on her? Bad enough he continued to fill her dreams, but seeing him everywhere she turned... It was embarrassing, even if no one else realized she kept doing it. *She* knew.

Their escort was staring off too, toward a group of boys that looked about his age. Sena smirked. "Go ahead. Just be back here in an hour's time, so we can go home together."

The boy smiled. "One hour. Thank you, Miss Sena."

Lark sent her eyes heavenward at Sena's determination for independence and let herself be steered through the large doors.

"Ah, Miss Randel." A gentleman approached with a smile. "How fortuitous I happened by. Might I assume you have my speech from your father?"

Sena presented it with a flourish. "I certainly do, Mr. Lloyd. I am sure, had I given him the chance, he would have sent me with a message of greeting to accompany it, but alas, he said the word 'trouble,' and I was off seeking it too fast to hear him out."

The congressman loosed a belt of laughter and accepted the papers. "Well, you may give him *my* message of thanks, and well wishes. How is your mother and the baby?"

"Both lacking in sleep but otherwise perfect."

Mr. Lloyd turned to Lark. "And good to see you again, Miss Benton. I trust your new friend is not leading you into any trouble from which she does not proceed to extricate you?"

Lark chuckled. Good humor seemed to flow wherever Sena went. Even here, where it surely wasn't the daily order of business. "Thus far, sir, though I daren't make any assumptions about the future."

"A wise young woman." He turned when someone called his name from down the hall. "Ah, I had better hasten back. Jefferson's determined to send out express riders to badger the missing delegates. Thank you again, Miss Randel, Miss Benton. I shall be by to see your father soon."

They exited the State House once more through its tall wooden doors, the sunlight reflecting off the new snow blinding Lark for a moment when it struck her eyes.

"Lark!"

She halted with one foot on a white marble square, one hovering over a black. The door behind her thudded shut. She blinked to refocus her vision, looked around. Sure that, whoever called her, it was not the someone she thought it was.

A theory that lasted only a second, before Emerson came bounding up the steps. "Lark! It *is* you. For a moment I thought my eyes deceived me, so set was I on greeting you at the Randels'. You cannot know how glad I am to see you."

He reached for her. Actually reached out, as if expecting her to put her hand in his or perhaps even rush to embrace him. Feeling each muscle in her face go tense and hard, she retreated a step instead. "What are you doing here, Emerson?"

"Emerson?" Sena's eyes went wide. Then, in true Sena fashion, she tilted her head and narrowed them again. "I would have expected horns and a tail. Or at the very least a pitchfork."

Perhaps, if she weren't numb with shock that Emerson stood towering over her when he should have been in Virginia, Lark would have taken the time to grin.

Emerson barely glanced at Sena, just locked that beseeching gaze on Lark. "I deserve your disregard, your anger. I know that. But please, darling, give me the chance to explain why—"

"You dare to call me that?" Fury built inside like steam in a kettle, more intense than any she had felt save that night in the library. "You dare to come here and pretend humility, to ask for *anything*, after the way you acted?"

"It is not pretense." He took a step toward her. She took another back. "Please, d—Lark. Hear me out."

"You cannot have anything to say that I wish to hear." She looked over her shoulder. Two more steps back before she reached the steps on the southeast side, opposite the ones they had come up a few minutes before.

"Your family misses you. Please, come home. For their sakes."

Oh, he was using all his skill, to be sure. The wide eyes, filled with emotion. The slant of his shoulders, conceding defeat even as he took another strong step toward her.

She was in no mood to be manipulated. This time she stepped forward and poked him in the chest. "You think I don't know what you are about? You may have never paid a jot of attention to me, but I know every trick of charm in your stockpile. I will not be talked into anything, no matter for whose sake you say it is. So *you* go home. I am going to stay right here, where people recognize I am something more than Wiley's quiet sister, until I am good and ready to leave."

What reaction had she expected? Surprise, most likely, as he showed on her birthday when she refused the diamonds. Perhaps anger. Maybe a bit of confusion. Certainly not the light that danced in his eyes, as if she were some great diversion.

She didn't just poke him now—she shoved. "Am I amusing, Mr. Fielding?"

The mirth took a sharp turn to something warmer, even as a smile played on his lips. "Sadly, I do not know, Miss Benton. But I would very much like to find out. Let me walk you back—"

She cut him off with a screech of frustration and spun away, running down the steps speedily enough to earn a hoot of approval from Sena.

He called her name, then a request for a pardon. Lark glanced over her shoulder long enough to see Sena had stepped into his path, and he was trying to sidestep her without knocking her down. All without taking his eyes from Lark.

He chose *now* of all times to keep his gaze on her? Well, it wouldn't do him any good. If Sena was going to risk getting tumbled to the ground so she could escape, Lark would make it count. She sped along a path through the snow-covered lawn.

"Lark, come now. Hold up."

She darted a glance back and saw him leaping down the stairs in a single bound. Her legs pumped faster.

"Lark!" His voice sounded incredulous. "Why are you running? I only want to talk."

"You had two years for that, Emerson." With a bit of impishness to her smile, she charged toward Cornhill Street. The only area of Annapolis in which she could hope to lose him was Market Place. Then, once he'd given up the chase, she'd return to Randel House and let Sena's father bar him out.

Behind her, he let out a half sigh, half laugh. As if he found her attempt to escape utterly ridiculous but was willing to indulge her. No doubt he thought he'd catch her within a few steps.

Little did he know she'd been getting such exercise daily.

She sped down Cornhill, dodging a carriage stopped before one of the two taverns on the street and weaving around a handful of chatting gentlemen. One of them tipped his hat to her and called out, "Good afternoon, Miss Randel...'s friend."

Lark would have laughed, had she the breath. Obviously the residents of the town would suppose it Sena flying past them. They wouldn't think twice about a young lady charging down the avenues.

Though they wouldn't be used to young men running after said young lady. She heard the same gentleman speak again. "Say, now. Hold up there, you."

Emerson's voice came out with a hint of frustration. "Step aside, I beg you, sir. She is my betrothed."

She caught something to the effect of "Merry chase" and "New meaning," though she was too set on seizing the chance to put distance between them to worry over the words between. Directly ahead lay the half turn where Cornhill and Fleet Streets collided, marked today by a snowbank. She could turn up Fleet and perhaps trick Emerson, if he didn't see it. But that would deliver her back to State House Circle, and he would surely catch her in all that open space.

No, better to stick to her original plan. She skidded into Fleet in the direction of Market Place and headed toward the bay.

Footsteps pounded behind her, but she wouldn't risk looking. She flew into the open market area, grateful the sunny day had brought the Annapolitans out in droves to stock up after the snowstorm.

"Lark, hold up."

Instead, she careened toward the thickest group of shoppers and used them as a blind for a moment or two. That worked long enough for her to take cover behind a grove of snowed-in barrels. She kept moving in a crouch. A peek from behind the barrels told her Emerson was near but had no idea where she was. He craned his head this way and that, brows furrowed.

Perfect. The moment he looked away, she made a dash toward the next large group.

The smell hit her before her eyes could register that this wasn't the kind of group she had expected. Bodily odor permeated the air, and now she could see the filth on the press of figures, the ragged clothes, the ropes binding ankles together, and the dark skin of each person surrounding her.

She'd run pell-mell into a slave auction. Which wouldn't have been nearly so terrifying if this group weren't obviously straight off a boat from Africa. One hurled a strange-sounding phrase at her and glared, another spat at her feet.

A whip sounded. "You treat your betters with respect, boy!"

A shriek escaped Lark's lips when another whip crack brought the black man to his knees. Why in the world did the auctioneer think *that* was the answer? The slave gazed up at her with pure hatred, his lips curled back to reveal vicious white teeth.

She pressed a hand to her mouth and stumbled backward. Of course he hated her—why wouldn't he? In his eyes she was naught but an oppressor, one blind to his plight.

A plight far worse than hers. "I am sorry. So sorry." She couldn't be sure he heard her over the rising voice of the auctioneer, or that he would understand her even if he did. But her stomach roiled, forcing her back another step. Not from the smell, not from the resentment he still leveled on her.

From the cruel-eyed white man behind him, with whip in hand and greed on his face.

A shiver coursed through her, and tears surged to her eyes. She must escape. She spun, ran as fast as she could without caring where it took her.

"Lark! Lark, watch out!"

The urgency in Emerson's voice brought her head around to find him, even as her feet kept moving. She saw the horror and fear in his eyes a moment before she felt her shoe slip on a patch of ice.

Snapping her attention back to what was in front of her, she realized nothing was—nothing solid, only the choppy gray waters of the bay. She screamed, flailed, but to no avail.

The icy water swallowed her whole.

CHAPTER TWELVE

A million images of terror flashed before Emerson's eyes. Friends walking barefoot through ice and snow in pursuit of the Redcoats. Men dropping unconscious before him from hunger or illness. Blood, cannon smoke, impending disaster. And always, always those screams of pain and fear.

Exactly like the one that spilled from Lark when the water first touched her, before it rushed over her head.

He must have screamed too. He felt it build in his chest, felt the burn of it in his throat, but his pulse hammered too loudly to hear it erupt from his lips. The world around him seemed to slow as he charged toward the slippery dock and dropped to his knees at its snowy edge.

"Lark!" He knew she couldn't hear him, just as he knew the weight of her dress and cloak would pull her relentlessly down. Lying flat, he thrust an arm over the side, hoping and praying his fingers would snag her hand, her clothes, her hair, *something*.

Nothing but water cold as ice wrapped around his hand.

No choice, then. He pulled off his boots and cloak, tried to discern her shape among the shadows of the dark water, and jumped near where he thought she was. Daggers of ice pierced every inch of flesh, but he had no time to acknowledge the pain. *Please, Lord, let me not hit her. Help me find her.*

Something brushed his foot. He had no way of telling whether it was Lark, but he dove under in the direction it had been. The water was too dark for him to see, but he waved his arms all around as he kicked himself deeper.

A strand of something smooth and long twined around his fingers. He grabbed the hair, tugged enough to slow her downward path, and forced himself lower until he found her head, her shoulders, her arms.

She lashed out, nearly striking him, but he managed to twist behind her and wrap an arm around her torso. And if he cursed women's voluminous gowns as he struggled to propel them back to the surface, he figured the Lord would forgive it.

They finally broke through, though he could feel the weight of her dress dragging them back down. He had no idea how he would manage to keep them both afloat, but before he could wonder about it, multiple hands appeared in front of his face, reaching for Lark. With one final burst of strength, he pushed her toward salvation and sucked in a deep breath of relief when two men hauled her up.

Hands reached for him too, and he accepted the help. Neither did he argue when someone draped a foul woolen blanket around his shoulder. Noisome or not, it would block the wind.

Lark was coughing, collapsed into a ball in the snow under a filthy blanket of her own. Emerson crawled over to her and pulled her close. "Fool woman. Tell me you are well."

He half expected her to slap at him, but the water must have stolen her spirit. She sagged against him. "I am s–s–sorry, Em–m–m…" Shivering took over her speech.

He must get her dry and warm, fast. She would probably prefer to be returned to the Randels' straightaway, but by the time he could carry her there on foot—he could fetch his horse. But then, if he were to go to Middleton's anyway, they might as well do their drying there. Especially since it lay directly across from them.

Lark still in his arms, he staggered up. The same hands that had pulled them from the water helped him gain his feet. He nodded to the roughly dressed men. "We are in your debt."

The man nearest him had a face creased with concern. "You had better dry yourselves, sir, before the cold steals into your bones."

"I have a room at Middleton Tavern. We can go there."

That was enough to disperse most of the crowd, but the near man picked up Emerson's discarded things and said, "I shall walk you over, in case your strength fails. That was quite a thing you did, diving in after her."

Emerson settled the shivering bundle of stubborn woman against him. "It was my fault she was running to begin with."

"You know the young miss?"

"She is my betrothed." They started across Market Place, and Emerson was glad for the company. Each step he took made him that much more aware of the failing strength of his limbs. Good to know there was help at hand, if he needed it again.

Lark turned her face up to him. Her teeth still chattered, but fury sparked in her eyes again. "St–st–st–op c–c–c–all—"

"Hush, love." He grinned down into her anger, unable to help it. Where had *this* Lark been all these years? Never, as she sat quietly in the corner of a room without demanding a word from him, had he expected a creature of such fire to be lurking under her placid surface. Had someone told him a year ago she would argue with him even while dangerously wet and cold, he would have laughed at them.

Had he been blind all this time, or had she hidden this side of herself from him? He had no idea, nor could he be sure she would give him a chance to make it right. But this he knew—had he never met Lark Benton before this day yet seen her as he just had, he wouldn't have let her walk away. He would have been too intrigued. And now—now he was driven to discover how spine and humility could coincide, how such a sweet-tempered young lady could toss aside demureness for defiance.

Her chin made an attempt to jut, though the chattering stole its effect. "Wh–wh–when I am w–w–w–arm ag–g–g—"

"When you are warm again, darling, you can tell me what you will do. For now, stop trying to talk before you chip a tooth."

Their guardian jogged ahead to open the tavern door, and Emerson sagged in relief. Truth be told, he could feel the shivers starting in him too, and his muscles burned.

Heat from the fire and many bodies embraced him the moment he stepped inside. The proprietress rushed up. "Oh, look at the two of you! Whatever happened? It looks as though you were both fools enough to attempt a swim."

"Next time we try it, it shall not be in January." Emerson leaned against the wall. Just for a moment. "I've a room where I can fetch dry clothes for myself, but if you could assist with the young lady, madam?"

"Of course! She will be dry and right as rain in half a wink. You bring her back here, young sir, and then the two of you can warm up in our private parlor." She took his things from their dockside helper and offered the man a pint of ale for his trouble. The stranger accepted with a nod and headed for the bar.

Emerson followed her through the tavern area and into what must be the owners' quarters. The woman indicated a small, neat room. He set Lark down upon a wooden chair. "There now, Lark. You will be warm soon enough."

She nodded, the fire gone from her eyes again, and shivered under the blanket still over her shoulders.

The proprietress shooed him out. "Hurry yourself into some dry clothes, sir, and then come back down. Henry will have the fire a-blazing in there"—she indicated a room to her right—"and I will bring you both some good, hot coffee. Maybe with a nip of brandy too, eh?"

As heat seeped in, it sapped his strength. He could only nod, then trudge toward the stairs and into his room. Josiah sprang to greet him with wide eyes. "Mr. Emerson! What—"

Emerson held up a hand. "One moment. I need to…"

Josiah helped him to a seat, clucking like a mother hen, and set out some dry clothes. A hot bath sounded just the thing too, but that would take time Emerson was unwilling to waste. He settled for changing into the fresh garments and then plodding back down to the parlor.

Henry had apparently been to work on the fire, because it crackled and snapped in the hearth and sent out blessed waves of heat. Emerson collapsed on the couch solely because it was closest to it.

After a short span, rustling in the hallway snagged his attention, and Emerson looked toward the door. Lark was led in by the proprietress and urged to a seat beside him.

"Allow me to fetch that coffee now. You two sit and thaw out before you turn right to ice."

"Thank you, madam." But Emerson didn't look at her. He was far too busy tamping down a grin at the way the coarse brown dress hung on Lark like a sack. She all but disappeared within its folds, which emphasized the delicacy of her frame and made him want to gather her close and keep her from making any other foolish moves.

As if she would allow *that*.

She sat on the edge of the cushion, huddled in on herself and straining toward the fire. Her cheeks were white as the moon, her lips purple-tinged. Emerson lifted a blanket from the back of the couch and draped it over her shoulders.

Her hair was no longer dripping but now hung free around her to dry. Between the sunlight from the window and the firelight from the hearth, it gleamed deep and rich as a fine port. He had never noticed the shine of it before.

"Thank you," she murmured, pulling the blanket around her. "And thank you for saving me."

"I expected rather you would berate me for being the cause of your new acquaintance with the bay."

Was it his imagination, or did her lips twitch up? "You were not. Not directly, anyway. Though I suppose it was hiding from you that resulted in my running into the slave auction, and *that* is what propelled me toward the bay." She shook her head, her eyes narrowing in seeming pain. "That was the second one I have seen since coming here. Why do we do it, Emerson? Is the coin it saves worth the cost of another's freedom?"

He opened his mouth but could find no reply beyond the trite. "It is a complicated matter." He cleared his throat and angled himself toward her. Best to change the subject. "Has rescuing you earned me the right to apologize?"

Lark let out a long breath. "I am hardly going to run again now. But Emerson." Her eyes looked both tired and determined. "Apologizing will change nothing. It cannot alter facts."

"I know that, but…" He halted when the proprietress rushed in with a tray of coffee and sweets.

"Here you are," she said cheerfully. "I put a dollop of brandy in it already, to warm you the faster. Not much, mind, just a nip."

She scurried out again even as they thanked her. Emerson poured a cup of steaming brew and handed it to Lark, then a second for himself. He took a fortifying sip and sighed. "Lark, I have no excuses for my behavior. I ought not to have acted as I did, and I certainly ought not to have flirted with your cousin. I have been a buffoon, and I can finally see that."

Lark cradled the cup between her palms and stared into the fire. "Your biggest mistake was not Penelope, nor the past two years." She turned her face, leveled him with a glare as piercing as a musket ball. "Your biggest mistake was ever asking for my hand when you had no warm feelings for me."

"Lark—"

"I knew you did not love me. How could you have, when you had been at war and away at school before that?" She shook her head and took a drink. "But I thought, when you asked, you must at least be fond of me. I thought our betrothal would see us draw closer, come to truly know one another." She shook her head again and returned her gaze to the fire.

Emerson stared into the black coffee in his hand. "I killed a friend of mine. In the war."

Her gasp was the only sound for a long moment. "Accidentally, you mean?"

"No." He breathed a laugh, though amusement had no place in it. "He was a Tory. We met on the battlefield. I might never have realized it was him had he not gasped my name as my bayonet…"

"Oh, Emerson." She shifted, and he looked up to see sympathy in her gaze. "I cannot imagine. But I don't see what—"

"It did something to me, Lark. The war in general, and then that—it was at Yorktown. We came home directly afterward, your brother and I, but that only meant there were no other images in the fore of my mind. No other battles lost or won, no other moments of excitement or dread as fresh in my memory. I dreamt of it every night. Every night."

She opened her mouth but closed it again without speaking.

Emerson sighed. "It must seem to have nothing to do with you and me, but it has. My mother thought marriage would cure me of all that ailed my spirit."

Lark stared openmouthed for a moment then surged to her feet, moving closer to the fire. "I suspected it was her idea. Why me, then,

Emerson? Why not some pretty, clever girl you had a hope of sharing interests with?"

Emerson ran a hand over his wet hair. How could he possibly answer that? His vow to be truthful filled him, but he knew it would hurt her. Still, he could hardly push her any further away. "I…I know this will sound terrible, Lark, but…I did not want involvement. I was willing to grant my mother had a point, but I had no desire to do anything to achieve it. Or to open myself up."

Silence. When he finally risked looking at her, her face had turned hard as stone. "So you chose me because your sisters would have told you I fancied myself in love with you, and you knew I would accept your proposal without a courtship first. You chose me *because* you did not care about me."

He was worse than a buffoon. He was an ogre. A monster. And he couldn't even refute it.

Lark placed her cup on the mantel with more deliberation than the action called for. "It would seem, though, that while that was reason enough to propose, your better sense kept you from going through with the marriage those two years. Why, then, did you not agree to end the betrothal on my birthday? You are surely healed by now. Go, fall in love. Marry someone else."

"No." He set his cup on the table at his side and stood. "I do not want to marry anyone else, Lark, I want to marry *you*."

"You do *not*." She spun as if to make for the door but then pivoted back to him. "'Tis only pride speaking, and perhaps guilt. You cannot abide the thought that I would run from you, that I would refuse you. And you feel terrible for the way things ended. But that is no more a reason to wed than your first one."

He shook his head. "Perhaps pride played a factor before. And perhaps guilt opened my eyes. But that is not what brought me here."

"No?" Incredulity dripped from her tone as the bay water had dripped from her hair.

Dare he take a step toward her? He made it slow, sliding, in the hopes she wouldn't notice. "No. I came because of what I saw once the blinders were removed."

She crossed her arms over her chest, pulling the blanket tighter with the action. "I fail to guess what you think you saw concerning me at that juncture, given I was nowhere nearby when the alleged removal of blinders took place."

His lips quirked up. Yes, she had certainly been in Randel's company—that sounded straight from one of their classes. "I saw a good deal more than I ever had before. Wiley gave me that letter you wrote."

For a moment she looked at him blankly, then her eyes went wide. "He *what*?"

"I think he wanted to be sure I understood what really drove you away. And he succeeded. Lark, I—"

"I have heard enough." She whipped the blanket off her shoulders and folded it with a series of sharp, angry motions.

He stepped between her and the door. "This particular anger is more for Wiley than me, isn't it? I had no way of knowing you did not intend me to read it. So if you would like me to deliver you home to Williamsburg so you can berate him—"

She slapped the blanket onto a chair. "I will stay right here, thank you."

Her anger was clear, yes. But more, there was stony determination beneath it. "You mean it. Even knowing how your family misses you—"

"Perhaps if my family had respected my wishes and canceled the wedding plans, then I would not *have* to stay away."

He studied the upward slant of her chin, the fierce burning in her eyes. She would not be budged. Which meant he had two choices. He could give up and go home, convince their families the betrothal was off. If he chose that option, then he would in effect being saying good-bye to her once and for all. Giving her her wish, which might be the gentlemanly thing to do.

But the light caught the depths of her hair, and her eyes shone like moonstone. Her dress hung in total disarray, but her spine was straight and strong.

Emerson dragged in a long breath and cast his lot on the second option. "If you will not come home, then I shall stay here."

She blinked, as if uncertain she had heard him correctly. "You... why in the world would you do that?"

His smile felt wry upon his lips. "Because if you are the woman I begin to see you must be, then you are worth the world."

For a moment he thought he glimpsed tears in her eyes, but then she averted them, and he couldn't be sure it was anything more than a reaction to the whiff of smoke from the chimney. Her hands fisted at her sides. "You have never lacked for lovely words, Emerson. But it is too late. Go or stay, it is no concern of mine."

He inclined his head. "Then with your leave, my dear, I shall stay."

With all the lack of concern of a British lady, she picked up her coffee and took a long drink. "Enjoy the town."

"I think I shall do so more this time than ever before. Given the company."

Her brows rose. "I know not what company you have in mind, but I promise you it shan't be mine."

He pressed his lips together against a grin. "Then I suppose you shall stay hidden in Randel House? Because I assure you, darling, I still have friends enough in Annapolis that if you step out to a ball or fete, I will have secured an invitation to it as well."

She looked as though she would have liked to dash the cup to the ground. Instead she raised her chin. "Very well. Enjoy the holiday celebrations too. But if you call me 'darling' again, 'tis the plank for you."

A smirk sprang to his lips before he could stop it. "You have pirates among your new acquaintances?"

"Scores of them." She sashayed past him with a smirk of her own, leaning close enough to say, "And Cap'n Mobcap's not one to be trifled with."

He let her by, mostly so she wouldn't see his lopsided smile. Getting to know Lark Benton might be the most enjoyment he'd had in ages.

CHAPTER THIRTEEN

"You failed to mention how devastatingly handsome he is."

"Did I?" Lark smiled at Sena and bent down to remove her slippers. "An oversight."

Sena chuckled from her place at the dressing table. "Oh, certainly. Admit it, Lark. Emerson Fielding looks at you, and you turn to pudding."

"Not under threat of torture will I admit such a thing." But she laughed and peeled off her stockings. "And I can say in all honesty there was no such reaction today."

"No, it seemed not." Sena sighed and turned away from the mirror to face her. "Still. I can see why you waited so long for him to set a date. 'Tis hard to let go of so fine a catch, hmm?"

"Especially when there is no good explanation for how I landed him to begin with." She sighed and rolled up the stockings for use tomorrow. The ones that had gone into the bay would have to undergo a serious laundering, but these she had only donned a short time before, after her hair had finally dried enough to walk home.

Accompanied, of course, by the undauntable Emerson.

Sena ran the brush through her hair one last time and set it on the dressing table. "I have no idea what you mean by that. You are a fine catch yourself. Lovely of face, graceful of figure, full of wit and verve, and from an excellent family."

Lark hummed and put on the thick socks she would sleep in. Her toes had yet to warm up. "But he admitted the only reason he ever wanted to marry me was because I was dull and silent."

Sena's brows rose. "You? Silent?"

Laughter bubbled up again. Naturally, Sena would take issue

with that rather than with Emerson's admission. "I thought the way to keep him was to obey all the lessons I'd had on propriety."

"I imagine if Mrs. Green were here, she would be able to provide some wisdom from Ben Franklin's pen to either convince you of your folly or assure you your reasoning was sound, depending on his mood."

"Sena, dear?" Mrs. Randel's voice came from the hallway. "Could you help me for a moment?"

"Coming, Mamma." She stood and pointed at Lark. "Do not dare think any pivotal thoughts about your Mr. Fielding until I return."

"I shan't, I promise," Lark said with a laugh. Then marveled at how much laughing she'd done about the situation this evening, when it had all seemed so dire and frustrating earlier.

As Sena reached the doorway, Alice filled it, outfitted in her new maid's attire. Strange how Lark barely knew the woman yet found the picture so very wrong. Sena, however, grinned and threw her arms around Alice with typical abandon. "Oh, you cannot know how glad I am to have you here! Are the children settled?"

Alice's scarlet curls danced as she nodded. "We will not stay here long, though—only until the roof is repaired. Which I would not have been able to afford to do, had your family not made this offer. I owe you much, Sena."

"Nonsense, it was pure selfishness." Sena winked and sidled past. "I would do anything to keep my friends in my house."

Lark took Sena's seat at the dressing table and picked up her own brush, though unease swept through her when Alice appeared in the mirror behind her. To any other maid she would have handed the brush without qualm. But this young woman should have been in a mistress's position, not a maid's.

Yet Alice's smile was pure serenity as she held out a hand. "May I? It has been ages since I brushed another's hair, other than little Callie's. My sisters and I once did this for one another every night."

Lark relinquished the brush. She and Violet had used to do so as well, the reminder of which made it seem more friendly. "How many sisters have you?"

"Four." The reflection of Alice's smile went bittersweet. "Two older, two younger."

"Do you see them much?"

She shook her head. "Not these last years, no. The family has all been forbidden to acknowledge me."

Though Alice showed no embarrassment over that, Lark felt it acutely on her behalf. "That must be difficult."

The brushstrokes hitched for a moment. "'Twas at first, yes. But I have grown accustomed to it. I knew when I made the choice to marry Matty that it would cost me my family."

Had her head not been anchored by Alice's hand, Lark would have shaken it. "How then? How could you make such a decision?"

Alice paused, met Lark's gaze in the mirror. "Not lightly, I assure you. Sometimes—sometimes we must do the difficult thing, when we know it is right." She broke the gaze and returned to brushing. "My father was in business with Matty during the war. He cheated him, and in a roundabout way caused the death of my husband's first wife, leaving him with a babe to care for on his own."

Lark sat up straighter. "Callie? But I thought..."

"I love her as if I *had* given birth to her." The strength of Alice's smile proved it. "But in spite of the romantic tale Sena is likely to weave about it, I was not so in love with *him* then. I was fond of him, I found him terribly handsome, but those would not have been reasons enough to make such a decision. Yet I could not shake the conviction that I was meant to make right their wrong. To mother this motherless child, to be a wife and helpmate to this honorable man. And I have not for a moment regretted my decision, especially given how deeply we have come to love each other."

Lark stared at the smooth, creamy plane of Alice's forehead in the mirror, unlined with worry or sorrow. Who was this young woman? How had she seen beyond a life of privilege to a sailor and his babe?

Never in her life had Lark felt so utterly selfish. She didn't even know with whom her father dealt in business, much less whether all his transactions were fair. She had only an academic knowledge of the less fortunate in Williamsburg, recognized only the poor who sold her goods.

Now everywhere she turned, she was faced with realities she had either ignored or been unaware of. Slave auctions and outcasts, ostracized Tories and social rebels.

And where did she fit in all this? Where did her problems with Emerson rank on this scale of desperation?

Alice hummed as she stroked the brush through a lock. "You have such lovely hair."

"Have I?" Startled, Lark frowned.

Alice chuckled. "Why do you sound so surprised? Look at it, all dark gloss, and it curls so nicely. I always wished for hair like this, rather than this awful red of mine."

"Oh, but your coloring is enviable!" Lark took a moment to study her own and had to breathe a laugh. "Mine was blond as a child, though it began to darken when I was about ten years of age. For years it could best be described as 'mouse brown.' I tend to think of it that way still."

"'Tisn't, though." Alice brushed a length of it forward, over Lark's shoulder. "Look, 'tis so rich and dark now. Rather close to Sena's, but with a touch of red to it, and more curl. You are so lovely."

Lark studied herself in the tilted mirror. Was she? Certainly she wasn't hideous, not even ugly. And perhaps, if one didn't know how beautiful everyone else in her family was, she would look appealing in a normal sort of way.

Emerson had looked at her today, truly *looked*, and when she was in an ill-fitting dress with dripping, salt-encrusted hair. He hadn't run for cover, but then, he couldn't have possibly based his determination to woo her on the picture she presented. Good, in a way, but…

But if it was spirit he suddenly wanted, hers dimmed in comparison to Sena's. If he admired strength, Alice's would put hers to shame. If sweetness could lure him, then someone like Kate would be her superior. And if he sought beauty, there were many young ladies in Annapolis that outshone her.

No matter what he might want, she would always fall short. She was naught but a spoiled young lady from a plantation, with no depth, no character to make her stand apart from the masses.

Sena returned, Annabelle in her arms. "You two look as though you are getting to know one another, which is splendid. Now Alice can help us plan the next step with your Mr. Fielding. Shall we make him writhe with jealousy before you admit you still love him? There are doting gentlemen enough to assist with the task."

Lark stood when Alice put down the brush. "Emerson has never shown the least attention to how I pass my time—or with whom I pass it."

"Nor has he ever chased you down the streets of town, I imagine." Habitual grin in place, Sena settled at the top of the bed, baby snug against her. "I *knew* he would come after you. So you ought to believe me on this too. He won't show so little attention again."

Why did that ignite a fuse of panic? Lark stood, grabbed her nightdress, and then halted when Alice stopped her with a raised brow and motioned that she should turn around. Sighing, she pivoted so her dress could be untied in the back. "'Tisn't so simple, Sena." Her voice came out softer than she had intended. "There is too much between us. Too much hurt, too much neglect. Better to each start fresh, apart."

"Is it?"

Lark looked to verify that the expression on Sena's face matched that in her voice—cryptic—then moved behind the dressing screen. "Is it not?"

Sena hummed. "If that were true, then Papa never should have gone to make amends with Edwinn."

"'Tis hardly the same."

"'Tis not so different. Except, of course, they had years of friendship behind them by the time they broke. And much longer apart than you and Mr. Fielding have. By your logic, then, they ought to have moved to separate continents."

Lark slipped the nightgown over her head. "But they didn't intend to marry."

Laughter filled the room, both Alice's and Sena's. "Granted."

Lark reemerged, plucking her wrap off the chair as she headed for the bed. She sat near the bottom. "It is not a matter of forgiving wrongs. It is a matter of trust, and I don't know that I can trust him. Not with my heart. Not again."

"Did you ever trust him with your heart to begin with?" Sena asked. Alice had moved to fold a discarded shawl but paused, obviously awaiting her answer.

Lark opened her mouth, but it took her a long moment to wrap her tongue around an answer. "I would have. I wanted to. But I could never hold his attention long enough to show him who I really am."

Sena pressed a kiss to Annabelle's head. "You have it now."

A turn as terrifying as his inattention had been frustrating. "But what am I to *do* with it? Now, when I'm not even sure I want it anymore?"

Alice laid the shawl upon a trunk. "Treat him like any other man you just met. Become better acquainted with one another and decide whether or not a union would work."

With a long exhale, Lark nodded. "'Tis as sound a plan as any other, since he's determined to dog my every step. I suppose I shall. Treat him like any other man."

Except he *wasn't* any other man. He was Emerson Fielding, the one she had dreamt of all her life. The one who had made her hope. The one who had made her ache as none other could.

"And if he hurts you again," Sena said with glinting eyes, "then we feed him to the sharks."

Lark grinned and pulled her wrap a little tighter. Cap'n Mobcap to the rescue.

Emerson drew in a long breath of the crisp, late morning air and gave in to impulse. A whistle spilled from his lips. Perhaps his melody was nonsense, perhaps he had no better tone than usual, but what matter was that? The day was new, the sun was bright, and in a few moments he would be sitting across from Lark at Randel House.

Yes, she was sure to frown at him. And if her reception was anything like her temperament when he delivered her back there yesterday afternoon, her only responses would be biting ones. Mr. Randel would do little but glare at him and send occasional, dagger-like questions his way. But neither Randel nor Lark had forbidden him from coming. Hope shone in that.

Look at him, turning into an optimist. Wiley would be so proud.

He reached the top of East Street and turned onto State House

Circle with a spring in his step. When he bumped into another passerby, his whistle faltered. "So sorry, sir! I beg your pardon."

The man stumbled, slipped in the snow, barely caught himself with a cane. He drew in a quick breath, then let it out with obvious relief. "Quite all right."

Emerson grimaced when another step from the stranger proved the cane was necessary, not for looks. "Are you certain? I feel terrible—I was paying no attention."

The stranger smiled. He was a young man, probably only a few years older than Emerson, and didn't look to be harboring any grudges. He looked rather like a man of some means and no cares. "No harm done. A fine morning for distractions, is it not? A sunny day in January is to be treasured, especially this year."

"Very true—still, I ought to watch where I am going when I round a corner."

"I had just stepped from the shop there." The gentleman indicated the haberdasher to their right. "You could not have seen me."

They seemed to have been going the same direction, so Emerson put enough space between them to give the man room to breathe, but held up so they might walk together as long as their paths coincided. "Good to know I am not completely addle-brained. Though I would not put it past myself this morning."

The young man laughed and ambled along beside him. His gait was mostly sure, though he leaned a fair amount on the cane. A war injury, no doubt. "My thoughts were elsewhere too. I am on my way to fetch my sister from her friend's house, and I was wondering what kind of giggling gaggle she and the other young ladies would have turned into today."

Emerson grinned. "As a man with three sisters, I can assure you it will be the most giggling gaggle of which you can conceive."

"Especially given the friends Kate is with." He shook his head, fondness in the squint of his eyes. "I do not recognize you, though that means less than it once did. Are you a visitor to Annapolis?"

"I am. Though I went to school here as a boy, so I know the town well."

"It is a lovely one to know." The man paused to extend his hand. "I am Edwinn Calvert."

Emerson put his hand in Calvert's and shook. "Emerson Fielding."

"Is that so?" Calvert's smile moved into a grin. "Of Williamsburg?"

He hiked a brow. "Correct. Have we met after all? I am afraid I cannot recall any Edwinns in the Calvert family."

"No, no. We have never met." Calvert indicated they should continue walking, his mouth still hinting at that grin. "We have, however, some mutual acquaintances."

"Have we?" He tried to recall hearing anyone mention a Calvert so near him in age, but his memory came up blank.

His companion chuckled. "I imagine we are both headed to them even now. I was a few years ahead of you at King William's, also under Master Randel. It was with his family recently that I heard of you."

A knot cinched tight in Emerson's stomach, effectively silencing the desire to whistle. "Then our other mutual acquaintance would be my betrothed, Miss Benton."

"Your *former* betrothed, if she tells the tale correctly. Yes."

The sun seemed to dim. Why exactly, he couldn't have said. Obviously Lark would have met new people in Annapolis. Obviously some of them would have been young men. And obviously Annapolis had its share of young men who looked so well put together and had such affable personalities.

But couldn't she have met those particular males *after* he arrived? When he could be sure no untoward looks were sent where they ought not to be?

He forced himself to smile. "I assure you I am making every attempt to remedy that 'former' and convince my beloved Lark to give me another chance."

"And yet her story revolved around the fact that she was *not* 'beloved.' From which sprang all the problems." Somehow, Calvert delivered this without a grain of judgment in his tone. Perhaps a few ounces of challenge, though.

Emerson's optimism fizzled its way into a bubbling concoction of frustration and shame. She had told these people what happened—even this young man who was naught but a stranger. Was she so hurt she could not contain it…or so close to him already? Neither option portended well for Emerson.

His glance moved from the man's cane to his placid face. He could hardly enter into a conversation concerning his heart with a man he literally bumped into on the street. Especially when the conversation could very well become heated, and he had no intention of dishonoring someone who still bore the mark of service to their nation.

So he stepped onto North Street with a strained smile in place. "I am glad she has found such staunch friends."

"Well of course she has." Now Calvert's tone sounded simply factual. "She is a delightful young woman who combines wit with a sweet disposition—not to mention her lovely countenance."

Emerson came to an abrupt halt. He wanted to insist her loveliness was no business of Calvert's, wanted to stamp his foot and declare like some petulant child that she was *his*.

But then the quirk of Calvert's brow reminded him the fault belonged to Emerson. He could not take his anger out on some other man for noting immediately what he had been blind to for years.

Still. That didn't mean he had to approve of the noticing.

Calvert gave him half a smile. "I must confess it. I wondered what kind of fool would let her go."

Emerson's fingers curled into his palm, and he bit back anger again. "Do you make a habit of antagonizing strangers?"

"'Tisn't my usual way, no." Calvert chuckled as he said it. "These are special circumstances."

"Are they." He wouldn't ask why. He had a feeling he didn't want to know.

They kept walking, silent now. But Emerson found plenty of reason to scowl, thanks to Calvert's contented little smile. What exactly had gone on between him and Lark? It had only been two and a half weeks since she arrived. Not enough time to form an attachment.

Naturally, countless examples sprang to mind of friends who had ended up betrothed to women within a few weeks' acquaintance. A few had even been maneuvered to the wedding chapel in that amount of time.

But Lark had more sense than to make a commitment to another so soon, did she not? How could she possibly trust any emotions she might feel right now? She was far too...

Oh, how was he to know if she was "far too" anything for anything? Blast his ignorance and idiocy. What if she *had* gone and fallen in love with the Calvert fellow, or someone like him? Was that what she meant yesterday when she said it was too late?

His companion whistled a spirited tune, in perfect pitch and timbre, no less, and seemed to lean less on his cane as he turned toward number 19.

Emerson huffed and followed him up the steps. The man might steal his music and put it to better use, but he wasn't going to steal his bride.

Chapter Fourteen

Edwinn smiled into Mrs. Green's welcoming face, especially when the housekeeper's sunshine turned to a thunderhead upon spotting Fielding. He had no doubt the man was accustomed to warm receptions everywhere he went—it would do him good to realize that in this house, the friends were all Miss Benton's.

If Fielding hadn't come for the right reasons, they'd soon discover it.

Edwinn drew in a contented breath. "Good morning, madam. I trust my sister is still within, or has Miss Randel stolen her away somewhere?"

Mrs. Green refocused her gaze on him and renewed her smile. "They have not escaped in pursuit of trouble so far as I know, though Sena has snuck past me before, heaven knows. Do come in, and I will show you to where they *ought* to be, in the parlor." She ushered him in then stepped before the door again to glare at Fielding.

Edwinn could hardly resist watching. He had been barred from this house long enough to know neither the housekeeper nor the master had any qualms about turning someone away.

"You." Mrs. Green wagged a finger at the visitor. "Mr. Randel may have said you might come, but be sure 'tis only so we can all keep our eye on you. You've quite a task ahead of you, if you intend to convince us you are not dear young Benton's one lapse in judgment."

Fielding looked at a loss for words. "I…thank you for the warning, I suppose, Mrs. …?"

"Green." The housekeeper huffed. "I was introduced yesterday, was I not? What kind of mind have you in that handsome head of yours? First you toss aside precious Miss Benton, then you cannot even recall a simple name like 'Green'?"

Edwinn coughed to cover his laugh.

Fielding shot him a quelling look, then sent an apologetic smile to Mrs. Green. "I do beg your pardon, Mrs. Green. Usually I have a fine memory for names, but I am afraid yesterday afternoon I was a bit distracted by seeing Miss Benton again."

She folded her arms over her ample chest. "A distraction that never would have happened had you not been a blockhead to begin with, sending her off as you did with your reprehensible behavior. What kind of tomfool has a picture of perfection like Miss Benton at hand all those years and does not marry her straightaway? Do you not know Poor Richard said, 'A man without a wife is but half a man'?"

Randel stepped from his study with a crooked grin. "He also said, 'Ne'er take a wife till thou hast a house (and a fire) to put her in.'"

Playful glint in her eye, Mrs. Green raised her chin. "'A house without woman and firelight is like a body without soul or sprite.'"

Sena bounded down the stairs, a book in hand. "Oh, I can play this game! 'An undutiful daughter will prove an unmanageable wife.'" When everyone looked at her, she grinned and lifted a shoulder. "Well, 'tis the one I hear most often."

Mrs. Green rolled her eyes and rounded on Fielding again, going so far as to wag that finger right under his nose. "For you, Mr. Fielding, it all comes down to *this* wisdom of Poor Dick's: 'The proof of gold is a fire; the proof of woman, gold; the proof of man, woman.' Our Lark's mettle has been proven. Now 'tis your turn in the fire, and we shall see of what *you* are made."

To his credit, Fielding's nod looked serious. "We shall. Let us hope Mr. Franklin was also right when he said, 'After crosses and losses men grow humbler and wiser.' I have lost what I ought to have treasured, and now I feel the burden. But I have learned from it, Mrs. Green. I have."

She conveyed a world of doubt and challenge in a single sniff. "We shall see, Mr. Fielding. Now, prithee, remove yourself from the doorway so I can shut out the wind."

Once the cold was forced back out, Edwinn unclasped his cloak and handed it to Mrs. Green, along with his hat. "Thank you, madam. Miss Randel, you have not sent my sister off on some adventure, have you?"

Sena arched a brow. "Would I ever do such a thing without accompanying her myself? Fie, Mr. Calvert. I am far too selfish."

Randel chuckled and indicated the parlor across from his study. "Everyone is gathered in there, if you would like to join them, gentlemen. Mrs. Green, you forgot something."

Turning a bit, Edwinn saw that Fielding stood with his hat and cloak extended, yet the housekeeper sauntered away.

"No I did not," she said over her shoulder. "Let the man keep them, so if he steps wrongly, we can boot him out the faster."

"I would dock her pay, but she is family. One must make allowances." Randel took Fielding's things, though his grin proved his approval of the slight. "Go on in, everyone, I shall join you in a moment."

Sena led the way, and Edwinn motioned for Fielding to precede him. In part because he disliked holding anyone up with his slower gait, but also, he must admit, because he relished seeing the reactions of those within when the newcomer made his entrance.

No surprise showed on the ladies' faces—they had undoubtedly heard the commotion at the door—but their expressions covered a range of emotions. Mrs. Randel beamed a welcoming smile as always, looking the ideal maternal image with the babe sleeping in her arms. Kate, upon spotting a stranger, focused her gaze on her hands and curled her shoulders forward.

But Miss Benton's face was the one he was most interested in, and the one that betrayed the most by showing the least. There was no surprise, no welcome, no acknowledgment at all. And hence no hope, no fears, no glimpse into her heart.

The Randel boys barely looked up. Johnny glanced away from his book long enough to nod, but Mark and Will were far too engrossed in their game.

"I am an eagle!" the youngest shouted, swooping through the open space as fast as his legs would carry him. "Beware, field mouse."

"Oh no." Will made a show of scurrying away, albeit ever so slowly. "No, eagle, don't take me to your nest."

"His what, now?" Randel entered the room with a raised brow.

The boys paused, both thinking. Will was the first to squeal, "I have it—eyrie! No, eagle, don't take me to your eyrie!"

Randel nodded his approval, and Edwinn shook his head. Though his friend came from a family with means enough that he could have enjoyed a life of leisure, the man was a born teacher. "Tell me, Randel, when you were leading your men on marches, did you test them on their knowledge of the local flora and fauna?"

Though Randel tossed him an amused look of reproach, Fielding laughed. "And if we answered incorrectly, he would make us carry those who answered aright on our shoulders for a mile."

"Nonsense. I only made you ford the streams first, that is all."

Laughter filled the room and warmed Edwinn to his core. It had been too long since he had heard the mirth of so many people at once, since he had felt a part of a gathering. He shared a smile with Sena as she handed off the book in her hands to her mother and took her seat, then found one of his own at Randel's invitation.

"I suppose introductions must be made." Randel settled at his wife's side and motioned toward Fielding. "This would be the infamous Emerson Fielding. Fielding, our good friends the Calverts—Mr. Edwinn Calvert, and his sister, Miss Kate Calvert."

Edwinn inclined his head. "We met on the walk over, as it happens."

"And I am pleased to make both your acquaintances." Fielding nodded at him and offered Kate a polite smile. He glanced over the rest of the gathering too, but then settled his attention on Miss Benton. "You look well today, Lark. I prayed you had not caught a chill from yesterday."

"Not at all." She offered a smile more mischievous than sweet. "Though perhaps I was warmed by the searing letter I wrote to my brother."

Fielding's smile was lopsided. "I feel no pity for him, even imagining how scalded he will be when he reads it."

Edwinn's question must have been on his face. Sena sent him her usual impish grin and bounced a bit on the cushion beside Kate. "Oh

Mr. Calvert, you would not have heard yet. Mr. Fielding happened upon us yesterday while we were out, and Lark dashed away like a veritable specter, flew down Cornhill Street, and tumbled straight into the bay. Mr. Fielding had to jump in after her to pull her out."

His breath hitched. "Dear Miss Benton, are you quite sure you have not suffered any injury? Those waters are brutal."

Her expression softened. "I am quite fine, Mr. Calvert. Thank you for your concern."

Fielding shifted in obvious discomfort. Well, let him be chafed. A bit of competition would do the man good, even if Edwinn knew full well his place was not by Miss Benton's side. He had been called to be her friend—and friends looked out for each other's best interests. He must discover if Fielding fit in hers.

The Virginian shifted, dredged up a smile. "The proprietress at the Middleton took most excellent care of her."

"Which would not have been possible without your quick action, Mr. Fielding." Mrs. Randel's soft smile lit up her corner of the room. "We all owe you many thanks for your heroics."

Though such words would flatter many of the men Edwinn knew, make their chests puff up no matter how humble the reply they made, Fielding looked genuinely uncomfortable with the praise. His shoulders rolled forward slightly, and his brows pulled down. "I am no hero, Mrs. Randel. Let us but thank the Lord I was there in ample time to do some good."

Though his speech halted, Edwinn sensed an unspoken "for once" hovering before him. Curious. Who was Emerson Fielding? This figure of contrition whose gaze didn't leave Miss Benton's face, or the passionless, unfaithful rogue Randel had described? He supposed it was possible for a man to have the potential for both inside him.

Edwinn rested his cane against his leg. "Well I for one will be thanking the Lord you came through the ordeal without injury or illness, Miss Benton. And I dare not consider what might have happened otherwise."

Sena sighed. "I knew I ought to have followed. Not that I would have been able to save Lark—we would have sunk to the bottom together had I tried it—but all the excitement I missed!"

"I would have gladly traded you places as I sat shivering afterward." Chuckling, Lark shook her head. "That particular kind of excitement I am happy to do without."

"I do not envy you that either. But the chase..." Sena drew in a long breath, the corners of her lips curving up. "Delightful. And I would have loved to overhear the two of you fighting it out at the Middleton."

Randel folded his arms over his chest. "As would I, to be sure there was a proper chaperone present. Really, Fielding, keeping her down there as long as you did..."

Fielding arched a brow. "Was necessary to ensure she was dry and warm enough for the trip back to your house, Mr. Randel." His lips turned up. "Though if you are concerned for her reputation, I am happy to make an honest woman of her. How does March seventh sound for a wedding, Lark?"

She narrowed her eyes to two blue slits as her cheeks flushed. "As my reputation is not in need of saving, it is irrelevant."

A ripple of laughter moved through the room. Mrs. Randel shook her head, amusement sparkling in her clear brown eyes. "You must have missed her immensely, Mr. Fielding."

His nod was serious. "More than words can express."

Lark's expression went far too sweet to be guileless. "Oh now, 'tisn't as though you saw me any less this last month than you did in the one before it."

Leaning comfortably into his chair, Edwinn smiled at her brewing temper. "In this case, his loss is truly our gain. I know I speak for all of us when I say we are pleased to be the recipients of your company, Miss Benton."

He couldn't help but look at Fielding to see the man's reaction—his jaw pulsed, his smile looked forced, and jealousy shadowed his eyes. Whatever the reason for Fielding's lack of attention in years past, he was obviously not disinterested in Miss Benton now.

Another slight movement caught his eyes, this one from Sena's direction. He glanced her way and frowned. Perhaps she meant it to look like she merely repositioned herself, but discomfort pulled at her posture, and something flitted across her face....

Someone might as well have struck him, for all his ability to draw another breath. She looked hurt. Distressed, though she covered it quickly with a beaming smile for Lark. Still, he caught the darting look she sent him, though her eyes snapped back toward the others when she realized he studied her.

Was is possible? Could she feel something warmer than friendship for him, something that would make his comments toward Lark upset her? Something that would make Randel's jest about a courtship feasible?

Uncertainty pounded through his veins. Sena was everything bright and bold, everything patriotic and loyal. She was without doubt one of the most beautiful women he had ever seen, and he knew her heart was beyond compare. But…but what was *he*? A lame, homeless Tory with no friends beyond this room. He had nothing to offer a woman like Sena.

He had just as little to offer any other woman, but one of a disposition similar to his would be more likely to accept him as he was, wouldn't she?

But Sena… He drew in a breath at last and felt a whisper move through him. Listen to him, admiring her so highly yet ignoring her most admirable virtue of all—her acceptance of persons based on their hearts, not their social status. Certainly she was *capable* of loving a man like Edwinn.

Not that she necessarily *did*.

Oh, blast. He'd set out to make Fielding give deeper thought to his feelings, not himself. Which just went to show that perhaps one ought not use devious means to achieve a goal. Shining a light on this stranger's heart was hardly worth risking Sena's, if feel something for him she did.

"Oh, before I forget." Randel stretched an arm out behind his wife on the sofa and sent Edwinn a half smile, then Fielding. "Upon my wife's insistence, I am hosting a gentlemen's evening this coming Wednesday. You are both welcome to attend; we shall convene at eight o'clock and carry on as long as the liquor holds out and Mrs. Randel's patience allows."

Edwinn's spirits rose…then plummeted. "What sort of gathering?"

"A resurgence of the Tuesday Club, or as close to it as we can manage." Randel waved a hand. "It shan't be the same, of course, but we shall do our best to combine our wits, sing our neighbors out of their beds, and trounce upon philosophies both sound and foolish."

Fielding leaned back in his seat with a nod. "Sounds entertaining. I shall certainly be here. Who else will attend?"

Randel coughed, glanced at Edwinn. "Oh, the usual crowd. Paca, Lloyd, Hamilton if he is in town. Jefferson has said he will try to be here, and Monroe will come if he does. I have heard tell a few other delegates are on their way who are always up for such a gathering."

Edwinn rocked his cane forward and back. "If you wish me dead, Randel, all you need do is find some shot. You needn't plan such a complicated execution."

Randel laughed, which loosened the knot of dread inside. It didn't unravel it completely, but it at least convinced Edwinn his friend's motives weren't underhanded.

"I did not want you to feel left out, Calvert. And it may be an excellent time to renew acquaintances."

He shook his head. "More like a sure way to ruin your gathering. I thank you for wanting to include me, but I shall take the path of peace and leave your evening free of Tories."

"Tories?" Fielding snapped forward, eyes gleaming. Not with hatred exactly, but with surprise. And perhaps disillusionment, though that made little sense. What illusions of him could the man have after a mere half hour? Then his gaze fell to Edwinn's cane, providing part of the answer. "You fought for the British?"

"Fought? No." Edwinn patted his bad leg. "This happened in a childhood riding accident. Though regardless, I would not have taken up arms."

Fielding looked genuinely perturbed, bordering on confused. "Did you really think the British in the right?"

He drew in a careful breath. "I thought the Patriot methodology in the wrong. I am glad these United States are now independent, do not mistake me. But I could not support the way they achieved it, and so I was branded an enemy."

"You agree with Dr. Byles's reasoning, then?"

Edwinn arched a brow. "Which? The man had quite a few witticisms."

Fielding tilted his head. "The one asking 'which is better—to be ruled by one tyrant three thousand miles away, or by three thousand tyrants not a mile away?' "

A smile teased the corners of Edwinn's mouth. "I thought that clever but unjust when I first heard it. Then my neighbors seized my property and still refuse to return it to me. It does beg the question of whether this freedom is to be as stingily granted now, from this government, as it was from the Crown. I have certainly not tasted of it."

Randel hooked an ankle over the opposite knee. "Surely you understand feeling torn, Fielding. You were in England when the war broke out. Staying with relations, even, were you not?"

"Cousins, when I was not at Oxford." Fielding's eyes seemed to darken, and his gaze didn't budge from Edwinn's face. "But there was never a question in my mind, no. I was a Virginian, an American, not an Englishman. I knew my duty."

"You always did," Randel muttered.

"Which is admirable." Miss Benton followed her assertion with a blush, as if remembering she didn't want to defend her former-betrothed. She swallowed and lifted her chin again, leveled her gaze on Fielding. "Oxford would be where you met Elizabeth, correct?"

Edwinn had no idea of what import this Elizabeth was, but he could see the effects of the name clearly enough. Fielding drew in a sharp breath, inclined his head, and stared down the woman across from him. "I imagine Wiley already informed you it was, yes. Which is irrelevant."

"Of course it is." She focused her eyes on the crown molding, somehow making it look as though she dismissed him, rather than that she gave up the argument.

Fielding visibly gathered his composure. "Lark, if you wish to discuss such bygones, I will happily comply when company permits. I cannot think everyone here would be interested in such history, though. Even Randel, who is so notoriously in favor of the subject when it comes to schooling."

She met Fielding's gaze again. Her countenance softened. "And why should he not be in favor of the subject as a whole? I always found history fascinating. The tides of kings and empires, of the common folk who rose above their means to make contributions we still remember today." She gave a happy, if exaggerated, sigh. "Sena and I have entertained ourselves with crafting stories these last weeks that utilize our lessons in history."

Sena smiled. "Absolutely. Knights-errant, tales of chivalry, the folklore of our distant kin... Really, history is so colorful there is little reason to ever embellish it. Is that not right, Papa?"

"Indeed, and we have seen the making of it yet again. Did you all hear that the Northern states have banned the import of African slaves? I know most statesmen from Maryland and Virginia hope to do the same, so that the dreadful practice of slaveholding will cease over time."

Fielding inclined his head. "Laudable, and I hope they shall. But many of the plantation owners I am acquainted with, especially those from the far Southern states, will not relinquish their labor force so readily."

Mr. Randel took up the debate, effectively moving the subject safely away from whatever dangers lay in the topic of this Elizabeth. When Miss Benton's gaze happened to swing Edwinn's way, he gave her a small nod of approval, which she acknowledged with a minuscule smile.

She would have had her reasons for bringing up the woman, perhaps a reflex to cover her defense. But she halted her interrogation rather than pushing the point and causing Fielding too much discomfort.

She still loved the man, without question. He buried a smile as he wondered if she realized it.

CHAPTER FIFTEEN

Lark pulled her cloak tight and surveyed the collection of congregants milling about West Street. Her hosts were surrounded by friends. This was the first week Mrs. Randel had ventured out in a long while, and they had been converged upon the moment they stepped from the theater-turned-church. They wandered a bit in the direction of home, but not quickly enough for Lark's taste.

She darted a glance behind her, where Emerson was fast approaching, then looked again to the Randels, who were barely moving. She could hardly escape Emerson at this snail's pace. She would have to circle around the milling bodies and come back to her friends in a moment.

Another step, and the subsequent slip from brick sidewalk to puddle of slush proved mortification was possible even at said pace. She barely had time for a squeak of dread before strong, familiar hands caught her elbows and pulled her back to safety. With a huff of frustration—more at herself than him—she glared at Emerson. "Will you stop?"

Amusement pulled up his brows and lips. "Stop rescuing you? I am afraid I cannot agree to that, Lark, lest you end up muddied or drowned."

She pulled her elbow free of his grasp and felt her face pull into a frown. "That is not what I mean. I refer to the fact that since you arrived on Friday, a waking hour has scarcely passed without you hovering."

His amusement didn't so much as twitch. "It would rather defeat the purpose of my presence here if I were not spending the time with you."

"So go home." She pulled her cloak tighter and turned away from him. Not that she had anywhere to go until the Randels were ready.

"No thank you."

A growl formed in her throat. She swallowed it down, but it still colored her voice when she said, "Then can you at least look somewhere else once in a while? Every time I glance up, you are staring at me."

As if it were the most natural thing in the world, he took her hand and tucked it into the crook of his elbow, then led her around a group of chatting Annapolitans toward a less-occupied patch of sidewalk. "For years I was purposefully blind. Now I find myself infinitely aware of all I failed to see before. And perhaps afraid if I take my eyes off you, you might run away again."

She had walked arm in arm with him often enough over the past two years. Into every dinner, every ball. But never when the occasion didn't demand it, when they were simply out and about together.

Perhaps because they had never *been* simply out and about together. Certainly he'd never felt the need to lead her around outside their own church.

Still, it shouldn't make that tingle of awareness shoot up her arm. She should be beyond that by now. The fact that she wasn't sliced her mood to a sharp edge. "I am not going anywhere, as I already made clear. Though feel free to take yourself away. You shan't be missed."

He splayed a hand across his chest. "You cut me to the quick, my love."

Yet he looked as confident as ever. "I am not your love, and I believe I asked you to stop calling me such."

"No, you said to stop calling you 'darling.' You said nothing about 'my love.'"

"I am saying it now."

"Very well." He chuckled and drew her to a halt beneath a bare-limbed tree. "I will have to think up some other clever endearment."

"No. You will not." She caught the curious gazes of a few young men she'd met at the New Year's collation and took her hand from his arm. "Everyone will think we're…"

"A couple? What a shame." The menacing glare he directed toward the gentlemen would have sent a thrill through her a month ago. "You seem to have gathered quite the collection of admirers, Lark."

"Which no doubt shocks you." Not that he had sounded as surprised by it as she had felt. "Apparently I *do* have some merits beyond being a Benton of Williamsburg."

Now his frown moved from jealous to pained. "You doubted that?"

"Why would I not?" She pitched her voice low and spread her hands wide. "No one ever sought out my company, Emerson. And the one man I wished *would* pay attention never did."

"He was an idiot."

"Yes. And now, for the first time since I entered society, no one thinks I belong to that idiot. For the first time I am allowed to be *me*, not just Wiley's sister or your intended."

He leaned in, crowding her without getting too close, simply because of his height. "I want you to be you. But there is no reason you cannot be you beside me, now that I have overcome my idiocy."

"Is there not?" She leaned back against the tree and surveyed the townsfolk milling about West Street. "Now seems as good a time as any for you to tell me about Elizabeth."

His spine went straight again, his hands clasped behind his back. "I thought we were talking about your current romantic interests, not my past ones."

She lifted her brows.

He sighed. "'Tisn't all that much to tell. I was young, and as much an idiot then as later. Her brother was a classmate, and he invited me to his home on several occasions. My reaction was predictable."

And yet hearing of it made a ball form in her chest. "She was beautiful?"

He hesitated a moment, then nodded. "Very, though I later realized it went no deeper than her skin."

A snort slipped out. "Sounds like someone else I know."

He grimaced. "Very much like."

The ball inside thumped against her rib cage. "You have a weakness for that type, then?"

"I…" After a moment's debate, his face went hard. "We shall discuss your cousin in a moment. For now, Elizabeth. She never seemed anything but sweet, at first. There was already ample tension between the English and the 'insubordinate colonists,' as her father called us, and her parents were never welcoming of my presence. I thought her willingness to disobey them meant she genuinely loved me. I thought I was the one she wanted to marry and her other beaux were a show for her father."

Lark watched the old emotions roll through his eyes. The hope, the faith, the fondness…followed by the hurt, the betrayal, the brokenness. All of which echoed within her, dissonant and unsettling. "If she is truly akin to my cousin, then obviously not."

"I question whether she was capable of loving." His eyes clicked back to blank. "I asked her to marry me, and she made as if she would, as soon as she convinced her parents to send her to an aunt's for a holiday, giving us a chance to run off together. As it happens, war was declared at that juncture, and I had to hasten home. So I asked her to come with me."

His silence said much, yet Lark couldn't allow the story to end there. "She did not."

A dry laugh slipped past his lips. "She could not bring herself to do it…given that she was carrying the child of another of my friends."

How could she help but wince for him? "Oh, Emerson."

"It was a blessing, though I did not realize it at the time. All I felt then, of course, was the anger and misery. But the Lord spared me what would have been a terrible marriage. She has apparently shamed the whole family since then by running out on her husband and children with some actor." He drew in a long breath. "Still. I suppose part of my mind viewed those days as idyllic. Before the war, before all the horrors that came along with it. Wiley asked me about her on your birthday, inquiring if I was still in love with her, and…I suppose it made me think about the days before I realized her nature. So when your cousin arrived, looking unnaturally like her, acting unnaturally like her…"

All emotion seemed to wash away, leaving her empty. Hollow. "You forgot the ending and thought only of the joys of the beginning."

Guilt looked to rest heavily on his shoulders as he nodded. "I am sorry. It is no excuse—even though it had nothing to do with your cousin, I was still not thinking of you when I ought to have been."

Lark wrapped her arms around her middle and made no reply. Perhaps she could forgive that—hadn't she, too, dwelt on thoughts of him even after their disastrous break? But it pierced. It proved yet again he had wanted anything, anyone but her. While her silly heart wanted no one but him.

She pushed off the tree. "The Randels appear ready to go."

"Lark." He caught her arm again. "Please. I know I hurt you every bit as much as she hurt me, but don't—don't fall into the trap of thinking the pain will vanish if you focus on another. It would not be fair to anyone."

"I am well aware of that." She stepped away, hoping he would take the hint and let go her arm.

Instead, he moved with her. "That Calvert fellow—he is obviously fond of you. You ought to tread carefully with him."

The suggestion at once eased the tension inside her and yet struck her as mistaken. Perhaps some of Mr. Calvert's comments had bordered on flirtatious, but she had seen the way he stared at Sena yesterday, as if all the answers of the universe rested with her. Lark pulled free of Emerson's grasp. "Do not presume to know anything about that. 'Tis no business of yours."

Obviously the wrong thing to say. His expression went from concerned to determined. "Of course it is. And I daresay your parents would consider it their business too—and you know as well as I how they would feel about you accepting a suit from a Tory."

She spun around to face him. "If after all you have been through you can still look at a man and judge him on nothing but his association, then I pity you greatly, Emerson Fielding. Now good day."

She stomped away. But the fact that Emerson didn't follow her this time did nothing to soothe the frustration now boiling inside.

Emerson handed his cloak to a bewigged manservant and stepped into the massive entryway of the Lloyd house. He couldn't help but look around with admiration. A magnificent staircase rose in front of him, graced upon its landing by elegant Palladian windows before it split into two perpendicular rises. Mahogany doors stood open, spilling music from their depths, and silver glinted everywhere in the golden candlelight.

Lark had certainly entered straight into the heart of Annapolis society. It had taken all his resources to secure an invitation to this holiday celebration, and he now owed several old friends a favor.

He could only pray it would be worth it.

Passing through the Ionic columns, he moved into the room that looked to be the center of activity. Here laughter rang out to vie with the music, dancing took up half the floor space, and rich colors met his eyes.

It took him only two seconds to locate Lark—and when had that become a talent of his? She was dancing, dressed in a gown of ivory and gold that drew out the luster in her unpowdered hair and the roses from her cheeks. Or perhaps such radiance could be attributed to her beaming smile, her laugh as her partner swung her around.

How had it escaped him all these years how beautiful she had become? She was no longer the child he had remembered, awkward and plain. Over and again he had heard comments about Violet being the beauty of the Benton family, but had all of Williamsburg perhaps continued to think so even after Lark came into her own, without stopping to examine the woman she had become?

Because seeing her now, moving about with such grace and energy that she put the other young ladies to shame, he couldn't help but think the perception mistaken. And it was a misconception obviously not shared by these Annapolis men, many of whom watched her as closely as Emerson did.

Which wouldn't do at all. He started toward the dancing floor.

"Emerson? Emerson Fielding?" A vaguely familiar laugh rang out a second before a vaguely familiar man stepped in front of him, jovial grin in place. "Well, what do you know? What brings you back to Annapolis? I have seen neither hide nor hair of you since our school days."

"Ah." He shook the proffered hand, returned the cheerful smile, and searched his memory until a name presented itself to go along with the face. "Good to see you again, Litchfield. Are you still living here?"

"I wouldn't go anywhere else, and rarely have since the war." He stepped to Emerson's side and surveyed the gathering as if it were his own. "Are you in town for the rest of the holiday season? There are parties planned almost constantly, making the most of Congress's presence."

"I imagine I shall be, yes." His gaze went back to Lark. At this point he couldn't be sure he'd have her home before the wedding at all—certainly it wouldn't happen by the end of January.

Litchfield followed his gaze, chuckled, and elbowed him. "I see that, as always, you are quick to spot the belle of any gathering. If you think to steal Miss Benton from us, though, you shall have a fight on your hands."

Emerson shot his old friend an arched glance.

Litchfield had never needed much by way of encouragement. He motioned toward Lark. "She is visiting from Williamsburg. Wiley Benton's sister, I finally realized—do you remember him? He was in our class. The two of you were friends, if I recall."

"We still are, yes." And Litchfield's memory obviously failed before he recalled they were also neighbors.

"She is staying with Master Randel and is fast friends with his daughter." He pointed to where Miss Randel also danced, a few paces ahead of Lark in the line. "A beauty herself, of course, but impossible to pin down. All of us have tried, but she refuses us with such wit it takes days to realize we have been dismissed. You ought to test out your charm on her."

Emerson chuckled. "And leave Miss Benton for you, you mean?"

"And why not? You may be just the man to convince Miss Randel to settle down. Miss Benton, on the other hand, is not at all your sort of girl."

His hand fisted. "What makes you say so?"

Litchfield leaned in, elbowed him again. "Because she is *my* sort."

Emerson chuckled again because it was expected, but he also recalled why Litchfield had never been more than a passing friend. "I wouldn't be too sure, Litch. She is Wiley's sister, remember, so she has a brain."

Litchfield held out his arms. "I admire that in a lady! So long as it isn't her only attribute, anyway. Come, this set is ending—let us see which of us she prefers for the next one."

Competing for his own betrothed. Divine justice for his treatment of her, he suspected. It undoubtedly served him right. And she would undoubtedly prove it by refusing him a dance.

He edged and slid his way through the crowd. The music went into its ending cadence, the dancers came to a halt, and Lark finally glanced away from her partner. Her gaze arrowed into him and held. At the smile he sent her, she looked more resigned than pleased.

Yes, divine justice. He recalled being the one feeling resigned on many an occasion as he made his way to her at a ball to claim his expected dances. Much as he still didn't love dancing, his pulse quickened now as he drew near to her, and hope battled the expectation of disappointment.

He and Litchfield were not the only gentlemen to gather near Lark and Miss Randel. Shouldn't most of them be giving their attention to the scads of young ladies without partners that lined the room? And thereby leaving *his* alone?

"Good evening, ladies." Litchfield at least had boldness on his side, which managed to part the company around them. Apparently because most of the gentlemen were his friends, and they welcomed him eagerly.

Come to think of it, several of them looked familiar. More classmates.

Before he could be caught up in renewing acquaintances, he sidled over to Lark with what he hoped was a charming smile. "My apologies for missing our customary first dance. Might I have this next one in its stead?"

She sighed. "No need to feel obligated, Mr. Fielding. I know how such expectations always taxed you."

Litchfield broke off his conversation with another young man—was that Woodward?—and sent Emerson a good-natured scowl. "Would you like an introduction, Fielding?"

"No need. I am Miss Benton's b—"

"Brother's dearest friend." Her interruption was pointed, her glare a warning. "And neighbor."

Litchfield's eyes went wide. "Of course! I had forgotten you came from the same town. Obviously you and Miss Benton have met."

She gave a sweet smile. "A time or two."

Emerson extended his hand and arched his brows. "For Williamsburg's sake?"

Her lips pursed, but there was a hint of amusement sparkling in her eyes. With a sigh, she placed her fingers upon his. "For Williamsburg's sake."

Litchfield chuckled and elbowed another friend. "I do believe that is the least enthusiastic acceptance old Fielding has ever received."

"My reputation is forever tarnished." He pitched his voice low, though he made no attempt to hold back his smile.

Lark laughed. "I think you shall survive it."

"Perhaps, if you keep looking merry." He stepped closer than necessary to her under the guise of squeezing past a few other would-be dancers. "You are lighting up the room with your smile tonight."

She slanted a disbelieving look at him. "Resorting to flattery, are you, Emerson?"

"On the contrary—I have been struck by the truth of it." He stopped them at the edge of the dance floor while the other couples ordered themselves. "How much begging must I do for you to promise me another set or two?"

For a long moment, she only stared at him. "You hate dancing."

"But you love it. Yet thanks to me, you have rarely indulged in it these last two years. You ought to have stomped on my toes and demanded I take you out more."

He feared bringing up the past would hang a cloud of gloom over her, but thankfully she grinned. "If I stomped on your toes, it would have given you an excuse to stay *off* the dance floor."

He made a show of considering this as he led her to an open space in the line of dancers and took his place beside her. "You may be right. But you could have stood on a chair to snag my attention and then made your demands. I would have acquiesced just to silence you."

Laughter spilled from her throat again as a minuet was struck up. His mother had made certain he knew all the dances so he could do his duty at a ball, but he had never really looked forward to one before. Now, though, he took the time to be grateful for the slower, elegant pacing. It showcased Lark's grace every bit as much as the more boisterous set had a few minutes earlier.

And she smiled at him as they bowed to each other, which did strange, unexpected things to his heart. "I have never considered a chair—but I confess I may have tossed myself to the floor, had I not feared being mistaken for a rug."

He took her hand, both of them facing forward now, and provided a pivot for her while she glided to the space before him. "I am glad you refrained. You would have made a lovely rug but been a bit of a tripping hazard."

Mischievous grin in place, she curtsied and swung back around to place her other hand in his. "Seeing a certain someone sprawl flat on his face might have made the risk worthwhile."

A chuckle rumbled in his throat. "It would have served him right, certainly." He released her hand again as she moved back to his side, then her other as he moved now in front of her. "I cannot fathom how you tolerated the dolt as long as you did."

"I am a saint, don't you know?"

He smiled but said nothing more, as some footwork was required. Simple enough, but he rarely tried to execute it while carrying on a conversation and didn't trust himself to keep from treading on her toes.

This was why he detested dancing. As naturally as it seemed to come to some, he always feared making a fool of himself.

"I never noticed that before," she murmured as they stepped to the side.

"Hmm?"

"You *cannot* dance and talk at the same time. I always assumed you just cared not to speak to me."

His chuckle nearly made him trip. "My true incompetence is a well-tended secret, and I thank you not to blab it. I have worked hard to hide it behind indifference."

She leaned a bit closer. "You missed a step."

And then she was moving away, toward the middle with the other women. Miss Randel was the one across from them, and so the one Lark now danced with. The young ladies whispered something as they pranced around each other, giggled, and grinned. Their friendship seemed to run deep for being so new.

He could hardly help but contrast them. The sparkle of their eyes had much in common, though their differences were easy enough to mark. Where Miss Randel greeted even these sedate steps with unnecessary enthusiasm, Lark combined spirit with delicacy. She was clearly not as dull and unassuming as he had let himself think, yet her vibrancy never overwhelmed. Like a vein of gold, one must know where to look for it, and then it would enrich the seeker.

And like a miner, he had been so close to these riches all this time, yet remained poor. He had given up his claim, only then to catch a glimpse of the fortune awaiting him.

Heaven help him, he must win her back.

She returned to his side long enough for another bow, then Emerson moved into the middle for the partner exchange and found himself facing a grinning Miss Randel. He offered a small smile.

"Are you enjoying yourself, Mr. Fielding?"

"I am, thank you. More than I expected to, as I feared Miss Benton would refuse to speak to me tonight."

They danced around each other, her laughter ringing out. "Well, our Lark is a fair-minded girl. Especially since you left your horns and pitchfork in Virginia."

"They are dangerous to travel with, you know. One unexpected bump, and…" He glanced over his shoulder at Lark. If her grin were any indication, she overheard without problem. He risked an unseemly wink and was rewarded with a blush and a glare.

Miss Randel chuckled. "So you are acquainted with Mr. Litchfield?"

Talk of his former classmates sufficed as they finished out that part of the dance, and Emerson drew in a breath of relief when he returned briefly to Lark's side before she moved forward to meet Miss Randel's partner in the middle.

It was several minutes later when all the trading-off was finished and they joined hands again. Emerson arched a brow. "Dare I beg you to promise me the next set as well?"

She inclined her head. "I don't know. Emerson Fielding dancing so much all at once? I have never seen such a thing. I cannot be sure you can suffer it."

"I know a way to find out."

He half expected her to refuse, but instead the amusement toying at her lips led to a nod.

The music unfortunately turned more lively, and Emerson had all he could do to keep up with the hops and skips Lark performed so beautifully. Still, he had no qualms trying for more of her time when finally they came to a halt. "Another?"

Lark shook her head at his request and fanned herself. A shadow had crept into her eyes—she must be in need of a rest. "I need a brief respite."

"Even better." He took her hand and led her off the dance floor, toward the end of the room where the refreshments were set up. "A lemonade?"

Rather than answer, she pulled away to stand before the partially open door, from which cold air made its way into the room a few feet before being swallowed up by the combined heat of all the guests within.

His lips quirked up. Had he ever tried to sneak off with her before? Of course not.

It was high time he did.

CHAPTER SIXTEEN

Lark breathed in one last gulp of the crisp air that didn't refresh her and was about to turn around when an arm caught her about the waist and propelled her through the door. The sudden cold stole her breath long enough for her captor to propel her out onto the portico and return the door to its original position.

She spun around, out of the arm. "Emerson!" And what had she expected? That some *other* man would have come up that quickly and kidnapped her from beneath his nose?

That seemed every inch as likely as this. She didn't know whether to laugh or shake her head. "Whatever are you doing?"

The impishness of his grin made her lean toward laughter. "You looked a bit overheated."

"I am cool now, thank you." Yet the words mixed with a chuckle. "We will freeze out here in about half a second."

He wiggled his brows. "I can keep you warm."

The shock wasn't from the suggestion so much as the fact that Emerson Fielding was making it—to *her*. "Have we met?"

"A time or two." He stepped closer again and held out a hand.

She, without quite knowing why, put hers into his. "Mr. Randel will have a fit if he finds us out here. We ought to go back in."

Emerson motioned to the lanterns glowing all along the rear of the house. "It was obviously anticipated that the guests might need a cooling breath now and then. Though if you fear for your reputation, I will yet again offer my promise that I shan't see it injured."

Where did the amusement come from? Where was the frustration of the days before? She chuckled and shook her head. "Is that your nefarious scheme? Force me into matrimony by sullying my good name?"

"Well, if it is the only way to win you." His grin proved him to be jesting. Perhaps that was why she made no protest when he slid his arm around her waist. But it wasn't mirth lighting the depths of his sienna eyes when his gaze roved her face. "Do you know how beautiful you are?"

A tremor started somewhere in her stomach. How many times had she dreamt of this? "Emerson…"

"I don't know when it happened, or if perhaps I have been blind all this time—a definite possibility. But watching you here, tonight especially…" He drew her closer, released her hand so he might trail his knuckles over her cheek. "You are magnificent."

The tremor spread to her limbs. Magnificent? *Her?*

His fingers caught one of the curls framing her face, and he leaned down. Close, then closer.

But she was not the magnificent one. She was not beautiful. She was not the one who made men's eyes go dark with longing, the one who inspired them to risk the wrath of chaperones for a few stolen moments. Violet was, perhaps. Sena could achieve it. Alice certainly had the ability.

And Penelope. Penelope obviously had no difficulty in luring a man away from the crowds.

His face was only a breath from hers, his intention obvious. But all she could see was his arms around her cousin's waist. All she could hear were the words of admiration he had spoken to another woman, another night. All she could imagine was Penelope seeing this same face, filled with the same desire, moments before he kissed *her.*

"No." She pushed him away, backing up at the same moment. Prayed her voice didn't sound as tremulous and tearful to him as it did to her own ears. "You had two years to kiss me, Emerson, two years when it would have been welcome and permitted. Why you think you can take such liberties now I cannot fathom."

She expected him to press, to reach for her again. But he made no move, and the lantern light caught a gleam of regret in his eyes.

Of course he would regret it. No doubt he couldn't fathom what had possessed him either.

He shook his head, his mouth taut. "I have hurt you again, when that was the last thing I intended to do. I'm sorry. Not for wanting to kiss you," he added with a shadow of a crooked smile, "but for failing to remember you are no longer mine to kiss. It is difficult, this starting anew when we have so much already behind us."

She opened her mouth but could think of nothing to say. A gust of wind blustered around the corner, though, giving her good reason to gather her thoughts. "I am going back in. I thank you to enter by way of another room instead of this one."

He glanced at the other doors cracked open and nodded, looking resigned.

Now *that* was an expression she had seen often upon his face. Whenever he turned to her, whenever he must play the role of her intended. Far more familiar than the interest he had shown all evening.

Before the tears in her throat could travel to her eyes, she rushed past him and slipped back in the door to the ballroom.

No one seemed to have noted her absence, and her reappearance caused not a stir. Good. She accepted a glass of lemonade from a passing servant. Putting to use her years of practice blending into the furniture, she made her way to the other end of the room before Sena bounced to her side.

"There you are! Where is Mr. Fielding?"

Lark ignored her friend's sly grin and took a sip of her drink. "I wouldn't know, we parted company several minutes ago."

"Oh." Sena's face went from sly to disappointed. "You seemed to be getting on well."

Too well, perhaps. She should have known better than to succumb to his charm. "I doubt I have scared him back to Williamsburg yet. But a couple dances make up for nothing."

Sena loosed a wistful sigh and linked their arms together. "I know, but 'tis so romantic. He came all this way the very moment he realized where you were. Chased you through town, has been haunting our house—and heaven only knows how he procured an invitation tonight. If ever I have seen a man more determined to win a woman's affections, I cannot recall it."

Lark sighed and put down her glass so she might discreetly rub her neck. Thus far she had done her best to ignore the tension coiling in those muscles all day and the twinge of pain behind her eyes.

She hadn't even noticed it when she was dancing with Emerson. But now that the warmth of the room chased away the chill of outside, it thudded to life again.

"Lark?" Sena turned to face her, brows knit. "Are you unwell?"

Lark dropped her hand and pulled out a smile. "A bit of a headache, nothing to worry about."

"Do you want to find a seat? We can—"

"No, not necessary." The last thing she needed was to rest and let that scene play through her mind again. "Let us see if we can find partners for the next dance."

But after another half hour of jumping and reeling, the pounding in her head would not suffer her ignoring it any longer. She slipped away with a wave for Sena and headed for the quieter rooms of the house.

A servant offered her a cake, but the very thought turned her stomach. She pressed on. The entire main floor of the massive house was open for the celebration, and it seemed as though people filled every inch. Where could she possibly find a moment's reprieve?

The drawing room was the likeliest option. It too was filled, but with a less boisterous crowd. She spotted the Randels in a corner, their friends around them. Hope filled her as she recalled that Mrs. Randel planned to leave before dinner, to return to little Annabelle. Surely that would be soon, and Lark could escape with her. Back to the quiet of Randel House, where there was no orchestra, no crowd, not so many glaring chandeliers. She could hide herself away in Sena's room for a few hours until the worst of the thumping subsided.

For now, she sank into an empty chair nestled into a corner. Her eyes slid shut. She lifted a hand to her neck again and wished she hadn't come tonight. She ought to have known better. Was she so silly a girl that without her parents to tell her to retire at the first hint of one of her headaches, she hadn't the sense to do it herself?

Apparently.

Had she obeyed her better sense, she would be resting even now. She would have been spared this latest Emerson pain. Oh, to have had such foresight two hours ago. But she had let herself get caught up in the excitement when Alice had exclaimed over the intricate brocade of her gown, the gold braid, the ivory lace.

Such trivial things. Hardly worth this price.

"Lark?" His voice was quiet, and coming from beside her rather than above her. Lark opened her eyes to find Emerson crouched at her knee. He frowned. "What is the matter? Are you ill?"

Her stomach churned along with the pounding in her head. "It is nothing."

He studied her long enough that she had to wonder what picture she presented. At the shake of his head, she suspected it was not becoming. "Have you one of your headaches?"

She found the ability to smile. A bit. "You actually know of those?"

"I am apparently not as oblivious as we assumed. I believe your parents usually insist upon rest and quiet."

"And darkness." She breathed a painful laugh. "I knew it was coming on. I should have stayed home, but I told myself it would go away."

"I am not the cause, then?" Relief tinged his tone, though it didn't eclipse the concern.

"No need to flatter yourself. I assure you, you are not the only cause of pain in my life." The moment the words left her lips, she regretted them. "I am sorry."

"I deserve it. Let me go and fetch—"

"Fielding, are you bothering my guest again?" Mr. Randel appeared with a smirk that soon evaporated. "Miss Benton, whatever is the matter?"

"She has one of her headaches." Emerson straightened and tugged his coat back into place. "We must take her home."

Mr. Randel studied her much like Emerson had, then nodded. "Martha plans on leaving in a moment anyway. Let me find Sena. We can all go, if—"

"No, you needn't force Sena away. Just let her know I went with her mother."

Mr. Randel sighed. Emerson straightened his shoulders. "I will accompany them back, sir."

"I suspect 'tis no use arguing with you, Fielding, so instead I will thank you for it. I was not fond of the idea of sending my wife home without escort, but I must stay so long as my daughter does." He regarded Lark again and held out a hand. "I called for the carriage, so let's find your cloak. I am sure Martha and Mrs. Green will do all in their power to assure your comfort."

She let her host help her up. When he then placed her hand on Emerson's arm, she made no protest. It was enough that they led her toward the door, explained to Mrs. Randel what was going on, and that Mr. Randel promised to seek out Sena and let her know Lark would be retiring.

Then she finally stepped outside, away from the bustle and noise. If only it weren't so cold, and she could lie down somewhere…

"Here we are, darling." Emerson helped her into the Randels' carriage, as carefully as if she were made of porcelain. She settled onto the seat and let her head rest against the padded back, her eyes sliding closed again.

"You poor dear." Mrs. Randel entered too, and apparently sat opposite. "You look miserable. Mrs. Green and I will make you comfortable as can be, and if the boys make so much as a peep, I shall send them straight to bed."

Lark tried to smile.

Emerson vaulted up and took the seat beside her. He sat closer than necessary, even went so far as to wrap an arm around her shoulder. She ought to pull away, but as the carriage rocked forward, she was too grateful for the support to do anything but bury her aching face in his shoulder.

They passed the couple minutes' drive in blessed silence and were soon back on North Street. Emerson helped Mrs. Randel out first, and then wrapped his hands around Lark's waist and swung her to the ground. "You will be resting in a moment, darling."

She hummed. He led her up the steps and through the door, where Mrs. Green was quick to grasp one of her hands. "Oh, sweet Lark. What can we do for you? A hot bath? A compress? Some tea? Or do you wish to lie down for a while?"

Lark unclasped her cloak as she considered. "Some tea might be good, then I will lie down."

"I have the water hot already. Mr. Fielding, will you take a cup with her? I hate for her to be left alone, but dear Mrs. Randel had to rush right up to take care of the babe, Alice is seeing to her own children, and I was about to fetch the boys their dinner."

Emerson nodded. "I would be happy to keep her company for a few minutes. If she makes no objection."

"I have none." Her voice came out no more than a whisper.

While Mrs. Green bustled off, Lark turned into the parlor where the comfort of the sofa beckoned. She heard Emerson follow but paid little attention to where he took himself, until he settled beside her. Then she sighed. "You needn't stay."

"I want to."

She breathed a dry laugh and closed her eyes again. Lifted a hand to her neck. Perhaps she should have sent him home, so she could take down her hair. "That takes a bit of getting used to."

"What does?" He brushed her hand away and put his on her neck instead, rubbing the sore muscles gently.

The action was probably improper, but it was exactly what she needed, so she didn't much care. "You wanting to stay with me."

"Ah. Does this help? When my sisters have the headache, they beg someone to rub it away for them."

He had to ask?

"See you keep it brotherly." Mrs. Green's voice, stern and yet soft, made Lark jump. Perhaps it was for her benefit he designed the question.

"Certainly, madam."

"And know if it were not so clear she is in dreadful pain, I would never allow such familiarity."

Emerson sounded like he was choking back a chuckle. "I understand, Mrs. Green. And if she were not in such pain, I would never attempt it."

The sound of the tea service sliding onto the table preceded Mrs. Green's huff. "I know young men better than that, sir. Now, I have to go and take dinner to the boys, but I will be back to check on you in a minute—so behave accordingly."

"Yes'm."

Lark opened her eyes long enough to watch the housekeeper leave, then gave in to exhaustion again. "It does help. At home, Wiley or Mamma does this for me."

"Well, I am happy to help in their absence." He shifted, sighed. "I'm sorry for ruining your evening, Lark."

"It would have been ruined regardless, with this headache."

"Still. I ought to have known better than to act as I did."

For a long moment she let the silence hold, let it soothe her while she replayed his flirting, his contrition afterward. "It was not so much your action as…as my memory of your similar actions that night. All I could see was Penelope in your arms."

His hand stopped its ministrations, fell away. And why did that make her feel as though *she* should apologize?

Perhaps she should. Perhaps it was a fault of hers, that she remembered what was best forgotten. Kate would surely forgive it. Sena would let it rest. Alice would gracefully move beyond it. Secure, all of them, in who they were and who others perceived them to be.

Why could she not be such? Why must she always fall short? Opening her eyes again, Lark turned toward him.

Emerson rubbed a hand over his face and sighed. "Why did you ever love me, Lark?"

Whatever intention she'd had vanished. "Pardon?"

He shook his head, then leaned over to press a kiss to her brow. "Let me pour your tea."

She said nothing as he stood and crossed to the table. She said nothing when he handed her a cup a moment later. She said nothing when he sat again, across from her this time. She had nothing to say. All her thoughts, all her consideration had been on herself, on why *he* had not loved *her*. But this, this question…it raised a whole other host of thoughts to plague her.

Why *had* she loved him to begin with?

CHAPTER SEVENTEEN

Wiley draped his legs over the arm of the chair—something he would never dare do outside his own room—and broke the seal on the folded paper. There had been two letters enclosed in the latest correspondence from Lark, and their parents were undoubtedly reading theirs even now with unbridled joy.

As for himself, he wondered if he ought to beware of poisons lacing the ink, or perhaps some deadly insect folded within, ready to bite.

Although he had to admit he'd liked to have seen sweet little Lark's face when she caught a glimpse of Emerson in Annapolis.

Smiling, he set his gaze upon the missive.

Dearest, Traitorous Wiley,

For a man who was as set on getting me out of Williamsburg as I was determined to escape, you have a remarkably short memory. Imagine my surprise when I stepped out of the State House and was hailed by none other than the man you promised to keep away from me.

Yes, I admit he is a humbler, more sincere Emerson than the one I knew. But that does not excuse the fact you didn't lift a finger to stop him from coming. Which I forgive. What you will pay for in some clever way I have yet to devise is the letter you gave to him. You knew very well that was not for his eyes! When I arrive home, you will have to watch your back, dear brother.

And here is where I sigh and say that, your treachery notwithstanding, seeing him again was not as bad as I feared. Other than the tumble I took into the bay, that is.

Oh, you want to hear about that? So sorry, I am all out of time. You shall have to wait.

As I told Emerson, I have no intentions of leaving Annapolis yet. He has said he will stay here, then. We shall see. But for now, know I miss you and all your troublesome ways, and I look forward to seeing you again. In the meantime, have a wonderful few months with our darling cousin.

Your sister, Lark

Wiley chuckled as he folded the letter back up. All things considered, that was far better than he had feared. Emerson undoubtedly received an earful or two, but Wiley wasn't going to pity him for it.

Although he *would* like to know what that bay business was about. Well, he would wait for her next letter, when she would surely tell him all about it, and otherwise praise heaven she and Emerson hadn't yet killed each other. Who knew? Perhaps they'd yet reconcile.

"Master Wiley, you had better get yourself downstairs for dinner."

Wiley tossed a grin his servant's direction and hauled himself to his feet. "Must I, Joe? I shudder to think what kind of dullard my cousin's about to present to us."

Joe chuckled and brushed some lint off Wiley's coat. "Now, you play nice with this boy, whoever he is."

The same admonition Old Joe had been giving him since he was a child. "Do I not always?"

Joe's only response was a guffaw. Wiley waved and exited his chamber, jogged down the stairs, and stopped outside the drawing room to pull in a fortifying breath.

He ought to be glad Penelope was taking her husband hunting seriously and pray the young man coming for dinner would be stupid enough to propose. But part of him wasn't sure he could let anyone go blithely into matrimony with that viper without a warning.

"Cheer up," he muttered to himself. "He will probably not believe me anyway, but my conscience will be clear so long as I caution him."

First, though, he would give Penelope time to scare the poor sapskull off on her own. Heaven knew she could bore a man to tears with all her prattle about fashion.

Squaring his shoulders, Wiley entered the drawing room, where the rest of the family was already assembled. His parents greeted him with a smile, but the Moxleys were far too engrossed in their precious daughter.

"But Savannah? Darling." Aunt Hester fluttered her fan. "I care not how charming this young man is, you cannot go so far from us."

Uncle Moxley nodded. "Your mother is quite right. There are young men enough in Philadelphia or Williamsburg, where you have family."

Wiley smirked and made sure to put a little threat in it when Penelope glanced at him. "True, cousin. We would be very happy to keep an eye on you if you stayed nearby."

She barely controlled her snarl. "Much as I appreciate the sentiment, Wiley dear, I can hardly make a decision on my marriage—my very happiness—because of where a man makes his home. Mamma, surely you understand I am in love with my darling George."

Wiley rolled his eyes and took a seat. He couldn't remember which of the victims she'd lined up answered to "George" and hailed from Savannah, but her love would have nothing to do with her choice.

Mother averted her face from sister and niece and indulged in a sigh and pained expression, which made Wiley grin. Apparently the prolonged exposure to Aunt Hester and Penelope wore on her too.

His aunt looked torn between her usual coddling and her own ambition to keep her daughter near. "We shall surely love him too, dear. But Savannah…"

"Yes, Mamma, Savannah." Penelope's tone went cool and low. "Half of which he seems to own."

"Half of *what*?" Aunt Hester snapped her fan shut. "'Tis hardly a city, barely more than a little frontier town. How long has it been there? Fifty years? You are not suited for the backwoods. Think how uncivilized it must be."

Penelope's face went sour. "If they have such outfitters in the backwoods as have dressed George, then I shall have no problems. Did you not see his coat at the fete last night, Mamma?"

"He could have gotten that here."

"He did not. I asked him."

She asked him. Wiley rubbed a hand over his face. His cousin was really so superficial as to ask a man where he commissioned his coat. And the blockhead still accepted her invitation to dinner.

Asa strode into the room and cleared his throat. "Mr. George Owens of Savannah and his mother have arrived."

"Show them in, please." Father stood, and Wiley and Uncle Moxley followed suit.

Georgie Porgie ushered his mother into the room with a smile. Not beaming, mind you, like an idiot would who was totally smitten with a lady within, but also not uncertain. In fact, Wiley narrowed his eyes when he saw the man's face and realized they'd had a conversation a week ago at a New Year's collation. Mr. Owens had struck him as an intelligent, even clever young man.

What in the world was he doing paying court to Penelope?

As the usual inane greetings were exchanged, Wiley took his seat and debated. Owens wasn't a bad-looking fellow, though he didn't think one would call him exceedingly handsome. What drew Penelope to him? His wealth, certainly. And quite possibly the fact that his wealth was housed so far away.

And wouldn't it be a shame if the distance precluded regular family gatherings with her?

A few moments' conversation proved the man to be attentive to Penelope, so his interest was obviously real...simply baffling.

Ah, well. If the gent stuck around, Wiley would try to figure him out. In the meantime he'd let himself dream Owens, or someone else, would indeed take Penelope far, far away.

Lark eased her weight onto her right foot, holding her breath lest the stair creak under her. Successful in her silence, she moved her left foot down to the last step.

Sena laughed softly behind her. "They cannot possibly hear us over that harpsichord."

"Shh." Lark glanced around with exaggerated trepidation. "You will be giving us away, Cap'n. And ye know what the penalty is for getting caught at espionage."

"Walkin' the plank, to be sure." Sena tiptoed past and motioned Lark to follow her into an alcove behind the stairs. "There ye be, matey. A fine view ye have from here of a fine-looking man."

Lark shook her head, though Sena would barely be able to see it in the dark. Sure enough, a glance through the door showed Emerson within her line of sight. A half smile played over his lips as he listened to the ribald tune one of the gentlemen pounded out on the instrument, and he laughed with the rest at the awful ending.

Sena leaned close to her ear. "Methinks yonder gentleman needs a few more lessons in music."

Lark pressed her lips against a laugh. "Aye, to be sure."

They had spied from the window an hour earlier as the visitors arrived, the dozen or more gentlemen all seeming in a mood given to revelries. Between the two of them, they had recognized most of them—congressmen, lawyers, judges, even the governor. Men who were determining the course of their nation...and who weren't to be stopped by their inability to carry a tune when it was time for entertainment, apparently.

Did Emerson feel at all out of place in such company? He looked perfectly at ease, but that was never an indicator with him. He looked perfectly at ease no matter where he was. That was one of the things she had always admired about him.

Admired...but hardly a reason to love a man, was it?

She rolled her eyes at herself. Her purpose in sneaking down here was not to figure out why she had ever fallen in love with Emerson Fielding. She wanted to see these statesmen flaunting their cleverness, that was all.

The laughter tapered off within the room. "A true demonstration of what music ought never to be." The voice was unfamiliar, though it carried an amused authority to it. "And as punishment for torturing us so, Mr. Foster, you are sentenced to a bumper. Fill it to the brim, Randel!"

Cheers went up, and Lark heard the sound of glass tapping glass. The voices raised in some kind of chant, getting louder and louder until there was a thud of glass on wood, and then another round of applause.

"Apparently the man can drink," Sena murmured. "Certainly worth cheering over, for 'tis such a rare feat these days."

Lark laughed softly. And paid absolutely no mind to the fact that Emerson looked more amused by his companions than participatory. Perhaps it said something about him, about his character, but she wouldn't be concerned. Not tonight. She had spent all day yesterday letting thoughts of him magnify her headache. It was time to think of other things.

"Well, we've a week before the vote for ratification is set. What say you fellows? Will our snowbound compatriots make it here in time to approve the Treaty of Paris?"

The speaker was out of sight, but one of the men whose back was to Lark shook his powdered head. "I can but hope so. Quorum seems out of reach at this juncture, but let us hope the seven-state ratification will suffice."

"Otherwise we can only pray for an extension of the deadline." Was that Jefferson? "I fear it will never make it back to France by the third of March."

"We could have sent it sooner had you not refused to give up hope for the nine states making it to town."

Jefferson sighed. "Similarly, if the other states had sent their missing delegates two months ago, we would not be in these straits. I maintain it is a dangerous trick we are trying, using only seven. What if King George refuses to honor it? He could demand new terms. Or start the war again."

"The express riders will surely convince the New England states to do their duty. I know they have a prodigious amount of snow, but this is worth uncomfortable travel." This speaker sounded vaguely familiar, but she couldn't place the voice.

"And if Beresford rallies enough to leave his sickbed in Philadelphia, he'll make South Carolina's delegation full."

"And if all that fails, Franklin will still manage to convince ol' King George not to renege."

Sena chuckled. "Because, as Mrs. Green would be the first to proclaim, Benjamin Franklin can convince anyone of anything."

Mr. Randel cleared his throat. "Let us hope so. And let us put aside our fears tonight and focus on the promise, on the wonder of what this treaty means."

A rare silence descended upon the library. Jefferson spoke again. "Randel is right, gentlemen. When the Treaty of Paris is at last ratified, we shall be established once and for all as a free nation. The war will be officially ended."

A chorus of "Hear, hear!" sounded, accompanied by the clink of many glasses.

Sena held up a hand as if cupping a tumbler in it. "To these United States of America," she whispered.

"Hear, hear." Lark tapped her invisible glass against Sena's.

"To the Treaty of Paris!" From the sound of it, the speaker surged to his feet. "That in the name of the most holy and undivided Trinity, it having pleased Providence to dispose the heart of the disturbed and tyrannical Prince George the Third—"

Laughter interrupted. "I believe that was 'serene and potent,' Lloyd."

"Hush, man, I am delivering it as it *should* have been written. That the disturbed and tyrannical Prince George the Third, who thinks himself king of much but is ruler of none, and the most noble and just United States of America, agree to forget all past wrongs the former did to the latter and pretend to restore a friendship we have not felt for decades. We shall establish good communication, et cetera, to procure peace and harmony and so on, forever and ever, amen."

More hurrahs rang out, and another gentleman took to his feet. "Article One. His Brittanic Majesty, the aforementioned disturbed and tyrannical George the Third, finally and fully acknowledges that these United States are free"—he paused for the cheering—"sovereign"—more hoots—"and *independent* states, and he will treat them as such, by heaven, and give up all his blasted claims to what is *ours*!"

Governor Paca stood. "Article Two—"

"Is boring, as is three. Article Four. Collect on your debts and take your sterling!"

"Article Five." The speaker paused to chuckle. "It is agreed Congress will *earnestly* 'recommend' to the state legislatures that all the property of the blasted Tories be restored. Not that we make any promises, mind you."

Lark didn't feel much like laughing along with the menfolk. "My, they sound sincere about honoring that one."

Sena stiffened beside her. "They've no intention of returning anything. Listen to them."

"It is not a matter of laughter, gentlemen." Jefferson's voice rose above the rest. "When we sign that treaty, we troth our bond to it. Including the provisions for the Tories, unpalatable as they may be to some."

The governor chuckled and took his seat again. "Speaking of which, Randel, that former student of yours keeps bothering my office about his house. If ever you see him again, advise him to give it up, will you?"

"Calvert?" Mr. Randel sounded not quite amused, though pleasant. "He will not. If you want him to stop bothering you, Paca, you had better give the boy back his property."

"Ha." Paca pointed a finger in Mr. Randel's direction. "He sided against us. Why should we do anything for him, before the law says we absolutely must?"

"'Tisn't as though he took up arms," Sena's father said.

"Not with that leg!" said a disembodied voice from the corner. Laughter sprang out again.

Lark and Sena exchanged a glance through the darkness.

"He would not have, regardless." The amusement had left Mr. Randel's voice.

"Easy to claim, Randel."

"Just as it is easy to claim otherwise, and to ascribe to a young man ignoble motives when you know nothing of him but one of his opinions." Mr. Randel's voice came from a different place now, as if he were pacing.

Paca waved it away. "You were the first to denounce him. And you, as well as anyone, know all we lost because of the blasted Redcoats and their conspirators." Paca turned toward Emerson, who had sat silently through this exchange. "You were a soldier, were you not, young man? Fields, is it?"

"Fielding, sir, and yes." Emerson's smile was as collected as ever. "I was."

"Well, and what does our brave, soldiering youth think of these British sympathizers?"

Emerson drew in a long breath and tilted his head. "I think it was a long and bitter war, sir. I think I lost many friends, all of whom were good, courageous men. I think our cause was just, and our nation has been established and blessed by the Lord Himself." He paused, offered that charming, rueful smile of his. "And I suspect men from the other side probably think the same thing."

A more muted, thoughtful round of laughter filled the room, and a few murmurs of agreement, including Jefferson's.

"There is one difference though," said a youthful voice whose owner Lark could not see.

Paca turned raised brows that direction. "What is that?"

"We were right, and they were wrong!"

The room erupted again, all attention focused on that corner. Except for Emerson, who looked toward the door and stared directly at their hiding spot.

Sena loosed a muted screech. "Do you think he sees us? Will he do anything?"

He lifted a brow.

Lark groaned. "He sees us."

Then he sent them a small, crooked grin.

"We had better go up," Sena said as the men within demanded another song. "If Papa sees him smiling at the doorway, he will figure us out in a heartbeat."

They climbed the stairs under cover of harpsichord music and shut themselves into Sena's room with a few giggles.

The mirth soon died. Lark shook her head. "'Tisn't right, Sena. I have no sympathy for the British, and I am happy enough that most of the Tories went back to England or to Canada. But the Calverts— they are different."

Sena sighed and sank onto her bed. "But as Pascal said, '*Et ainsi, ne pouvant faire que ce qui est juste fût fort, on a fait que ce qui est fort fût just.*'"

"'Since we cannot make the just strong, we make the strong just.'

We justify ourselves." Lark leaned against the closed door and stared at the darkened window. "But that never really makes it right."

"No. It does not."

Much like acknowledging it didn't change anything. But what else could they do?

Snow pinged against the window, the wind creating a swirl of white amidst the blackness. How complicated things had gotten since she came here. They seemed simple in Williamsburg, before her birthday. Tories were evil, social standings were set in stone. She would marry Emerson, live out her days as neighbors with her family.

But now…perhaps the lines had always been so blurred, and she had just been too blind to notice. It was as though by taking that one step, away from Emerson, she had entered a world removed from the one in which she'd grown up. Here, nothing was certain. Not peace, not fairness.

And least of all her own future.

CHAPTER EIGHTEEN

Emerson sloshed through the melting snow and didn't know whether to sigh or smile when he spotted two young ladies stepping from the stoop of number 19. On the bright side, they held up when they spotted him. On the other hand, if Lark and Miss Randel were off for a morning of errands, they would not want him tagging along. Though he saw no escort with them, so surely they had no plans to venture outside the residential section of town.

"Mr. Fielding, good morning." Miss Randel offered him a grin so sunny he had to wonder if he should be suspicious. "We were headed to the Calverts'. Would you join us?"

Yes, suspicion was warranted. "Ah." He cleared his throat and glanced at Lark, who looked as surprised by the invitation as he felt. "I cannot think Mr. Calvert would welcome my addition."

"Oh fie, he is the friendliest, most hospitable of hosts." And Miss Randel was surely the most mischievous of young ladies, with that gleam of trouble in her eyes. "Join us, please. I had a game in mind in which you would love to participate."

His brows rose. "Is this game, by chance, 'Lynch the Virginian'?"

The girls laughed, and Miss Randel shook her head. "Of course not. We owe you a favor for not turning us in to Papa the other night, after all."

He made a dubious hum and looked at Lark again. She rolled her eyes. "You might as well join us, Emerson. Whatever Sena has planned, she will no doubt make it entertaining."

"Very well." He offered Lark his arm and was a bit surprised when she tucked her hand into it without hesitation. Perhaps they were making progress, in spite of that kiss incident on Monday, and the days in between when they'd barely spoken.

Miss Randel bounced to the other side of Lark and led the way around the corner and down Tabernacle Street.

Emerson used an icy patch as excuse to pull Lark closer to his side. "You are feeling better? You certainly look well this morning."

"I have had not so much as a twinge since Wednesday."

"Excellent. I wanted to check on you yesterday, but with the ice storm… I might have braved it, had I not been fairly certain you wouldn't have sneaked down to spy on us Wednesday night if you were still ill."

She smiled up at him. "You acquitted yourself fairly well for being the youngest there."

"I was not—Monroe and Hardy are both my age, and yet entrusted with the representation of our fine state of Virginia."

Her laugh might be the loveliest sound he'd heard in days. "Oh, do forgive me. I did not see them."

Emerson grinned. "It was intriguing to be privy to the conversation. I had not realized Mr. Jefferson was so anxious about the ratification of the treaty. Or that so many of the statesmen are as incapable of carrying a tune as I."

She laughed again, as did Miss Randel. "I hope you wrote Wiley and bragged of your inclusion. He will be green with envy."

"Well, what else would I have done while iced in yesterday?"

The girls launched into a tale of how they'd spent their day, which, to hear them tell it, involved stumbling across a pirate den in icy Annapolis and being instantly transported to the Caribbean. He smiled at their obvious delight with the game they had devised for the Randel boys, and their supposed escapades kept him entertained until they stopped before a town house on West Street.

"Here we are," Miss Randel said as she bounced up to the door and rang. When it opened, she beamed. "Good morning, Mrs. Haslip. We have braved the remnants of ice for some company. And we even brought a guest for Mr. Calvert."

The old housekeeper smiled. "Come in out of that cold, dears. I have coffee on."

They all did their best to remove ice and snow from their shoes and pattens, then handed off their cloaks and hats and followed the housekeeper's wave into a parlor. No Calverts were within, but Emerson no sooner took a seat across from the chair Lark chose than he had to stand again. Miss Calvert and her brother entered together and sat.

The girls dove headlong into chatter that sounded meaningless to him, which left him and Calvert staring rather blankly at one another. His host cleared his throat. "Did you attend Randel's gentlemen's evening on Wednesday, then?"

Emerson nodded. "It was an enjoyable time. Your name was mentioned."

Calvert winced. "I can only imagine. Let me guess—the governor complained of my requests for my property to be returned."

"Very astute. Randel said the best way to quiet you would be to do as you asked."

With a chuckle, the man shook his head. "I have a feeling that will do naught to convince him. But I am grateful to Randel for saying so."

Miss Randel looked their way. "Do not dare launch into any talk of the political situation. We are going to play a game."

Calvert made a face. "Miss Randel, your games are always—"

"Brilliant. I know. Here are the rules for this one. I shall begin by asking a question of someone in the room. A deep, probing question of course, otherwise what would be the fun? The person must answer in all honesty, and the reward for their answer is that they then gain the floor and can ask someone else whatever deep, probing question they most want to know."

Emerson and Calvert both groaned, Lark looked dubious, and Miss Calvert paled and sent her friend a beseeching glance.

"You needn't fear, Kate—you have no secrets to hide." Miss Randel's lips curled into that impish grin of hers, and she looked directly at Emerson. "My question is for Mr. Fielding."

He raised a hand to his forehead. "I don't think I like this game. You swear it will not lead into 'Lynch the Virginian'?"

She laughed. "We are a peaceable company, I assure you. Now. What really happened that night with the villainous, dastardly Penelope?"

Lark's uncertainty slid into discomfort. "Sena—"

"An easy question to answer, actually." He kept his gaze fastened on Lark. "After Wiley went up to check on you, I found myself in a bad temper. I wanted to escape our fathers for a while, so I headed to the library—Wiley had mentioned a book he thought I should borrow. But I no sooner gained the room than your cousin slipped in. She said she was looking for a book to pass the evening with—"

"Ha!" Lark folded her arms over her chest. "She has probably never read an entire book in her life."

"Which I had no way of knowing at the time." He drew in a quick breath. "I selected one for her, handed it to her, and the next thing I knew she…" He shrugged.

Lark's stance didn't soften. "You did not look to be fighting her off."

"And that is where my guilt lies. I am sorry for it." When Lark averted her gaze, he glanced at Miss Randel. "My turn?"

She nodded.

"Excellent. My question is for Lark." Though she still didn't look at him, he smiled. "What is your favorite book?"

"Oh, come now!" Sena bounced in her chair. "That is neither deep nor probing. You could learn the answer in *any* conversation."

He kept his smile in place. "It is of the utmost importance I learn the answer now, so if ever *she* asks me for a recommendation on what to read, I can offer a learned opinion. Lark?"

She heaved a sigh. "*Don Quixote.* And now 'tis my turn, so I will ask something of Mr. Calvert. What was your first reaction when you learned your house had been seized?"

They all looked to their host, who offered a small smile. "I prayed. First of all to thank the Lord for His wisdom in urging us to our plantation for the duration of the war. Who knows what would have happened had we been there when they demanded the property? And then for direction in where to find housing."

Emerson could only stare. Did the man honestly expect them to believe that? That his first response to such news was *prayer*? But the ladies all seemed convinced of his answer. And he sounded sincere, granted.

Which was unfair. How was he to compete with a man so blasted perfect he harbored no ill will toward anyone?

"My question, then." Calvert arched a brow at Emerson, which made him want to groan again. "How did you manage to maintain an engagement to Miss Benton for two years without ever getting to know her?"

Though Emerson started to sigh, he realized midbreath the question wasn't as hostile as it could have been. He didn't ask why he had wanted to, or what was wrong with him to have done so. He asked how he had managed it. Emerson settled his gaze on Lark yet again. "I am not sure. I admit I made no attempt to remedy it, that at first it was even what I sought, that lack of involvement. But as I come to know her now…I have to think had I seen *this* Lark at any point in those two years, I could not have maintained my indifference."

Her eyes went wide, her arms went to her sides. "Are you saying this is *my* fault?"

He grinned. "I believe the next question is mine, Miss Benton. But I will use my turn to ask you what is on your mind, which I assume is whether I am laying the fault for our failure at your feet. The answer to which is that of course I am not. I know well had I asked you a single question *then*, you would have been happy to provide the answer. I am merely pointing out that had you acted at all during the last years as you have since coming to Annapolis, I wouldn't have *had* to ask anything to glimpse that beautiful nature of yours."

Miss Randel huffed. "Absurd. Not the fact that Lark has a beautiful nature, which we all know, but that she needed to do anything differently to show it. I cannot think she had a complete change in personality merely by arriving in our fair city. And I happen to know if she kept to herself, it was because she felt she *must*. And whose fault is *that*, Mr. Fielding?"

The housekeeper entered with a coffee tray, but no one did more than glance her way. Calvert gave Miss Randel a muted grin. "For this being your game, Miss Randel, you are terrible at obeying the rules. The question belongs to Fielding now, 'tisn't to be asked of him."

He nodded. "Thank you, Mr. Calvert. And since your fairness is obvious, I will put my question to you. Unarguably the fault is mostly mine—I would never claim otherwise—but I have given much thought to this over the past few days, and I would like your opinion. Can two people remain perfect strangers because of the choice of one, when they are in the same company day in and day out for years?"

Calvert frowned as he considered. "I confess my initial reaction is that they cannot."

"Edwinn!" Miss Randel squeaked.

Calvert grinned. "Can you not wait your turn, Sena?"

She glared. "No, and I thank you for asking and thereby making the question irrelevant. And now I will demand you tell us, Mr. Calvert, whose side you are on!"

"Theirs." He spread his hands, palms up. "It is obvious they care for one another, but how will they ever mend things if they do not examine the issue from all sides?"

Emerson's eyes bulged. Calvert was not against him?

Miss Randel held her glare while the housekeeper passed out the coffee. "Certainly 'tisn't by blaming anything on Lark. Lark—tell these idiot men why you remained aloof, if in fact you did."

Calvert sipped his coffee. "You at least had the floor this time, but was that supposed to be a question?"

"Yes," she snapped. "Lark?"

Lark looked caught between a smile and panic. "I…only did what I had been taught a lady must, and what I thought he wanted. After all, that was how I had always acted before he proposed, and I assumed he had a reason for asking me to marry him to begin with." Her gaze went sharp and pierced him. "What else was I to do, Emerson?"

"Perhaps exactly what you have been doing since—reprimand me for my idiocy and refuse to hide that bright spirit of yours, as the Lord Himself cautioned us about."

Calvert buried a chuckle in his coffee, which earned him the glares of all three young ladies.

Lark all but growled. "Sometimes the idiocy is so great it precludes reprimanding a man for it, until some other event has first knocked the stubbornness out of him."

"I will be gracious enough to take that observation into consideration before forming my next question." He paused for a sip, then set his cup upon its saucer. "If indeed I was such a prodigious idiot—which, again, I will not deny—then I must ask again the question I put to you the other night, Miss Benton. Why did you ever love me to begin with?"

Lark turned a lovely shade of pink. "Do you really think that an appropriate question to ask in company?"

"No, but neither have any of these others been. And it begs to be asked."

Her jaw clenched, her fingers dug into the arm of her chair "We are *not* talking of this here. I have a question for Miss Calvert."

"Ah, but the floor is mine." He sent her an innocent smile, then said, "I have a question for Miss Calvert." He looked at the lady in question, then at Lark again. "What is my question?"

For a moment she continued to glare at him, then the amusement crept in. All at once, the group burst into laughter. Through it, he caught the encouraging nod of Calvert, who in a single glance managed to say he'd done well.

Emerson wasn't certain of that, nor of what to make of the other man's support. But perhaps Lark would consider the question. And perhaps she would come to see that foolishness was not his only characteristic. Unless she were as superficial as her cousin, he must have *some* virtue to have won her regard.

He picked up his coffee again as the girls declared the game finished, and tried not to wonder what he would do if his question turned on him. Tried not to fear that Lark, like Elizabeth and Penelope, had been interested only in his looks, his wealth, his charm.

Because if that were the case, his chances of winning her back were minuscule. If she'd never truly loved him, she wouldn't care enough to forgive him.

He sighed into his coffee. It would serve him right, to be falling in love with a woman who would as soon toss him back into the bay as give him another chance.

Emerson might not be as devout as Calvert seemed to be, but that was enough to spur him to desperate prayer.

The moment the door to Kate's room was shut, Lark spun on Sena with wide eyes. "What in the world were you thinking with that game, Sena Randel?"

Her friend laughed and took a seat on Kate's bed. "It seemed like a good idea at the time. Though I confess, I did not expect Mr. Calvert to take Mr. Fielding's part so much."

Kate chose a seat on the plush couch and smiled. "It was good to see him and another young man being companionable."

"And shocking, given that these two particular young men are both interested in the same young woman." Sena arched a glance at Lark.

She rolled her eyes. "Mr. Calvert is not interested in me, Sena."

"Of course he is. Tell her, Kate."

But Kate inclined her head. "He may have entertained a few notions, but I think his true heart rests closer to home."

Sena looked none too amused. "Don't fill my head with nonsense. Your brother has never shown the slightest preference for me...and even if he had feelings, he would never act on them without my father's approval. Otherwise I might have been tempted to throw caution and family opinion to the wind like Alice did."

"Did your father not tell you?" Kate leaned forward, eyes twinkling as she began to relax. "When he came to speak with Edwinn while your mother was in her child-bed, he said he wouldn't be opposed to Edwinn's courting you, if ever he inclined that way."

"What?" Sena jerked upright, but then her face went sober. "Then back to my original point—he must *not* be inclined."

Lark took a seat beside Kate and enjoyed the respite from her own romantic woes. "Come now, Sena. I barely know Kate's brother, yet even I can be sure he is only taking some time to divine your feelings, and perhaps be sure your father meant his words. His inclination is certain, otherwise he never would have argued with you as he did during that game of yours."

"By that logic, then, your Emerson is completely smitten with you."

Lark winced, though she'd brought that on herself. "We have plenty to argue about. You and your Edwinn, however, do not. I think you must give him some encouragement. Right, Kate?"

With some relief, Lark saw Kate's reticence had disappeared.

Looking perfectly at ease, she nodded. "He will need it, to be sure. And even then, he may hesitate until he succeeds in reclaiming our property. It is difficult for him, feeling he has no place. And I imagine any man who feels displaced will not be confident in asking a woman he loves to share his exile with him."

"Well." Sena rolled over onto her stomach and propped her head on her hands. "I shall bat my lashes and flirt as needed, and we shall soon see if he responds. In the meantime…"

"No." Lark groaned and fell into the back of the sofa. "Let us focus no more on me, Sena."

"It must be done," she replied with feigned sobriety. "You are the most interesting thing to happen to us for ages. Kate, what say you of the menfolk's claims? Does Lark share in the blame for the distance between herself and Mr. Fielding?"

Lark's eyes slid shut. "You questioned me on that before. You asked if I had truly shown him my heart."

"And I was satisfied with your answer, but they obviously saw it differently. You behaved exactly as a young woman is taught to behave. I, however, have little experience doing such, so I figure Kate can give us a better perspective. She is dutiful and obedient too. Kate?"

At Kate's thoughtful hum, Lark opened her eyes again to study this other new friend of hers. Surely if anyone would take her side, it would be gentle, bashful Kate, who didn't seem to have a contentious bone in her body.

But Kate's eyes didn't look particularly indulgent. "I suppose I must wonder what kept you silent all that time. As Sena pointed out, you can't have changed overmuch within. You obviously *had* such spirit during your engagement. Why did you not show it?"

Lark smoothed back a loose hair. Part of her wanted to ignore the question, but this was the longest speech she had ever heard from Kate, and she hadn't the heart. "I think I have changed more than you may realize, having been exposed to more in this past month than all my life beforehand. Still, I had opinions I never shared. I…I suppose I was afraid I would scare him off. I had been in awe of him all my life, so I had always been meek and silent in his company, and when he proposed—well, I assumed he *wanted* a quiet, unobtrusive wife."

"And so you would have resigned yourself to that for life?" Sena looked at her as though she were a simpleton. "*Could* you have? Did it never occur to you he would find you out eventually?"

Lark could only bury her face in her hands and mumble, "I don't know."

Kate put a reassuring hand on her shoulder. Strange how the touch could be so encouraging simply because it was so out of character. "Let us, for a moment, examine the fear. He is your brother's closest friend, right? Then what is your brother like?"

She sighed and lowered her hands again. "Wiley is...Wiley. Clever, lighthearted, a bit of a joker. Optimistic, but with a fierce streak if you back him into a corner or injure one he loves."

Kate nodded. "As I thought—not so unlike you. So then, if this is the sort of personality Mr. Fielding is drawn to..."

The parallel was too obvious to miss. "I should have shown him from the start I could be like that too. Instead, I cowered in a corner for years, too afraid of losing him to truly win him."

And yet the same fear was still there, nibbling away at her innermost self. It was one thing to be rejected by a man who was a stranger to her true self. But if she showed him all of who she was, and still he tossed her aside for another, how much worse would it hurt?

Kate gently squeezed her shoulder. "Lark, fear is not of the Lord. Trust me, I know this better than anyone. Never does He work through discouragement and apprehension, but rather through peace and edification. It seems to me God is doing a great thing in both of you, something you might not have seen or embraced without going through what you did. But in order to find His perfect will for you, you must seek it. Seek the perfect love of our Father, not the affection of man."

Sena grinned. "She is as able as Reverend Lake. And though her sound advice is always hard to follow, in this case you ought to do well. I am all but positive you have secured the affections of your man this last week anyway."

Kate smiled. "He does seem set on capturing your heart." After removing her hand, Kate leaned her shoulder companionably into Lark's. "Do you love him, Lark?"

The question of the week. "I don't know. I thought I did, but... did I? *Do* I?" She could only shrug.

One of many questions for which she had no answer these days.

CHAPTER NINETEEN

"You are going."

Edwinn ignored Randel and kept sharpening his quill.

"Calvert, this is a monumental day. For the entire country, to be sure, but also for *you*." Randel leaned over Edwinn's desk, as he had done many a time back in his school days, and glared. "The treaty will be ratified. Peace, true peace, at long last. Official, legal peace—and with it, the promise to restore your estate. How can you *not* be there to witness it?"

"Because I know well *they* will not honor it. Not that part." But he put down the feather with a sigh. "I will not be welcomed in the State House."

"They have said anyone might witness."

At that, Edwinn loosed a dry laugh. "By 'anyone,' they did not mean *me*."

"Hence why it would be a statement." Randel straightened again. "You will never succeed in your goals by sitting here in this rented study and writing letters. Stand up and come *do* something for once."

Edwinn shook his head in wonder. "And this is how the dedicated scholar made the transition to an army commander. You are a study in contradictions, my friend."

Randel picked up Edwinn's cane and held it out. "Now, or I shall rap your knuckles with it."

"Have it your way." Edwinn took his cane and used it to help him stand. Perhaps afterward he would visit at Randel House, manage a few moments with Sena. Assuming he lived through the first order of business. "If you have to defend me against a mob, you have only yourself to blame."

Randel rolled his eyes and plopped his tricorn back onto his head—he hadn't even bothered taking off his cloak. "Have you a blade hidden within that thing, at least?"

"No, but it can double as a club in a pinch." He followed Randel out the door of his study and went to collect his cloak and hat.

The moment they gained the outdoors, the cold worked its way into Edwinn's leg. He had long ago given up coddling it, but this winter had been a terrible one for pain. "Did the missing delegates brave the snow for the occasion, or will it be ratified by only the seven states, rather than the nine needed for quorum?"

Randel grinned. "The express riders Jefferson sent out on the third did their jobs. The delegations from New Jersey and Connecticut both arrived yesterday, and Beresford made it this very morning. We have the full nine votes, praise the Lord. Now we have to pray for safe passage back to Paris."

"I envy not the couriers the trip across the Atlantic this winter, for certain."

Randel shuddered. "Franklin writes that it is as terrible a winter in Europe. Bizarre, but he has a hypothesis about it being tied to the volcanic eruptions in Iceland."

"Really." Edwinn let that swirl through his mind as they reached the corner of West and Church Circle. "I have never heard of such a theory. Something about all the gases released, perhaps? I have read that much of Northern Europe is still experiencing toxic fogs associated with Mount Laki's activity."

"'Tis an interesting possibility, at any rate. There is surely *something* to explain this winter. I have never experienced the like. It has been enough to make a man want to move to the South."

And talking of scientific theories was far preferable to thinking about the welcome Edwinn would soon receive. He deliberately kept the subject on climate and volcanoes until they stepped onto State House Circle a few minutes later. At which point, he let silence reign.

As it was, no one paid any attention to him as they made their way inside and to the senate chamber. Fielding was already there and waved them over to a few feet of floor he had reserved. He offered a smile. "Randel succeeded in convincing you, I see."

Edwinn faced forward, where the congressmen were milling

about. "Only after he threatened to cane me. With my own cane, no less."

Fielding laughed. "He does excel at ironic punishments."

Randel took off his hat and slapped Edwinn on the arm with it. "Watch yourselves, you mouthy pups, or I shall let neither of you through my door again. And given the young ladies I have under my roof…"

"He has also mastered the art of effective threats," Calvert said in a stage whisper to Fielding.

Fielding nodded, but Mifflin called the congress to order, so they all fell silent.

As a matter of course, the president read through the articles of the treaty, which took a good while. Edwinn paid strict attention, though, especially when Article Five was reached.

Mifflin read that section in the same even voice as all the rest, but there were a few snorts through the audience, and some of the members exchanged amused glances. As if the very inclusion of the provisions for Loyalists were only a joke.

He shouldn't have come. His presence here today would accomplish no more than his letters. These men would not grant him the rights they had fought for, the ones they had espoused in their Declaration of Independence. How was he to pursue happiness among men who considered him a traitor? Where was his liberty? How many of them would even take from him the right to live?

Maybe he ought to give up the fight and content himself with a quiet existence. Let the officials forget about him so he didn't bring trouble upon his or Kate's head.

At long last the reading was complete, and with great flourish the congressmen signed it on behalf of their states. Mr. Jefferson took the floor. "Mr. Dunlap will be printing thirteen copies of a Peace Proclamation that will include these articles, to be sent to each of the states. This proclamation will also stress that each and every sentence was approved by us, by whose authority the people's existence as free men is bound up. Hence, *every* stipulation must be obeyed."

He looked at some of his colleagues, his friends, then glanced at the audience. Did he look at Edwinn, or was it his imagination? "I move Congress pass a resolution immediately, earnestly recommending each state comply with all provisions, especially those concerning restitution of seized property."

"There, see?" Randall mumbled around his smile.

"No, but I shall believe it when I do."

While Congress returned to the matter at hand, some of the audience began drifting out. Edwinn motioned toward the exit. "I am heading home, Randel. You?"

"Not just yet."

Edwinn nodded and sidled through the crowd. Though he thought he glimpsed Fielding exiting too, he didn't hold up. Not right now. He wanted only to go home, out of the cold, and pray. Turn this mess over to the Lord yet again.

He made it outside and down the steps before someone recognized him.

"Hey! You there, Calvert. What the deuce are you doing here?"

To stop, or to keep going? He debated a moment, before the option was taken from him. The acquaintance who had hailed him leaped in front of him, practically snarling. "You came to hear your precious king acknowledge us, did you? Well good. Now that you have heard once and for all that we are right and just in our independence, perhaps you shall pack up and return to England where you belong."

Edwinn sighed and leaned on his cane. He recognized his accuser but couldn't recall his name. "I beg your pardon, sir. I rejoice in the independence of these United States along with everyone else, and am, most of all, glad the hostilities have ceased, as *that* is what I took issue with to begin with."

"Ah, right." The man held out his arms and laughed. "He is a hater of war, that's it. A turn-the-other-cheek sort. Well then, Mr. Righteous, let us give you something to forgive."

Before Edwinn could shift away, the man's foot flew out. Edwinn felt the impact on his cane, felt it shudder and slip as if time had slowed. In that fraction of a second he wished, willed, prayed it would hold firm. But the icy bricks betrayed him, as did his support. He went crashing down, his bad leg screaming as it struck the cold, hard pavement.

He gripped the head of his cane as his throat closed off with anger. For nearly twenty years he had come to terms with the knowledge that he couldn't fight even if he wanted to, but in this moment he was tempted to risk a sure thrashing just to demonstrate to this idiot that seeking war didn't guarantee one would win it.

Before he could do more than pull himself up to a knee, another figure charged forward and knocked the instigator back.

"Fielding, unhand me!"

Fielding? Edwinn blinked and shook his head.

Fielding made no other move, just extended his arms to keep anyone from moving. "Have you not tired of fighting yet, Litchfield? The war is over. Let it rest."

Litchfield, yes, that was his name. He muttered a curse and waved a hand at Edwinn. "I cannot suffer it, Fielding. These cowardly Tories—"

"Think of them what you will. But *I* cannot suffer you marring this day of peace with such behavior."

Another vaguely familiar young man rushed forward and placed a restraining hand on Litchfield's elbow. "Fielding has a point, Litch. Leave it for today. Besides, there is no glory in thrashing a cripple."

Much as he wished he could leap to his feet and prove that word did not apply to him, the throbbing in Edwinn's leg was too great.

Litchfield looked about to argue but at length made a dismissive gesture and turned away. "You are right, Woodward. He is hardly worth it."

Edwinn waited for them to saunter away, thanked the Lord when their parting gift of spittle landed an inch from his boot rather than in his face, and only then struggled up, losing his cane again in the process.

Fielding picked it up, held it out to him. Fearing what he might find in the man's regard, Edwinn nevertheless met it. And sighed in relief. No pity, no apology. Just a nod, a simple understanding.

Respect.

It was enough to square Edwinn's shoulders and give him the strength to withhold his wince until he had turned toward home.

Lark tilted her head to better examine the detailing on the miniature dress. She was passable with a needle, able to mend and stitch, but embroidery that fine made her miss the servant at Endover who was so very skilled at it. "I would never be able to duplicate it."

"Nonsense." Alice peeked under the skirt of the fashion baby to see the back of the stitching. "'Tis simple enough. If you've a mind to add such embellishment to one of your dresses, I would be happy to help you."

"Do let her, Lark. Alice is brilliant with a needle and lacks the excuse to use it as much as she would like." With a glance over her shoulder, Sena took the doll from the shelf and turned it over in her hands. "Though I maintain you could become a prosperous dressmaker if you put your mind to it, Alice. Marie Antoinette's could not hold a candle to you."

Alice laughed and took the fashion baby from Sena's hands, replaced it on the shelf. "I haven't the time, not with Hugh and Callie and, Lord willing, more children in my future. Speaking of whom, we had better head back. I would like to be there when they wake up from their naps."

Though Sena loosed a sigh, Lark tamped down a smile. It had taken quite a bit of convincing to get Alice to accompany them to Market Place at all. She had finally been won over by Sena's argument that her presence as a respectable married woman lent them the propriety everyone insisted she needed more of.

As if anyone or anything could ever make Sena entirely proper. Lark certainly hoped not.

"Very well. For the children." With her usual energy, Sena led the way out of the aisle of fustian and then the shop entirely.

For her part, Lark was content to remain a step behind, beside Alice, as their intrepid leader flounced through Market Place and headed up Fleet Street, back toward State House Circle. She couldn't help but note that Alice's countenance reflected a peace it hadn't since she came to Randel House. "Have you heard from your husband, Alice?"

"Hmm?" Alice looked her way, beamed a smile that no amount of homespun could make look common. "No. But I feel now that all will be well. Matty will come home. He must, if he wants to meet his next child."

"His next—Alice, I had no idea."

"I had been uncertain, until just the other day."

Sena held up to draw even with them, her eyes wide. "Did I just overhear what I think I did? Alice, what a blessing."

At least it would be if the absent Mr. Mattimore returned. Assuming he returned with goods or sterling enough to keep them.

Lark shook off those thoughts, determined to be as happy for her new friend as Alice obviously was. "Well, I think we know what our next sewing project must be. Forget the latest from Paris—we must dedicate ourselves to gowns of a smaller scale."

Talk of what blankets and gowns Alice would need kept them occupied from Fleet to Cornhill Streets, and as they stepped onto State House Circle. But when Lark spotted Emerson standing on the walkway, his posture tense and his gaze toward a figure limping in the distance, thoughts of Alice's expanding family fled.

"Emerson?"

He spun, his expression softening into a smile, though his eyes still betrayed concern. "You mean to tell me you ladies were not eavesdropping on the assembly from the gallery?"

"Not today." Sena's response lacked its usual good humor as she looked to the same place Emerson had been. "Is that Mr. Calvert limping so terribly?"

The worry took over Emerson's face again. "Litchfield accosted him a few moments ago. I stepped in, but he had already been knocked down."

If Lark had doubted Sena's feelings for Mr. Calvert before now, she surely could not in the face of the fury and agony that possessed her friend. "Is he injured? I have never seen his limp so pronounced. If that idiot Litchfield… I must go to him."

"You must *not*." Emerson stayed her with an outstretched arm. His gaze demanded understanding. "He was stripped of enough pride today at the hands of Litchfield. If you went to him now, Miss Randel, it would make him feel worse, not better. Let him salvage his dignity."

Sena glanced from one of them to another, obviously exasperated. "I cannot do nothing! He is in pain, he is—"

"Hush now, Sena." Alice stepped forward and wrapped a supportive arm around her shoulders. "Mr. Fielding has the right of it. What we shall do is repair to Randel House with all haste, and you and I shall make up a poultice. We shall then deliver it covertly to his staff in the kitchen, then go around front and ring for Kate. You know well she will tell us how he fares, but without further damage to his pride."

Sena let Alice lead her away, her silence speaking to the depths of her distress.

Lark watched them go, tucking her hand into the crook of Emerson's arm. "You are a good man, Emerson Fielding. Guarding his pride as you just did, and stepping in with Mr. Litchfield."

Emerson sighed, though he covered her fingers with his own. "I did little enough."

She smiled up at him, an ember of warmth blossoming inside the portion of her heart that had long been his. "You did what you always do. You took the role of hero."

He led her along toward North Street at a slow, leisurely pace better suited for a warm spring day, but she made no complaints. Then he angled a grin down at her that had a hint of the rogue in it. "So Lark Benton likes a man who can play the hero once in a while, does she? You know, there was once a time I rescued a little girl from a sure fright when her brother tried to drop a frog onto her head."

Laughter tickled her throat. "Mmm, so you did. Though if recollection serves, you first gave the devious brother the idea for the prank by wondering how shrilly said girl might scream in such a situation."

He chuckled too. "You were not supposed to remember that part."

"It wouldn't be nearly so dear a memory without it." Memories of simpler days, of shared history. A reminder that their past was not only betrayal and heartbreak, but many golden days spent together as well. Perhaps, if she focused on those, then a shared future wasn't so inconceivable

Perhaps.

CHAPTER TWENTY

Wiley barely refrained from rolling his eyes at the way Penelope pranced and preened, holding out her wrist at all times lest anyone lose sight of the sapphires that shackled her. She had been acting a complete ninny ever since Owens took her outside for a walk yesterday and then brought her back branded as his.

Well, more a ninny than usual, that is.

"I want a spring wedding, of course." She twirled around and admired the blue gems. Again. "Spring in Savannah—which would be March, I suppose."

"Savannah?" Aunt Hester snapped to attention, her indulgent smile evaporating. "Why would you want the wedding to be *there*? Is it not enough you will be moving so far from me? You must wed near your family, either here or in Philadelphia."

"Gracious, Mamma. Not with this winter, I shan't. Do you not want to escape the cold? Yet I have my doubts all that snow will be gone from Pennsylvania until May."

A smile flitted across Mother's lips, then away. "But March, dear... 'tis Lark and Emerson's wedding. You would have to wait until afterward, but then your cousin will be on her wedding trip."

Penelope fluttered her lashes like an innocent and smiled like a devil. "Now, Aunt Margaret. We have all refrained from pointing this out, but we also all know Lark has no intentions of keeping her promise. Why, that silly girl has no care at all for your feelings, for all she's put you and Uncle Benton through. 'Tis time to give up on the hope she will do what is right and let those of us who have honored our parents have our day."

Why that little...

But Mother narrowed her eyes. "I know not who you think to be fooling with this act of yours, Penelope, but I assure you, 'tisn't me. Whatever you did to come between Lark and Emerson—"

"I?" With the expert performance of an acclaimed actress, she blinked back tears from her wide eyes and pressed a hand to her heart. "Aunt, you injure me. What could I have possibly done?"

Mother's chin rose a notch. "Knowing you as I do, it is hard to say. But I find it no coincidence that an engagement proceeds without bump for two years and then falls to pieces the very *day* you meet Emerson."

Not exactly without bump, but Wiley had no desire to interrupt this display in defense of mere facts.

Aunt Hester puffed out her chest like an angry bird. "And why is that Penelope's fault? She can hardly help it if she is a more alluring girl than that dull, sullen daughter of yours. If Emerson was smitten with her, 'twas Lark's fault, not Penelope's."

"How *dare* you!" Mother surged to her feet, the tower of her hair doing its usual wobble. "My Lark is the sweetest, loveliest girl I have ever met. It is *your* little doxy of a daughter who leaves insult and destruction in her wake wherever she goes!"

Wiley pressed his lips down on a smile and looked to Aunt Hester, whose face had gone red. She, too, took to her feet. "You were always jealous, Margaret. Jealous of me, and now jealous I have a daughter capable of making whatever match she pleases."

"Jealous?" Mother looked a hairsbreadth from vibrating with rage. "Why in the world would I be jealous of your sour temper, or of a child so indiscreet you must leave your home in the dead of winter to avoid scandal because she dallied with a—"

Penelope's screech drowned out the sordid details, though Wiley strained forward, hoping to catch them.

He could have sold tickets to this.

"Perhaps my Penelope gets carried away with her feelings now and then, but at least she can keep a man's interest, unlike Lark."

Mother sucked in a long breath and looked as though she wished for a dagger. "I do not care for her method of keeping a man's interest. And if the entire coast were not locked in snow, I would toss you both out on your backsides."

Aunt Hester tucked a now-crying Penelope to her side. "Rest assured we will be out of your miserable home as soon as Mr. Owens can arrange travel for us to Georgia."

"Which will not be soon enough." With a regal pivot, Mother stormed from the room.

Aunt Hester and Penelope left too, the elder murmuring phrases meant to soothe while Penelope increased the pressure of her crocodile tears.

Well. That had been entertaining. Wiley almost hated to see it end so soon. Though when Asa announced Mr. Owens's arrival a minute later, he supposed it was a good thing the theatrics were over.

He stood to greet the guest. "Good morning, Owens."

"Likewise." Owens looked around, brows up. "Is Miss Moxley about anywhere? She knew I was coming this morning. I am taking her to meet my grandmother here in Williamsburg."

"Ah." He tried to fight his grin. Truly he did. "She is collecting herself. Some minor disagreement about where the nuptials should take place, you see. I believe she convinced her mother of the merits of Georgia, though."

"Excellent."

Wiley motioned to the furniture. "Have a seat. It may take her a few moments to properly preen for you."

Conscience niggled as Owens sat. He really ought to leave well enough alone and let the man take Penelope away for good, but... Wiley sighed. "Have you any idea what you are about by marrying her?"

Owens lifted his brows and rearranged his coattails. "Certainly I do. I am taking the most beautiful woman I have ever met home as my bride."

He sounded far from naive as he said it, but... "How can I put this delicately? Owens, beauty, in this case, comes at a price. Penelope is the nastiest, most selfish creature I know. She will make your life miserable."

Yet Owens chuckled. "Now Benton, 'tis all a matter of whether I can handle her or not. And I assure you, I can." He leaned forward, amusement and determination on his countenance. "I am a wealthy man, I will not equivocate about it. That is undoubtedly why your cousin is interested in me. And since I am interested in her solely because she will look charming on my arm, I do not mind her superficiality. I intend to be the pillar of Savannah society. To do that, I need a wife who will awe the masses with her beauty."

Wiley frowned. "Will it not undermine that position, though, when she turns on you? Discretion and loyalty are not my cousin's virtues."

"I daresay the allowance I give her will keep her in line."

Well, Wiley had to give the man credit—he knew her well for so brief an acquaintance. And at any rate, he had issued the warning, so his conscience was clear. "I wish you all joy, then. Even if I cannot fathom how you may achieve it."

"'Tis all a matter of one's expectations." Owens made himself comfortable, but then stood, his gaze on the door.

Wiley followed suit, though he was more than a little surprised to see Penelope back so soon, and without a trace of tears.

"There you are, my darling." She rushed forward as if her life had not begun until that moment. It would have been enough to make Wiley ill, had it not been so amusing. "Let me fetch my cloak, and I shall be set to meet your grandmother."

Owens smiled and patted the hand she had thrust at him. "Oughtn't you be dressed first, my love?"

Her laugh rang out as she brushed her free hand down the straight skirt of that barely-a-dress she was so fond of. "Oh, you silly man. This is a new fashion. Of course I don't wear it to the balls—"

"Certainly not, everyone would think you forgot to put your real gown on." Owens somehow said it with a charming smile. "Now darling, Grandmother is an old-fashioned sort, still wearing powdered wigs for all occasions. She wouldn't know what to make of this... *lovely* style. I am sure you do not want to shock her."

Penelope paused only a moment. "Of course not, darling. I will run upstairs and choose something else."

"I do appreciate your consideration." His smile was almost childlike. And therefore all the more cunning. "I am sure you will exercise as much thoughtfulness among the society of Savannah, who are a bit behind the times in their fashions as well. You can lead them forward, but it will have to be in small steps. All the ladies shall look up to you, but you will not want to appear too foreign to them either."

"Oh…well…"

"The first order of business when you arrive at your new home will of course be to visit the dressmaker. I imagine the two of you can put together a stunning new wardrobe to impress everyone."

Apparently the promise of limitless new things was enough to mollify Penelope. She pulled away with a beaming smile. "I shall make you proud, my darling."

"Of course you shall. You are the most beautiful young woman I have ever seen. Now run along. We mustn't be late, or Grandmother will be put out."

As Penelope sped from the room, Owens turned back to Wiley with hands spread. "See there? Easy enough, if one's purse is deep enough and one's tongue well accustomed to flattery."

"You are a man above men." Wiley took his seat again, chuckling. "And yet, I envy you not in the slightest."

Lark set down her quill and blew the words dry. She hadn't used the journal Kate had given her as much as she had expected, but this morning had seemed a fine time to put down her thoughts.

I am to blame too. That was the insight with which she began her musing, and it still made her insides tense up to admit it, even if only to herself.

> *I am to blame too. For the failure of my engagement, for the distance that caused it. All along I thought it was Emerson, his lack of feeling, his fault. But how could it have been? Yes, he did wrong. But I never challenged him to do right. I never invited him to do right. I just sat there and let my hopes dissolve. I was content to leave the direction of my life up to him.*

Lark paused, tapped the feather of her pen against her chin. At home, it had been so easy to play the part she was expected to play, yet was she ever satisfied with that role? Only with Wiley had she ever felt truly comfortable, and only now did she realize it was because he challenged her to be more than what was expected. Emerson was right. Had she acted from the start as she did now, their relationship would have been very different.

She bent back over the diary.

> *And now we are here. My eyes have been opened to parts of this world, this life I had never imagined. I am forced to examine what the consequences of my decisions will be. If I do not marry Emerson, where will that leave me? Not in straits so perilous as Alice's, to be sure. But nevertheless serious.*
>
> *And if I do marry him? What then? Will he love me, truly love me? Can I love him as he deserves to be loved, or has my devotion heretofore been based on qualities too superficial?*
>
> *Perhaps it was. Perhaps I fancied only his face, his pleasing manners. Now, though, I see that those things that drew me are rooted in qualities that run deep within him.*
>
> *Still, I hesitate to trust him, not knowing what he may do with my heart. But I do not want to be like the delegates, who risk all they fought for because of the threat of inclement weather. If I have stood up, demanding to be loved for who I am, then how can I refuse to take a step toward the hand now outstretched?*

She sighed and put the quill in its holder, staring long at the words. The world seemed at once so stark, yet so blurred. Right and wrong begged for recognition in political matters, yet clarity there showed her nothing about how to apply it to her life. Still she was unsure whether she had the strength to take a risk for what she believed.

For the Calverts. Or for Emerson.

Her eyes slid shut. Kate had said that she must give her direction over to the Lord. Had she ever done that? Certainly she had the roots of faith within her. She knew that Christ had shed His blood in atonement for her sins, she knew that God formed the world. He was Providence. He was Heaven. But had she ever thought of Him as Father, as the Calverts did?

Drawing in a long breath, Lark rested her head against her

clasped hands. "Please, Father, show me Your will for me. And give me the strength to follow it."

Unable to think of any other words to suit the churning within her, Lark rose from her seat and turned to look out the window. She smiled. The boys had crossed Tabernacle Street and descended upon the lawn in front of Bladen's Folly to throw snowballs at one another, and apparently while she was lost in her musings, Emerson had joined them.

She leaned into the window frame and watched him slip and slide around, lob a white ball at Johnny, and dive to escape retaliation. It had been years since she had seen him play. He and Wiley had once sought out any mischief to be found, even into their adolescence. But since the war, there had been no snowballs, when a rare snow descended. There had been no water fights in the summer. There had been no boyishness, only the responsibilities of men.

She admired the men. But she missed the boys.

More youngsters soon came upon them and apparently lured the Randels into another pursuit. Emerson waved them off and headed toward the house. And why should that make her heart race? She'd seen him nearly every day for weeks now.

Perhaps she *could* risk loving him, and letting him love her. Perhaps she *must*.

Sucking in a long breath and pressing a hand to her stomach, she whispered another prayer that consisted of little but "Dare I, Father?" and headed downstairs.

Mrs. Green and Emerson both stepped through the front door, though the woman stopped him with a scowl. "You will stomp off that snow before you step foot in here, young man."

Emerson grinned. "I certainly shall. But as Poor Richard would say, Mrs. Green, 'Clean your finger, before you point at my spots.'"

The housekeeper narrowed her eyes then widened them and looked down at her own feet. Her pattens were packed with snow, and her guffaw of laughter made Lark grin.

"So he would, Mr. Fielding, so he would. Miss Benton, be a dear and take these packages so I might clean myself off, would you? I would have come in the back way, had I not seen your young man approaching and thought to let him in."

Lark accepted the basket of goods from Mrs. Green and smiled at Emerson as the housekeeper took off her pattens. That was another of his admirable features—the ability to know what to say to win over anyone. She had always attributed it to charm, but it was more than that. He had to first understand someone to know how to speak most effectively.

He sent her a wink and then cleaned off his boots, removed his snowy cloak. A minute later Mrs. Green bustled away with the damp wool and her basket, and Lark motioned toward the library. "Mrs. Randel and Sena are in there; Mr. Randel is out."

Emerson nodded, but rather than stepping forward, he grinned and held out a rectangular package wrapped in calico.

She stared at it for a long moment. The last time he had offered her any sort of gift, it hadn't signaled a great day. Granted, this didn't look to be the family diamonds. "What is it?"

His grin went lopsided, dry. "Nothing my mother foisted upon me for you, I promise you that."

Oh, she wished her hands wouldn't tremble as she reached for it. She ought not to be fearful, not given how attentive he had been lately. But it came so naturally.

When her fingers closed around it, though, relief swept through her. "You brought me a book?"

He clasped his hands behind his back. "It struck me as one you would enjoy. Though if you prefer a gift of jewels, I have a very nice set of emeralds in my room at the tavern."

A chuckle slipped out as she untied the twine and exposed the cover. "*Gulliver's Travels*."

"If *Don Quixote* is your favorite, this ought to be to your liking too. Have you read it?"

She ran her fingertips over the embossing in the leather and shook her head. Such a lovely copy. Such a thoughtful gift. So very perfect. "Wiley has spoken of it, but he has been unable to locate a copy for me."

Her voice broke, and tears stung her eyes. She might have laughed it off as being a silly female tendency, crying over such things, but Emerson had already reached to frame her face in his chilled hands.

"Oh, darling, I'm a dunderhead. Even when I try, I make a mess of things. Please, do not cry."

She chuckled and looked up into his face, more handsome than ever when creased with concern for her. "You have made no mess at all. The opposite."

"Ah. These are *those* kind of tears." Yet he didn't release her. Instead, he thumbed away the moisture that had spilled onto her cheeks and drew a fraction closer. "I suppose if I am going to make you cry, I want it to be from happiness. But I confess, I prefer to see your smile."

She blinked rapidly, drew in a breath she hoped would steady her foolish emotions. But what was she to do? This was the Emerson she had always dreamt of, the one she had wished so long would love her. This was the Emerson she had given up on ever seeing come to life in her company. Yet here he was, gazing deep into her eyes and tracing the contours of her face with soft fingers.

"Lark." His voice was only a rumble, but his eyes spoke much, and eloquently.

She ought to pull away from the intent she saw so clearly. Someone could happen by at any moment. They were no longer engaged. And really, what had changed since he tried to kiss her before? Nothing.

Everything.

He dipped his head, keeping his eyes on hers, so slowly she would have had ample time to resist. Instead, she held the book to her chest with one hand and reached to touch his cheek with the other. Tingles raced up her arm.

The first brush of his lips was only a feather's breath, light and sweet. Yet that was enough to make those rampant emotions surge again. He cradled her face as if she were precious, kissed her as though she were beautiful. Whispered her name as though he loved her.

For the first time in her life, she thought maybe she was. Maybe he did.

At the exaggerated "ahem" of a voice behind them, they jerked apart. Lark spun around, but then sighed when she saw it was only Sena.

Her friend sent them a fierce frown and planted her hands on her hips. "If you expect me to pretend I did not see that," she said in a deepened voice that borrowed her father's cadence, "you will be disappointed. What are your intentions, young man? You had better be willing to marry a girl if you stand around kissing her."

Heat flooded Lark's face, but Emerson laughed. "I believe that speech needs to be aimed at Lark, rather than at me. I want nothing more than to marry her—the question is whether she is yet inclined to have me."

Wishing the blush would fade, Lark raised her chin and clutched the book to her chest. "I am not as disinclined as I once was."

"Well." He took one of her hands, kissed the knuckles. "Where there is progress, there too is hope. Whenever you are ready for those emeralds, my love, just say the word."

The flutter of her heart was far too immediate for her peace of mind. So she grinned, trying to look as flippant and bright as Sena could. "For now, the book will suffice."

He seemed to gaze straight through her light tone and down to that last thread of uncertainty. But he nodded. "Yes. For now it will."

Chapter Twenty-One

Edwinn knew the moment he winced it was a mistake. The female chatter he'd been ignoring died away, and two concerned gazes bore through him.

He sighed and put aside his book, stared down first his sister, then Sena. "Will the two of you desist? Yes, my leg hurts. Just as my leg always hurts when it is cold and damp, as it has been incessantly this winter. But I am not dying, I am not in any more pain than usual, and I wouldn't have dared wince had I not been sitting too long in one position for fear that if I moved, your clucking would start again."

Kate's lips twitched into a smile. "You needn't be testy, Edwinn. We are only attentive because we care."

"Attentive I appreciate. Obsessed and coddling is insulting." That last part he directed to Sena, who had come by every day since the State House incident. Oh, she was all innocence and pretended to come only to see Kate, but he was no idiot. She had obviously heard about the scuffle. And while he had thrilled at the devotion in her eyes, it didn't change the fact that he was tired of being watched like a child.

Sena narrowed her eyes. "Perhaps if you would be honest with us instead of hiding your every feeling and pain behind a wall of stoicism, we would not *have* to obsess over each wince and movement."

"Forgive me." Perhaps his tone didn't convey any apology, but after a week of them jumping every time he flinched, what did they expect? "Like every gentleman of worth, I was raised not to show discomfort to company."

Sena let out a huff of exasperation. "So after all these years, I am still considered *company*?"

Obviously that had been the wrong thing to say, though he couldn't think why. "Ah." He looked to Kate for help.

Kate's eyes flew to the clock. "Oh, look at the time. No wonder I feel peckish. I had better see if Mrs. Haslip will have our luncheon ready soon."

"Very subtle maneuver, Kate," he called as she scurried out the door.

Sena wrapped her arms around her middle. The uncertain gesture was so out of character that Edwinn pushed to his feet and crossed to sit beside her before he could think better of it. "Sena...I know not what I said, but I did not mean to hurt you by it. You must realize that."

She wouldn't even look at him. "Of course—Edwinn Calvert would never hurt *anyone*."

He frowned. Was that emphasis the key to her upset, then? "You are more than 'anyone.' You know that, do you not? So if I call you 'company'—"

"I do not want to be *company*." Her arms released her middle, her gaze flew to his. "I want to be *family*. I want you to trust me with your hopes and fears, with your pains and feelings."

Given the glistening depths of her eyes, he had to assume she didn't mean she wanted to be his sister. Strange how her declaration at once exhilarated and weighted him. He reached for her hand and held her fingers lightly in his. "I *do* trust you. But I also want you to respect me—"

"Prithee, Edwinn, do not be a fool." She clasped his hand and covered it with her other one. "I respect you more than anyone else in the world."

He sighed and wove their fingers together. And, yes, noted how well hers fit in his. How small and delicate they seemed, though he knew it an illusion. "I don't know how you can, Sena. I have lost everything—"

"Why this self-pity lately?" She shook her head and drew in a fast breath. "Edwinn, you are still a Calvert. You still have a family to be proud of, and a sister who adores you. You have a roof over your head and a plantation to your name. If you want to see someone who has lost everything, look at Alice. Yet she is happy with her lot."

The arrow hit its mark. Was he putting too much stock in regaining Calvert Hall? In spite of all the times he told himself he would leave it to the Lord, did he still identify himself by his home?

He raised her hands, pressed a soft kiss to her knuckles. "You are right, of course. I am fortunate. I have all I need, and then some."

Sena held his gaze for a long moment. "And yet...?"

One corner of his mouth pulled up. "And yet I worry. There are still those who refuse to buy the Briers's crops because of my allegiances. I have to keep enough sterling set aside to sustain it if profits are down or this winter stretches too far into the planting season. I must also be certain to maintain a legacy for Kate. In short, Sena, so long as my greatest asset is in the hands of the state, the rest of them are in peril. I...I am afraid of what the future holds for me."

"I had not thought of all that." She looked down at their hands and seemed to fight back great emotion. When she looked up, her eyes shone with unshed tears. "But I would face it with you. I know 'tis unseemly for me to say such things when you have shown no interest, but Edwinn, I love you. Please do not keep me distant any longer."

"Darling Sena." He put an arm around her, pulled her close. Slid his eyes shut when she rested her head on his shoulder. "I dared not show interest. You deserve better than me."

She splayed a hand over his racing heart. "If there is a man better than you, I have never met him."

He must have done something right to be given so precious a gift as her love. He covered her hand. "My heart is yours, Sena. But I have a feeling your father would agree I must have my affairs in better order before I can have the honor of making you a Calvert."

She straightened with a growl. "I hate politics."

"As do I." He grinned and smoothed a curl away from her face. "But whether they like it or not, our leaders have signed into law an agreement that they will either return my house or pay me its value within a year."

"A year." To see the dismay on her face, one would think those twelve months to be sixty.

He felt a shift within, a redirection of his determination. Until now, he hadn't bothered asking for the house's value, because it was the house itself he wanted. And the house, he suspected, the politicians didn't want him to have, as it was such a symbol within the town. But a future with Sena was worth more than Calvert Hall. "Perhaps they will act more quickly if I settle for the monetary restitution."

No wonder he loved her, given the sadness that flooded her expression on his behalf. "But 'tis the house your grandfather built. Your family home."

"Ah, but 'tis the family that makes the home." He smiled and held her close again. "Your father invited me again to the gentlemen's gathering this evening. I shall come this time, my love, and try to win their favor. And as soon as I have it—or enough of it, anyway—"

She silenced him with a kiss.

Emerson listened partially to the familiar story of Gulliver in Brobdingnag, but more to the melodious sound of Lark's voice as she read. And if he paid more attention to the delight that lit her features as she laughed at a humorous line than to the line itself, he figured no one would blame him. *Gulliver's Travels* he had read before—her face while *she* read it was new and fascinating.

He sat as close to her as he dared. If he scooted so much as an inch nearer, Randel would lower his *Gazette* and glower at him. All well and good. If the warmth in her expression were any indication, she would marry him one of these days. Perhaps she would need a bit more time than their seventh of March date would allow, but he could wait. However long it took, he would wait. So long as eventually he had the guarantee they could spend all their days together, and no one would mind if he leaned over and kissed those perfect lips.

Those lips that now paused in their reading, attempted a firm line, yet quirked up in the corners. "Mr. Fielding, you seem to be paying more attention to *me* than to the book."

He grinned and met her amused gaze. "You are far more interesting."

She somehow looked both put out and pleased. "Then why did you ask me to read it to you—nay, in fact forbid me to read it but when in your company?"

"Ah." He lifted a finger, as if presenting an argument in class. "Well you see, I am greatly enjoying your enjoyment. And I have this nefarious scheme, that you will become so enthralled in the story that you will seek out my company all the more so you might continue reading."

Eyes twinkling, she lifted her chin. "Perhaps if I am so caught up I shall read in secret, after you leave."

"Well, what would be the fun in that?"

The rustle of newspaper drew Emerson's attention to Randel, who arched a brow their way. "I believe I preferred it when you two did nothing but argue."

Emerson chuckled. "Should you not be starting classes again soon, Master Randel?"

"How I wish it were so." He flipped a page in his paper. "None of the students are traveling in this weather, it seems. Though let it be noted none made a fuss about going *home* through the snow. And how they expect me to believe them unable to reach Annapolis when *you* made it here easily enough..."

Emerson leaned toward Lark and spoke in a stage whisper. "He is warming up to me."

She laughed. "How can you tell?"

"He used to ignore my presence altogether, then insult me the moment I left. Now look at him—he cares enough to insult me to my face."

Randel made as if to reply, but the slam of the front door interrupted. He sighed. "My daughter must be home."

A moment later she burst into the room, still whipping her cloak off her shoulders. Emerson glanced at Lark; he appreciated spirit, but he was yet again reminded of how much he preferred her version.

"Papa, something must be done."

"I do agree." Randel went back to his paper. "The manners of the youth these days are simply atrocious. Parents ought to make better use of the rod."

Miss Randel sent her father a scowl. "Well, if you want me off your hands, I know the way to do it. We must convince the governor to give Edwinn his house back."

"Unless *you* intend to then take it from him, I fail to see how that will result in my being relieved of you."

"Papa." Obviously not affected by Randel's banter, she went to perch on the arm of his chair. "I am going to marry him."

"Are you?" He didn't sound surprised by the suggestion, though Emerson's jaw dropped. "Strange, I have not been approached on the subject, and I believe my approval is necessary, as you are not yet twenty-one."

"You and Calvert?" Emerson shook his head. "Why did no one tell me things leaned that way? I wouldn't have wasted my time being jealous of his attention to Lark."

Lark put a marker in the book and sent him a high glare. "Who says it was wasted?"

Randel grunted a laugh and turned another page in his paper. "Sena, my sweet, I still fail to see what young Calvert's intentions have to do with harassing my friends."

"Then you are not thinking, Papa, because 'tis clear as that ice I slipped on earlier. He is uncomfortable speaking to you before he knows where he stands with his holdings, and with one of his greatest assets in the hands of the state and the other facing loss because of sentiments against him…"

Randel actually put down his paper. "I do see his point. But there is no need to fret over it, dear; the Treaty of Paris has been ratified. They now *must* return to him what is his."

Miss Randel stood again and paced the length of the room. "Must they? What if they say they are not bound to uphold the articles until King George ratifies it? And what if it is late getting to Paris because of this wretched weather, and the king refuses altogether? What then? Will they keep it indefinitely?"

Randel pinched the bridge of his nose. "Sena—"

"No, Papa. 'Tis wrong what they do to him, and even if they begrudgingly do what is right, how long will it take? Am I to wait forever to marry the man I love?"

Her father sighed. "Sena, a protracted engagement is no great cause for distress."

Emerson looked to Lark as she looked at him. She gave him a small smile, but it faded as she focused on her friend again.

Miss Randel drew in a sharp breath that spoke of tears. "There *is* cause for distress. A grave injustice is being done to a perfectly good man, and no one will lift a finger to help him. Even his supposed *friends*."

She stormed from the room, pounded up the stairs. Randel sighed and stood. "Sena!" He took three steps to the door and then spun to them, pointing a finger and a glare at Emerson. "I will be back directly, and you had better be on your best behavior in the meantime."

He held back his grin. "Yes, sir."

Lark didn't look to be in the mood for stolen kisses anyway. A crease scored her brow. "Poor Sena. But surely she is right that something can be done. Mr. Randel is friends with those who have the power to change things."

Emerson sighed and took her hand. "Those men are the ones who led the fight for independence, darling, who shed blood and tears to win our freedom from Britain. They cannot be expected to feel favorably toward a man who told them they were wrong to do so."

She turned tempestuous blue eyes on him. "But that is unfair. He only held himself to the standard Paul gave the Romans, to submit oneself to one's rulers."

"And if he remains here, then his rulers are these men Miss Randel would have her father oppose. By his own argument, ought he not to submit to *them*?"

The rhetoric did nothing to soothe the irritation in her eyes. "And so he does. He will bear whatever yoke they strap upon him. But that does not mean 'tis right for them to treat him this way, and they surely know that or they wouldn't have put stipulations for Loyalist property into the treaty."

"They included it because they had to." He sighed and stroked her knuckles with his thumb. "Darling, they are good men. They will do what they must."

"What they must." She moved her gaze to their hands and stared at them for a long moment. "What if that is not enough?"

"It will be. We must have faith in their honor." He tilted her face back up with a finger under her chin. "These men founded a nation. They deserve our respect and trust."

"I know they do." She leaned into his hand for a moment then sighed and stood up. "They are noble, honorable men. But what is one to do with noble, honorable men when they are not acting so nobly or honorably?"

He sighed and rubbed a hand over his face. "They will eventually forgive, and they will keep their word."

"Will they?" Her chin quivered a bit as she stepped over to the window. "Would you?"

Emerson stood too, moved over to stand behind her, and watched snow swirl down outside the pane. Heavy clouds had obliterated the afternoon light, bringing evening before its time. "Of course I would, if I were them."

"When?"

"Pardon?"

She turned her face toward him, her fingers gripping the windowsill. "*When* would you move forward and keep your word, Emerson? When the first opportunity arises, or when you are forced into it by that very bond you put your name to?"

A gust of wind blew the snow into a feverish dance against the pane. "Are we still talking of the statesmen and the Calverts' plight? Or of my failure with our engagement?"

The shake of her head wasn't encouraging. "You seem to understand them well, to look up to them even when they act the parts of fools. Even when they deliberately put off what they promised they would do."

Emerson spun away, though that did nothing to cool the frustration burning inside. "Yes, I understand them. What is so difficult to grasp? They have lost the luxury of being idealistic, Lark. They have fought a war, they have had to try to turn philosophy into a system that will run a country. Do you suppose that to be easy? Do you think it simple to come back to society after six blasted years in the field and blithely pick up where you left off? We may call it a Glorious Cause all we like, but that cannot change the horror of war. And it cannot change the fact that nothing—*nothing*—is the same when we come home."

She looked caught between the desire to comfort and the desire to fight, to reach out or to shrink away. She sighed and made no move whatsoever. "You certainly know that better than I. But if nothing is the same when you come home, 'tis because those of us at home went through our own kind of war. The fear of losing all you have, all you are. Of falling into enemy hands, or never seeing those you love again. Of being powerless, completely powerless." She shook her head and folded her hands over her chest. "I cannot fight these men, they would never listen to me if I tried. But I wish I could. I wish I could take such a stand, make such a defense. I wish someone else would do it where I cannot."

Wished *he* would, she meant. Wished he would endanger his standing—*their* standing—for this cause not their own. He pointed toward the door, toward the problems waiting beyond it. "They are your friends, and I know you want the best for them. But we must stay out of it."

She extended her hands out at her sides, let her arms fall against her skirt. A gesture that at once spoke of helplessness and the rejection of it. "Is that how it will always be, Emerson? Will my thoughts, my beliefs be forever subjugated to your duty and pride?"

For a moment he stood there, mouth agape, and stared at her. "You make me sound like a tyrant. Have I not proven since coming here that I respect your opinions?"

With an incredulous breath of a laugh, she shook her head and strode from the room.

He was quick on her heels. "Lark, stop. We have not finished talking about this."

"Yes. We have."

"No." By the time he caught her arm, they were in the entryway, dim from the lack of lamplight and the snow, howling now outside the windows. "You cannot run away every time you come up against something you don't like."

She pulled free of his grasp, eyes ablaze. "I do *not*—"

"Twice, Lark, you have fled rather than face me. Twice."

Mouth set in a line of fury, she whipped a cloak off the coatrack and onto her shoulders. "Well, try, try, and try again."

CHAPTER TWENTY-TWO

The snow pelted her face and hissed against the bricks, but Lark didn't slow. Couldn't slow. The fire inside raged too hot, a bubbling cauldron of fear, anger, and determination. A confused mass of her past and her friends' future, Emerson and the statesmen.

Though ice crystals stung every bared inch of flesh, Lark sucked in a breath and ran across Tabernacle Street.

"Lark! Where the devil are you going?"

She ignored Emerson and picked up her pace, slipping and sliding her way up the hill. Bladen's Folly hunkered down at its crest, a dark shadow of misty gray in the vortex of white.

He caught up to her, tried to stop her with a hand on her arm. Thrown off balance, she slipped to her knees. Tears burned her eyes. Why did she always stumble when he was around, always make a fool of herself?

"This is madness." He pulled her up, but she fought free again and kept moving. She heard his growl swirl through the snow. "Return to the house, Lark, before this turns to a blizzard and we both are lost."

"You go." Though she spun to face him, she kept moving toward the abandoned mansion. "Go back to your comfortable parlor, where war is but a memory. Go back to your comfortable thought that the men you admire can do no wrong, and that doing what one *must*, *when* one must is enough."

He surged forward and gripped her shoulders. His eyes gleamed like embers through the storm. "Stop it. This is not about me, nor is it about you."

"Is it not? If they trample the liberties of one man, who is to say where it will end?" She turned again toward the building and scurried forward until she saw the outline of its shallow moat.

He muttered a curse and pulled her back. "What are you doing now, fool woman? You could slip and break your neck."

"I will not. Sena showed me—"

"Life is not a pirate story, Lark!" He gave her a small shake, his grip on her arm tight, though she couldn't tell if it were from fear or anger. "And you are not Miss Randel, praise be to heaven."

"Now you insult my friend?"

He grunted and pulled her clear of the moat, his face hard as the stones that made it up. "I only mean you have sense to temper your spirit, and I am grateful for that. And I only wish you would employ it and see that this is not about treatment of the Tories, 'tis about my treatment of you. Yet you run every time the battle gets too heated. Sound a retreat instead of facing me."

"I wouldn't have to if I had felt I had the freedom to be who I am with you. Just as I wouldn't feel someone ought to fight with the politicians if they would let the Calverts live free."

He threw his arms up and spun away from her, into the mounting storm. "What must I do, Lark? What *can* I do to prove to you I am no longer the idiot I have been since the war? I can give you your dreams back, if you but let me. If you but *want* me to."

She shook her head and brushed the snow from her lashes, not even sure she knew what those dreams were. "How can I trust that? What happens when I disappoint you, Emerson? What happens when you disapprove of something I feel is right? Like this?"

"Then I love you anyway." Spinning back to her, he planted his hands on her waist and drew her close before she could dart away again. Through the shadows of evening and snow, his eyes smoldered dark and intent. "I want you to be free with me. I want you to know I love your spirit, I love your heart. I love this Lark I have seen since coming here, and I am sorry, truly sorry, I failed to discover her before. But 'tisn't too late for us."

He held her so close even the snow couldn't blow between them, dipped his head until his lips touched hers. She let him deepen the kiss, let her senses swim and swirl like the blustery crystals around her. Closed her eyes on the storm and nestled in the warm oasis of his arms.

But none of the feeling that pulsed through her could change the truth. He might say he loved her, just like the men who ratified the treaty might say they held it in the highest esteem. But she was still the same girl he had ignored for two years, just as Calvert was still the Tory that had offended them. Promises, they all made promises. But making them didn't mean they would keep them.

She pulled away, backed up a step so the nearly blinding snow could veil her from his gaze. "I love you, Emerson. I always did. I love you for your honor and nobility, for your strength and dedication. I love you for the very things that have always, *will* always take you away from me."

"I will not—"

"You *will*." Though hardly able to see anything before her through the raging snow, she stumbled away, following the downward slope of the land and trusting it to take her in the general direction of home. "I showed you a glimpse of who I am on my birthday, of this spirit you say you love now. And it scared you into Penelope's arms. You may admire it when it only leads to jests and stories, but when it comes to making a decision, you will never choose me. Certainly not over your heroes."

"At least face me when you accuse me of being bound to abandon you." He halted, forced her to as well. She heaved a breath when he moved in front of her but refused to look past his chin. "You have gotten a taste for fighting, I see. Just like Wiley—when the heat of battle is upon you, you forget everything but raising your musket and charging ahead, even when that means running straight into enemy fire and risking your very life. And for what, Lark?" He shook his head.

She folded her arms over her middle and raised her snow-blurred gaze to his nose. "Say all you like that they have lost the luxury of being idealistic, but it was ideals that made them fight to begin with. And ideals they mustn't forget if they want this country to be anything but another tyranny."

He turned half away, hands fisted on his hips. "This is madness."

She lifted her shoulders. Finally, she raised her gaze, though now it was he refusing to meet it.

At length he faced her again, the snow blanketing his shoulders making them seem all the wider. But the flakes slowed now, the wind died down. Calmer, quieter, but somehow more threatening for its lack of bluster. Emerson drew in a long breath. "Your brother saved my life a time or two in battle because of his heroics. But I saved his just as much, pulling him out of the scrapes his recklessness led him into."

"I cannot think it reckless or mad to do the right thing. But regardless, I need to know you will love me, even when you deem me such. 'Tis all I ever wanted. If you cannot, do not…then there can be no future for us."

Instead of pulling her close again, he backed away. Instead of softening, his face went cold as the wind that blustered around them. Without another word, he pivoted on his heel and stomped off through the new-fallen snow.

She watched him cross Tabernacle Street, hoping against hope he would turn back. But he didn't. He walked away, never even glancing over his shoulder.

She lowered her arms but couldn't convince her fists to relax. This was it, then. The first disagreement, and he forgot his claim of minutes before, that he loved her for her spirit. He didn't, evidently.

Of course he didn't. Why should he? Spirit might be a battle cry, but it wasn't what one wanted to found a family, a nation on. It led one into war, but it was the steady that brought them back out. He might like spirit in his friends, but when it came down to it, it wasn't what he wanted in a wife.

She wasn't what he wanted. Would never be what he wanted.

Her knees buckled, and the ground rushed up to greet her. Snow burned her bare hands like fire when she caught herself.

Pushing herself to her knees, she looked up through the last few flurries of snow, straight at the towering trunk of the Liberty Tree. Its branches reached so high, all the way to heaven. Spread so wide, beyond her periphery. A symbol to all. A rallying cry.

Freedom. Liberty.

Her eyes slid shut. It was just a tree. One of many, nothing but a meeting point. Easily chopped down, easily burned up.

But it hadn't been, not this one. It had survived. The frozen ground under her knees beckoned, and she opened her eyes again, focused on a bump in front of her. Half-dazed, she brushed at the snowy lump until she caught sight of the root that had broken free of the soil at some point.

That was how it stood. It had its roots deep and wide. Otherwise, these winter winds would have toppled it. This bitter cold would have frozen out its life.

So what of her? Where were her roots?

She looked across the street, but Emerson had disappeared into the encroaching night. He couldn't be her foundation. Nor could her family or these new friends who had quickly become dear.

Drawing in a deep breath of the frigid air, Lark rested her hand on the root and focused her gaze on the tree. "My liberty is in You, Lord. Only in You. If I am to be rooted, it must be in Christ. If I am to seek purpose, it must be Yours. So tell me, please, what You want me to do. Will I ever be enough for him? Or is my love the sacrifice I must make for the freedom to hold to my beliefs?"

The empty street seemed to be her answer.

Emerson stomped up the stairs and rang the bell for number 19 with more force than was necessary. Soon enough, he would have to bury his feelings once more under the trained facade of a gentleman. Soon enough, he would have to smile and laugh.

And wait—wait for the chance to speak a lot of rot and foolishness, to offend those he most respected, just to earn the affection of a woman who ought not to give it with such strings.

A woman for whom he would make a fool of himself a thousand times over, if that was what it took to win her.

As he stood on the snowy stoop, he shoved a hand into his pocket and fingered the emerald he'd gone back to his room to fetch. She would see. When he made her points for her and was laughed out of polite society, she would see he loved her above all. More than duty to them, to his state, to his country. She would see that he sought her more than respect itself.

He would draw her aside, draw out the ring, and tell her she could make whatever stands she wanted. He'd be there. Right beside her, ready to charge in on her behalf, as he had always been beside Wiley in the war. She demanded proof? He would give it.

Blast it all. He *did* love her, loved every flash of fire in her eyes, even as he knew it would light a powder keg. That didn't mean he was looking forward to the explosion. It didn't mean he was to be blamed for wanting to return to Virginia and the quiet of his plantation. To enjoy their freedom without thinking they still had to fight for it every minute of the day.

He had fought for six endless years, had killed enemies who had once been friends. Why did she now insist he fight for friends who had once been enemies?

The door swung open, and Mrs. Green stood aside to let him in. He expected a berating from her, but she only gave him a sympathetic smile and took his cloak and hat. Exhaling the pent-up frustration left him deflated. "Has Lark returned yet?"

"More or less." She motioned toward the rear of the house. "She has been pacing around out back, ignoring me if I tell her she shall turn to an icicle if she does not come in. Mr. Fielding." She pressed her lips together for a moment. "Do you know why I am forever quoting Mr. Franklin? Because he lives his life by one principle: go straight forward in doing what is right, leaving the consequences to Providence."

Something settled within him. Unable to voice what, or the proper thanks for it, he nodded.

Mr. Randel stepped into the hall. He motioned Emerson in, then leaned closer as he drew near. "Calvert is already here, waiting in the kitchen for my signal to join everyone else."

The front door opened again, admitting no fewer than half a dozen men.

"Glad you could make it, gentlemen," Randel said. "Go on in and warm yourselves by the fire. I think this is the whole gathering tonight."

Emerson went into the library and took the same seat he had last time. Largely, yes, so he could watch for certain sneaking females. The other men followed, already laughing and jesting. Monroe nodded at him. "Have you heard from home lately, Fielding?"

He forced a pleasant expression. "I had a letter from Wiley Benton this morning."

Monroe smiled. "I have seen his sister at several of the balls recently. A lovely young woman. Are the two of you still…?"

Oh, for all that was holy. He slipped a hand into his pocket and fisted the ring. "Yes. We most certainly are."

Jefferson looked up from the harpsichord. "Given this weather, you had better return to Virginia as soon as you are able, Mr. Fielding, if you intend to be present for your own wedding. One would not expect it to take six weeks to travel so short a distance, but who knows but a blizzard might strike and keep you immobile for a fortnight."

"A point we shall most certainly consider as we plan our return." Assuming she would believe even this show he planned, would *ever* believe his love enough to wed him.

Governor Paca chuckled. "Look at the wistfulness on his face. You know, Fielding…" His voice trailed off, his smile melted into a frown. "Randel. What is the meaning of this?"

Emerson looked to the door along with everyone else, though he knew exactly what he would see. Randel had ushered Calvert in.

To his credit, Calvert achieved the perfect stance. His spine was straight, shoulders back, but his chin at a respectful angle. He neither gripped his cane too tightly nor leaned on it overmuch. He looked exactly as he must to have a chance at winning the regard of these men—humble but not weak.

Randel's smile looked more than a little forced though. "Gentlemen, I trust you all remember my former student, Edwinn Calvert."

Paca narrowed his eyes. "Hard to forget the most notorious Tory in Annapolis. After all your family contributed to this nation, young man, the fact that they all sided with the Crown was a terrible blow to our cause."

Calvert inclined his head. "My family made their decisions based on many factors, sir, which led most of them back to England.

But my reasons were my own, and my love for my home not affected by it."

"Love for your home?" Paca's jaw ticked. "If you loved this land that had birthed you, you would have taken her side. Yet now you think to stay here and cause trouble?"

"I think I have proven these past two years I intend to follow the justly appointed leadership of my state and country. I intend to remain in Annapolis and raise a family here, but in order to assure their comfort, I must beg—"

"Raise a family here?" Another man of middling age scoffed. Emerson couldn't recall the fellow's name, but he was the same one who had made the rude jest about Calvert's leg at their last gathering. "And what father in his right mind would wed a daughter to *you*?"

Randel cleared his throat. "That would be me."

A moment of silence ticked by, followed by several exclamations of surprise, the loudest coming from the governor. Randel shrugged. "They are in love, and Calvert is a good, godly man. Why should I oppose it?"

"Because he is a traitor, a Tory!"

Randel directed his sigh toward the bilious man. "It is time we forget all that, Mason. The war is over, and if we intend peace to succeed, we must forgive and move forward."

At that, Emerson had to nod. They must indeed. And he had no personal issues with Calvert. He understood his reasons, even if he didn't agree with them. But they could not simply force the leaders to see things their way by insisting they were right.

"Move forward we shall, but forgiveness…" Paca shook his head and folded his arms over his chest. "When the treaty is signed into law by King George, then we will have no choice but to give you restitution within a year. Until then, I advise against asking anything of a people who would still be quite happy to see you expelled from our country, Mr. Calvert. And my condolences to you, Randel, for gaining such a son through the foolish choice of your daughter."

"Now, see here!" Randel lunged forward, but Calvert stopped him with a hand on the arm.

"Randel, relent," he said softly. "It *is* a foolish choice, and we all know it."

"We do not." Randel shrugged off Calvert's hand and tugged his waistcoat back into place. "As you yourself pointed out, Paca, I was the first to decry the Calverts. And now I shall be the first to say for all to hear that I respect Edwinn Calvert for holding true to his beliefs. Freedom, gentlemen, must be given freely."

Emerson shifted and toyed with the emerald in his pocket. The man raised a valid point. He himself intended to prove his love for Lark was not conditional...and shouldn't justice claim the same?

Paca grunted and turned fully toward the exit. "I have heard quite enough for one evening. We shall do our duty when we must, Mr. Calvert. Until then, I bid you farewell."

Emerson frowned. He knew well what one gained by doing only duty when one did not truly believe it, and not doing that until one must—nothing. But Lark was right. Their country could not stand on that. It was not what these very men had founded it on. And now was the time to prove what these United States stood for, not to provide a precedent for forgetting it.

He pushed to his feet. He would make Lark's point. Not for her, not to prove anything. But because it was right, and now was the time to say so. "Governor Paca, if I might speak?"

Chapter Twenty-Three

Lark sat on the icy back step of Randel House, lost in shadows that felt far deeper than the night. The garden of the court shared by a few other houses lay enshrouded with snow. Lovely, yet merciless.

The door squeaked open behind her, but Lark didn't turn to see who came out. Not until the newcomer sat beside her.

She sighed as she glanced at Alice's profile. "I have made a mess of things. With Emerson. Am I wrong, Alice, to demand he choose me over his duty to men who are barely more than strangers?"

Alice offered a small, lopsided smile and leaned in until their shoulders touched. "He ought to choose you. Yet you ought not to demand it."

A tear tickled her cheek as she nodded. "It all seems so muddled. I want to do what is right, want *him* to do what is right. Because for so long neither of us did, when it came to each other. Perhaps I thought…perhaps I felt it would prove we have changed enough to build a solid life together if we could take the Calverts' part. Yet I can do nothing, and I have forced him away by insisting he do what I cannot. He is probably on his way back to Williamsburg even now."

"Oh, Lark." Alice chuckled and stared into the dormant garden. "He is in the drawing room, and when I peeked in a few moments ago, he looked ready to surge to his feet and demand justice."

Lark's heart fluttered, only to fall to a ball of lead in her stomach. "Because of my ultimatum, no doubt. Now he will forever resent me for forcing him into the bad graces of those gentlemen."

"Does the fact that he would do so not prove he loves you?"

It should. It ought. So why did she still feel stifled with uncertainty? Toying with the hem of her cloak, Lark found no reply.

Alice angled toward her. "You are so fortunate. You know that, I hope. You have a gentleman in there who is considered a catch by all, who looks at you with adoration, who will do anything for the honor of making you his wife."

"But I am not what he really wants."

The silence brought Lark's gaze up, and she found incredulity upon Alice's face. "Prithee, why would you speak that way? He has proven his devotion, Lark. The only thing remaining is for you to accept it. For you to realize that it is not with *him* you must reconcile, but with yourself." Alice pressed her warm fingers over Lark's icy ones. "You must let yourself believe you are worthy of his affections. Once you do that, you will see that such love does not make demands, nor does it seek argument. You will see that being bound by such love is the most freeing thing in the world."

Points of ice pinged against brick and stone, but an ember of warmth bloomed within her. How had she failed to see that? That liberty and love were not at odds, but rather joined hands. Of course, it was love of their homeland that led the Patriots to fight for her, for the freedom to be Americans. It was love that brought Christ to earth to offer liberty from their sins.

And so, if one were to love a person, to love him truly and fully as Scripture said one should…

New life pulsing within her, Lark sprang to her feet and pushed through the door, Alice close upon her heels.

"Lark?"

"I must get his attention, let him know I am sorry for asking him to do this." She whipped off her cloak, flew down the hall. The Calverts deserved help, yes, and Lord willing, they could find a way to offer it. But she had no right to ask him to ignore his sense of duty, when it was that very quality that made him the man she loved. No right to demand her own freedom and deny him his.

She spun into the hallway and found Sena in the shadows, clutched to her mother's chest. Though her tears were silent and slow, they told Lark clearly how the meeting had gone thus far. But when she approached, Sena managed a smile and nodded toward the door.

Emerson was standing, his face confident and earnest as he said, "Thank you, governor."

"No need for thanks." Paca's gruff voice came from beyond Lark's line of sight. "You have proven your loyalty by fighting for your nation, Mr. Fielding. You fought for the right to be heard."

Emerson nodded, looking more handsome than ever with the fire of justice bright in his eyes. "I did, yes. But more, Mr. Paca, I fought for *his* right to be heard."

"What rubbish!" came a voice from the corner of the room.

"Hush, Mason. Let the boy speak." Mr. Randel sounded calm, perhaps even amused.

Alice moved off, undoubtedly to check on her sleeping children. Lark hoped her smile of thanks could be seen in the semidarkness.

Emerson smiled, too, at the gentlemen within. "I am sorry if I offend any of you—heaven knows I have only the deepest respect for you all. Mr. Jefferson, your ideals and eloquence have given words to the cry of all our hearts. Monroe, we served together in the army, but rather than dedicating yourself to the concerns of youth upon our return, you went on to represent our fine state. Mr. Lloyd, you outdo so many of us by loving the confederation of states as much as your own. And Governor Paca, you have long been a leader of Maryland in whatever capacity it most needed you."

That Mason fellow grumbled again from the corner Lark could not see. "You think to flatter them into giving this traitor anything?"

"I think to hold a mirror before them, so they might be reminded of who they are." Emerson straightened, surely commanding the respect of them all by giving it so fully. "Gentlemen, we fought to be free of tyrants—not to become them ourselves. If we extend the freedoms for which we shed our blood only to those who agree with us, then how are we any better than King George?"

Paca paced into view, face red. "He is a self-professed Loyalist."

"He did not take up arms against us. He did not oppose the cause of liberty, just our method of obtaining it." Emerson slanted a half smile toward where Mr. Calvert presumably stood. "Do I agree with him on that? No. But I maintain he has a right to his beliefs, and he ought not to be punished for them. He has a right to disagree with me, just as I had a right to disagree with the Crown."

Paca's mouth moved without sound, and he paced to the window. For a long moment he stood there, lips pressed together and hands clasped behind his back. The twitch of his fingers was the only sign of internal tension, the only indicator of what must be racing thoughts. Then he spun back around. "Randel has told me you suffered injury at Yorktown. You gave of yourself for our cause, you fought for your liberty. Would you truly now extend it to those who did not?"

Emerson inclined his head. "If I failed to do so, then the liberty we won would be worthless."

Paca's breath eased out in a long, slow stream. "Perhaps. Perhaps it would be." He turned his scowl toward Mr. Calvert. "Though one ought not to think that even if I am convinced, it will make any great difference. The state of the treasury being what it is, we may not be able to make recompense even if I were so inclined."

"Then return to him the house itself, Paca." Mr. Randel's voice now sounded nearly bored, though Lark knew him well enough to think he could not be.

Paca glowered, then sighed. "I will consider it. That is the best you will get from me tonight." He glanced back toward the window as if it offered salvation. "Gentlemen, the ice is accumulating quickly out there, and I for one do not intend to be kept here until the morrow. Again, I will bid you all a good evening."

The mention of the weather signaled a veritable stampede toward the doors. Lark drew into the shadows along with Sena and Mrs. Randel.

Within the room, Mr. Calvert clasped Emerson's hand. Though he didn't smile, high emotion radiated from his countenance, and he nodded.

Emerson nodded in reply, tacking on a half-smile.

Mr. Randel clapped a hand on Mr. Calvert's shoulder. "That went as well as I could have hoped. Come, Calvert, I will walk you out." When the men stepped into the hall, the Randel women converged on them. But Emerson had lingered within, so Lark flew around the others and into the room.

Directly into his arms. "Emerson, I am so sorry. I should not have asked you to do that—you were magnificent, but I ought not have demanded such a thing. I am sorry, so sorry."

He held her close and chuckled into her hair. "I am sorry too, my darling. You were right. I thought to make your argument only to appease you, but you were right. It needed to be said. Who knows if it will effect any change, but we must stand up for the ideals we fought for."

She pulled away enough to look up into his precious face, nearly overwhelmed by the pure flame of love within his eyes. It burned away the last echo of doubt. Filling her. Freeing her. She rested her cold palm against his warm cheek. "I love you, Emerson Fielding. I love you."

He pulled her closer, the heat in his eyes shifting as he inclined his head.

Mr. Randel had apparently come back in, for his cleared throat broke them apart. When Lark looked over at her guardian, she found amusement in his eyes. "I do hope you had no intentions of embracing my ward, Mr. Fielding."

Lark laughed and settled for tucking her hand in her beloved's arm. "Rest easy, Mr. Randel. You can always force him into marrying me to salvage my reputation."

A corner of Mr. Randel's mouth quirked up. "I have little choice, given such behavior."

"Well, if you are appealing to my honor as a gentleman..." Emerson reached into his pocket and pulled out a familiar green gem, gleaming with promise and history. His teasing grin leveled into sobriety. "My darling, I ask you this time for the right reasons. Will you be my wife?"

She held out her hand so he could slide the ring onto its old place on her finger. "For all the right reasons, Emerson, yes."

A squeal from behind them proved that Sena had come in. When Lark turned to smile at her, she was clinging to the arm of a grinning Mr. Calvert.

Mr. Randel cleared his throat. "Well, I am glad to have that resolved. Now then, gentlemen, I fear Paca was right about the ice. Get yourselves home. You may come back tomorrow to engage in all the nonsense of plans."

Emerson lifted her hand to his lips and pressed a lingering kiss on her knuckles. "Tomorrow."

Yes, tomorrow they would plan. And then in a little over a month she would become his wife. Six and a half weeks. Forty-five interminable days.

Not that she was keeping account.

Lark admired the emerald on her finger as if it hadn't been there for two years. It felt, for all their past, as if finally the future's promise lived within the green depths of the stone. She looked up to smile at Emerson.

His returning smile was a bit sheepish. He had been looking out the window with a frown.

She reached for his hand. "What is worrying you?"

He shook his head and looked outside again. "There seemed to be an abnormal number of grumbling men outside the State House this morning when I walked by. Unusual for so icy a morning."

Mr. Randel looked up from his book. "Unusual indeed. Could you hear any of these grumblings?"

"No." His smile started as forced but then thawed. "I ought not to let it bother me. We must plan our return to Williamsburg, darling, for whenever you are ready. If you wish to tarry here longer, the winter would make a postponement of the wedding perfectly understandable—"

"Not necessary." Lark rested her hands in her lap. "The first break in the weather, I am in favor of heading home. Though we will need a chaperone, of course."

Mr. Randel set the tome upon a table. "My daughter has already convinced me that she and I are obliged to see you home so she might attend the nuptials. Since it seems my students have no intention of returning until the last cloud is gone from the horizon, it was easier to agree than to argue. And I would enjoy seeing your brother again."

"And he you. I thank you, Mr. Randel. That would be delightful and is so kind." Lark gave her host a smile.

He cleared his throat and waved it away. "Someone must be sure young Fielding behaves himself, and I have the most practice at it."

Emerson chuckled, though it faded away and darkened to another frown as he glanced out the window. "Is that not your maid rushing up?"

Lark turned to the window, mouth falling open at seeing Alice fly up the walk in a way only Sena was usually wont to do. Perhaps Mr. Mattimore had finally come home—that would warrant the rush.

But no, Alice's face was not filled with joy. Rather, with fear.

Leaping to her feet, Lark rushed to the front door, since that seemed to be Alice's destination, and threw it open. "Alice, what is it?"

Alice glanced over Lark's shoulder, breath heaving. Lark turned to find that Emerson and Mr. Randel had followed her out, that Sena even now rushed down the stairs. The redhead sucked in air. "Calverts' house. There is a mob. I think—they looked as though—"

Neither Emerson nor Mr. Randel waited to hear more. They both snatched up their cloaks and squeezed past Alice. Emerson called over his shoulder, "Remain here."

"Does he really expect us to obey that?" Sena shook her head and grabbed their cloaks, passing Lark's to her with trembling hands.

Lark gripped her friend's fingers and squeezed. "If your Mr. Calvert were here, he would tell us to pray before we do anything."

Sena looked bent on arguing, though at length she nodded. "We should. Could you? I do not think I can find any words."

There was no time for awkwardness or nervousness. Lark reached for Alice's hand, too, and shut her eyes. "Dear Father, we know not what is happening at Calvert Hall in this moment, but we thank You for bringing Alice here to warn of trouble, and for the quick reaction of Emerson and Mr. Randel. We ask that You help them resolve the situation, that You give them peace and wisdom in dealing with these men. And if there is anything we can do, Father, please show us. Most of all, keep everyone involved safe, we beg You, and please preserve the Calverts' home as well. Amen."

The others echoed her amen, then turned without another word to the still-open door. Icy wind gusted over them, piercing the wool of Lark's cloak and making her shiver. Or perhaps that was as much from anxiety as the cold.

Neither of the men were within sight by the time they gained the sidewalk. Sena motioned across Tabernacle Street. "We had better hurry. I have such a terrible feeling about all this."

Pulse pounding in her ears, Lark nodded and followed her friend across the snowy street. Only a single line of wheel tracks marred the pristine white—obviously most Annapolitans had better sense than to be out and about on a day like today. So what had drawn some to the State House, and then to Calvert Street?

Whatever the answer, it would equal trouble.

They traveled the length of Tabernacle, a turn of Church Circle, and stepped onto Northwest Street. "There they are." Lark pointed to where Emerson and Mr. Randel turned the corner ahead of them. When the men broke out in a run, Sena did too.

Lark glanced over at Alice, who sighed. "We had better keep up as best we can."

Not having taken the time to put on pattens, Lark's shoes were encrusted with ice and snow, and attempting to turn the corner with any great speed sent her reeling. Alice steadied her, nearly fell herself. They righted each other.

Any other time, it would have warranted laughter. But Lark felt no mirth when she saw the score of men gathered on the lawn of Calvert Hall. Men armed with muskets, and a few with flaming torches.

Her blood ran cold as the frozen waters of the Chesapeake.

Alice gasped and gripped her arm, tugging her to a halt away from the fracas that Sena had already run into the middle of. Their friend jostled her way through the crowd, shouting, "Stop! What is the meaning of this?"

"Silly, rash Sena." Alice shook her head and held tight to Lark's arm. "She will not help matters here."

Lark patted Alice's hand, fearing she spoke truth. Though a few of the faces were familiar, a few of the suits of clothes and cloaks of high quality, the majority of the men assembled looked rough and dirty, the creases on their faces not made by smiling. What care would they have of Sena's sensibilities? Even less than Sena herself had, which was pitiful indeed.

One of the men made a growling response that Lark couldn't make out, but which seemed to ignite Sena's wrath all the more. Her voice carried easily. "I will *not* get myself home. *This* will be my home, just as soon as—"

A roar covered the rest of her speech. Lark could hear phrases like "Tory lover" and "traitor" but little else.

A well-dressed gentleman finally stepped to the front of the path, though he looked none too pleased with Sena either. "Randel, control your daughter."

The voice was familiar—the Mr. Mason who had been at Randel House just last night. Alice gasped beside her.

Even as Mr. Randel called Sena's name and tried to reach her, Sena spun on Mason. "You! You are naught but a warmongering, bitter man who seeks trouble where peace would reign."

A poorly clad thug stepped forward, arm pulled back. Lark pressed a hand to her mouth. Surely he wouldn't raise a hand to a gentlewoman, one whose father was so near. Surely he wouldn't...

Sena's scream pierced the air as the back of the man's hand came across her cheek. Mr. Randel was there in the next second, pulling Sena up and against him. Emerson rushed forward and plowed a fist into the attacker's face.

Dear, strong Emerson, so ready for peace, yet so bound by his duty to protect those who were weaker. He shouted something at the man, something about the fellow's lack of honor, but then four more men surged forward and knocked her beloved to the ground.

Instincts battled within her. She wanted to rush to tend Emerson, to plow her way through the crowd. To assure herself he was well. Yet fear rooted her where she stood, fear and better sense.

What could she do in the face of such men?

Mason sneered. "Who is the brave war hero now, Fielding? So respectable, so eloquent, are you? Well, Paca may have been swayed, but I am not. If the governor tries to return this house to that swine, he will find no house left to return!"

Emerson was back on his feet, thank Providence, though being restrained by four sets of grubby hands. He wore the proud defiance on his face of one who knew he was right and was willing to pay the price for saying so. A Patriot, tried and true.

Lark could not swallow, could not breathe. Could do nothing, nothing but stand there and wish it were otherwise.

Alice's grip on her arm tightened, and a whimper came out. "That is my father."

"Your... Alice. *Him?* And yet still Mr. Randel invited him last night, knowing how he has treated you?"

"One cannot ignore certain associations that have been so long-standing." But Alice trembled, and her face had lost all hint of color. "Did I mention that he said he would sooner kill me than ever look on me again, when I married Matty?"

Lark spun, putting herself between Alice and Mason. "Then you must go, before he sees you. It is only a matter of time before he looks this way."

"I cannot leave Sena here like this." Yet fear and desperation saturated her voice.

Was it possible? Courageous Alice, so afraid. Spirited Sena, hurt and crying. She could only hope that sweet Kate had been urged by the Lord to pray. Pray that Lark, who wanted little more than to tremble and cry too, could be now what they could not.

She gripped Alice's shoulders and gave her a gentle shake. "You have your children to consider, Alice. Callie and Hugh, and the life yet unborn. You must go. Go to the Calverts, and tell them to pray. You can be there in two minutes."

Alice's eyes lost some of their panic. "Yes. Yes, of course, I must go tell them. And you must come with me."

She shook her head. "No, I will see how this ends. But I intend to stay out of sight. Go. Go, now."

After a mere moment's hesitation, Alice nodded and grabbed up her skirts to better run. She headed down a drive and into what was presumably an alley that would put her out on West Street.

Making good on her promise, Lark followed at a slower pace, pausing when she reached the rear of Calvert Hall. From back here, the voices of the men were disjointed rumbles and shouts, low throbs of threat and indignation. When her knees wobbled, she reached out to grip the closest thing at hand, though it looked like little more than a frozen clump.

Her fingers dislodged the snow and closed around wrought iron. 'Twas the stair railing, sturdy and strong. Unbent, undamaged, though covered by a winter's worth of ice and snow.

Lark closed her eyes and drew in a deep breath. *Dear Lord, help me find the iron within me. Help me find a way to help.*

Sleet hissed down, hard and fast, stinging her cheeks, her hand, any other inch of bare skin it could find. She raised a hand to shield her face, though it did little to protect her from nature's attack. Opening her eyes again, Lark's gaze landed on the door. She raced up the steps and a moment later tried the latch, amazed when it gave under her fingers. She couldn't imagine why it was unlocked but wasn't about to question good fortune. Stepping inside, she closed the door against the ice and absorbed the silence of an empty house.

She followed the main hallway toward the front, toward the voices that slowly seeped back into her hearing. She had just stepped into the entryway when a rock crashed through the window beside the front door.

In swept cold air, hate-filled shouts, and a flaming torch.

A scream caught in her throat, but Lark swallowed it down and rushed forward, toward that flaming rod. It landed on a stretch of bare floor, and she snatched it up before it had time to light the wood or leap to any of the cloths covering furniture.

Only then did she pause to breathe and to look at the black mark that already scorched the floor. Safe. For now. Though if the first torch failed at its job, a second would surely follow, and was probably ready even now to be tossed.

And why? For what? Bitterness, bitterness and hatred. A decision not to understand, not to forgive. A choice to cling to war when peace hovered on the horizon.

Warmth flooded her, bringing her chin up. She strode to the front door, threw the bolt, and wrenched it open. When she stepped out onto the stoop, the ice swirled into a gust of snow, then abruptly ceased.

Lark thrust the flame into the air. Silence fell, and she felt the gazes of every man upon her.

So long she had been invisible—but not now. So long she had held her silence—but not now. No, now she met every gaze, those of strangers and those of the same young gentlemen she had danced with at the holiday balls. Litchfield and Alderidge, Woodward and Griffith. Men whose jaws dropped upon spotting her. And in the back, a few more of the older men who were supposed to be leading these others.

She then looked at Sena, still huddled against her father's chest.

A few of them followed her gaze and looked sheepish as they

noticed the Randels. Those who knew them, no doubt, who respected them. Those who only now paused to see what their thirst for vengeance had wrought.

And finally, she looked to Emerson, who stared at her in disbelief. Fear creased his brow, but pride still shone in his eyes.

Lark drew in a long breath. "I daresay none of you much care to listen to the philosophy of a mere woman, so I will make no attempt to reason you out of this despicable show. But I will say this, gentlemen. You shame us all with such behavior. The time for destruction has passed. You have a nation to build."

Shaking her head, she shoved the torch into a snowbank. Its hiss of death filled the air, and a ribbon of smoke curled upward.

Conviction descended upon their faces, one by one. Not because of her words, certainly, but thanks to their own consciences.

But Mason pushed forward, rage upon his face. "And who do you think you are, to tell us what we ought to be doing? Another Loyalist doxy? Another weak-willed Eve trying to undermine man's authority?"

For some reason she couldn't fathom, Lark felt her lips pull up into a smile. "And who are you, Mr. Mason, that these men should follow you? A man who cannot rule his own house without revolt? A man whose business dealings are so suspect his daughter must make amends where he will not? I daresay the Mattisons would question your authority."

A few guffaws of laughter filled the air. And one of the burlier, ill-clothed men turned on Mason with folded arms and a glare. "You be *that* Mason? The one what cheated good Matty?"

Several more men rounded on him, none of them looking too pleased with him now. One crowded so close Mason could probably smell what exactly befouled the man's clothing. "The miss has a point—why ought we follow *you*? You, who cheat us whene'er you can? I say any man who's an enemy of yours be a friend of mine!"

The gentlemen all slunk away, leaving their supposed friend at the mercy of the rabble. Lark's attention, however, was snagged by Emerson, who rushed up the steps until he framed her face in his hands.

She couldn't tell if he was pleased or angry with her, the way he stared so hard into her eyes.

"Emerson, I know you said to remain at Randel House, but—"

"Have you any idea how terrified I was when I looked up and saw you here?"

She covered his hands with hers. "Perhaps as much as I when I saw them attack you."

"More, surely. For you know I can handle myself in battle. But you?" Finally, the corners of his mouth pulled up. "I pray God our children have your spirit, Larksong. Charging out with a flaming torch as you did...I am proud of you, but you scared a year off my life."

"I will have to find a way to give it back, then, as I want it only lengthened." She grinned up into his handsome face, into those warm brown eyes she intended to lose herself in for years to come.

He dropped his hands to her shoulders and pulled her close, chuckling against her hair. "I had better see you back to Randel House. You are like ice."

She nodded, even let him tug her down a step before she craned her head around to look at the house behind her. "Are they really giving it back?"

"So it seems—or at least the governor is speaking of doing so. I imagine it will take some time for all the details to be determined."

"You convinced him, then." She tucked her hand into his elbow and leaned on him more than necessary as they continued down the walk.

"We are apparently quite the persuasive pair." Grinning, he turned them down Calvert Street. "Wait until we tell your brother about this."

Laughter tickled her throat at that. She looked over her shoulder at the now-empty street, and the last drop of anxiety vanished from her soul. Though hard-won, at last peace blanketed her. She could hardly wait to share it with her family.

EPILOGUE

Endover Plantation, outside Williamsburg, Virginia
7 March 1784

Wiley meandered around the edge of the gathering without a care as to where he headed. It hardly mattered. The house was filled with friends from near and far, all here to wish Lark and Emerson well. Laughter rang out, violin music danced on the air, and smiles wreathed every face.

None so bright, of course, as the wedding couple's.

Wiley allowed himself to grin as he caught sight of them, Emerson unable to take his eyes off Lark even while she joked with Miss Randel and Isabella a few feet away from him. Yes, it was worth that dreaded month of uncertainty, to see those two in love.

"She is a charming bride."

Wiley spun at the voice, his posture snapping straight of its own volition. But General Washington wasn't talking to him. Wiley had merely wandered near where he stood with Mr. Jefferson and Randel.

Jefferson chuckled. "I hear she has the spirit of any Patriot soldier too. She talked a crowd away from following the bilious Mr. Mason."

"She did, at that," Randel said. "I was there."

"Perhaps we ought to send her to Paris to provide support for Franklin, if he needs it to convince King George to sign the treaty." General Washington clasped his hands behind his back and smiled out at the assembly.

Jefferson sighed. "Let us pray such recourse is unnecessary. I received word just before I left that New York's harbor was finally free enough of ice for the two couriers to set sail."

"I praise the Lord for that." Randel, too, looked over the room, his gaze directed at his daughter. "The thaw finally brought the husband of my daughter's friend home, which brought rejoicing to our household. I was very glad to hear it finally released the Treaty from its icy hold as well."

Jefferson nodded, still serious. "There is no hope the treaty will arrive by deadline, but hopefully Franklin's pleas for an extension will be granted."

"I shall pray Providence softens King George's heart." Washington's voice was soft. "We are a nation ready for peace, Mr. Jefferson. Desperate for it."

Wiley turned away from the group and their sober talk and meandered from the ballroom into the quieter parts of the house.

"Ah, Master Wiley." Joe smiled and held up an envelope. "I must have missed this in yesterday's post. I was just taking it up to your room for you."

The feminine script on the envelope caught his eye. Had Lark beaten one of her own letters home? Given this winter, it wouldn't surprise him. "Let me see it." But upon closer inspection, it wasn't Lark's hand at all.

Curious now, he unsealed the missive and glanced at the bottom as his servant ambled away. And nearly choked on his own breath. Penelope? What the devil was she doing writing him? His gaze flew back to the top.

Oh Wiley, I must beg you for help. George and I were married a week ago, and he has shown himself to be a veritable monster!

Wiley pursed his lips. Owens hadn't struck him as particularly monstrous, and blast it, he didn't want to have to feel guilt over his cousin's folly. She deserved whatever fate handed her. Though no one really deserved a monstrous spouse, did they? Sighing, he read on.

Within days of marriage, his true nature showed. He tossed out half my wardrobe—half!—and insisted I commission these wretched, outmoded rags in their place, which do not flatter my figure at all. And then—oh, forgive the tearstains—

then when I complained, he threatened to lessen my allowance if I persisted in wearing the styles I prefer. He is a tyrant, and my parents are no help at all, refusing to see my points. Please, Wiley, write to him and tell him to be kind. He respects you, he told me as much, and since it is largely your fault I was foisted upon him...

Wiley snorted and took great pleasure in tearing the letter in two.

"Bad news?"

He turned to smile at Emerson, who stood a few feet away with Lark tucked under his arm. "In Penelope's eyes, it is. Her husband is set on forcing practicality upon her, and knows just which strings to pull—those of his purse."

Emerson widened his eyes and made a gasp of horror. "The blackguard! And what does she intend you to do about it?"

"Intervene with him on her behalf, since 'tis all my fault she wedded the beast." With more delight than it probably warranted, Wiley crumpled up the two halves of paper and tossed them over his shoulder. "Memory apparently is not her strong suit, if she appeals to me for help."

"In which case, she will forget how horrible he is as soon as he drapes some pretty bauble around her neck." Lark grinned and motioned toward the ballroom. "You left as we were looking for you to wish you farewell."

"Stealing my sister, are you, Emerson?" Try as he might, he couldn't convince his smile to shrink. "I know not what I shall do, Larksong, you being a whole mile away at Fielding Hall."

Emerson snorted a laugh. "Says the man who sent her all the way to Annapolis."

"For which you thanked me repeatedly." Wiley chuckled. "Eventually."

They headed back toward the guests, Emerson's grin still in place. "I am man enough to admit when I was a fool."

"Ha!" Wiley gave his friend an amicable shove in the shoulder. "Took you long enough to see it. And so you do not think yourself too perfect, let me assure you you are *still* a fool, Emerson. A love-struck one."

Emerson didn't seem to take offense. His eyes, in fact, went dreamy as a schoolgirl's as he looked down at Lark. "'Tis a good kind of fool to be."

She smiled, blissful as she was resplendent in her silk. "You ought to try it sometime."

"There seems to be quite enough of that going around, thank you. Some of us must keep our wits about us."

Emerson dropped a kiss onto Lark's brow. "Well, may your wits keep you company, my friend."

Wiley chuckled at the pretty blush that bloomed in Lark's cheeks. Mrs. Fielding at last.

And finally the headache of seeing his sister happy was over. He loosed a happy sigh and couldn't resist one more poke at his friend. "I don't imagine you will be stopping by tomorrow for our usual chat, given your wedding trip the next day. Shall I come to you, then?"

For a moment, Emerson's casual smile actually gave him pause. Until, that is, he put a seemingly friendly hand on Wiley's shoulder that was far too firm in its grip. "Wiley, old friend. Don't even think about it."

Ah, yes. All was right in the world.

AUTHOR'S NOTE

When I decided to set a book in historic Annapolis, there were some things I knew I would include, and which I couldn't wait to highlight. The Liberty Tree, where the Sons of Liberty met. Bladen's Folly, the abandoned governor's mansion that later became McDowell Hall, the anchor building for my alma mater, St. John's College. The State House in all its Colonial splendor, the charm of the bay, the picturesque beauty that I associate with the city I called home for five years.

But as I sat down to research the Annapolis of 1783–1784, when it was capital of the nation while DC was being built, I discovered quite a number of things I hadn't realized but couldn't ignore. For starters, the treatment of Loyalists in those years directly following the Revolution. Though most Tories fled to Canada or back to England, some chose to remain in the US and underwent an epic battle to regain the property and assets that the Americans had seized during the war. Though stipulations for the return of property were included in the peace agreements, they were largely ignored for years. Many Tory families returned to Annapolis as soon as peace was declared, however, and adapted to the new circumstances. Historian Walter B. Norris observes that "it is creditable to the patriots to notice that the wounds of such a bitter difference of opinion were not long in passing away" (*Annapolis: Its Colonial and Naval Story*. New York: Thomas Y. Crowell Company, 1925, p. 108). Within a decade, such differences were forgiven as all rallied under the banner of being Americans.

In Maryland, one of the first families to regain its holdings was the Calverts, who had played such a pivotal role in the state's founding that respect for them eventually outweighed resentment of them. Because of that legacy, I chose to create a fictional branch of the

Calvert family to represent their struggle and share some of their reasons for remaining loyal to the Crown. The threat of vandalism to an ancestral Calvert home is fictionalized, but at that point Loyalists were still so hated that it's a reasonable inference.

Though my beloved Annapolis was by all accounts past its prime after the Revolution and was considered a backwater again by 1790, memory of its golden age still would have been strong during the so-called Long Winter of 1783–1784. Perhaps those days-gone-by filled the minds of the statesmen as they wondered if their fellow representatives would brave the snows in order to guarantee a peace that seemed tenuous at best.

Though the couriers with their two separate signed peace documents did not in fact reach Paris by the agreed-upon March 3 deadline (they were iced into New York harbor until February 21), King George surprised them all by graciously extending the deadline. Perhaps because the winter had been just as brutal in England, or perhaps because he was more tired of war than he let the Americans believe. But on March 29, 1784, Benjamin Franklin finally welcomed the signed Treaty into Passy, France, and peace was soon after settled once and for all.

Those at home pressed ever onward, the battle for freedom finally won. Of course, the path of the nation had yet to be determined. Those same great men we get a glimpse of in this book had years of debate ahead of them before they struck upon a Constitution and a form of government that soon revolutionized, not just a collection of thirteen colonies, but the entire world.

ALSO BY ROSEANNA M. WHITE

BIBLICAL FICTION

A Stray Drop of Blood
Jewel of Persia
A Soft Breath of Wind
Giver of Wonders

CULPER RING SERIES

Ring of Secrets
Fairchild's Lady (free e-novella)
Whispers from the Shadows
A Hero's Promise (free e-novella)
Circle of Spies

LADIES OF THE MANOR SERIES

The Lost Heiress
The Reluctant Duchess
A Lady Unrivaled

SHADOWS OVER ENGLAND SERIES

A Name Unknown
A Song Unheard
An Hour Unspent

YOU MAY ALSO ENJOY...

The Portraits of Grace Series
by Cara Luecht

Soul Painter   *Soul's Prisoner*   *Soul's Cry*

Twilight of the British Raj Series
by Christine Lindsay

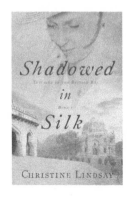  

Shadowed in Silk   *Captured by Moonlight*   *Veiled at Midnight*

CPSIA information can be obtained
at www.ICGtesting.com
Printed in the USA
LVHW03s1918120718
583537LV00004B/775/P

9 781946 531087